YES, AND...

ARTS AND LOVERS

RACHEL CAREY

Yes, And... Copyright 2025 © Rachel Carey

Cover design by Dar Albert at Wicked Smart Designs

Published by Oliver-Heber Books

0 9 8 7 6 5 4 3 2 1

"MY NEW, PURIFIED SPIRIT"

IMPROV COMEDY IS SUPPOSED to be unplanned, but from what I've learned in the last few weeks, there are rules to it, and they include the following:

1. you are not supposed to start kissing someone during an improvised scene, and
2. whatever happens between you and your scene partner, you aren't supposed to take any of it too seriously.

LET ME PAINT A PICTURE FIRST. Imagine a group of grown adults standing around after a few glasses of wine, pretending to be something they're not. It's a typical night out in your thirties, perhaps, complete with white lies about the fun jobs people pretend to have, the trips they didn't really enjoy, the romances that aren't quite living up to expectations.

Then imagine that everyone is doing this cheerful prevarication as a planned activity. They are gathered in a snug living room in a remote city in Canada, willfully lying to each other for their own entertainment. That will give you a picture of the Newfingers, Newfoundland's premiere (only?) improv group, getting together for a practice.

Mark, Lisette and I arrived at Paul's house at 7:30 sharp that evening for improv practice in his living room. Paul is in his mid-thirties, a couple of years younger than me, and his place is very typical of downtown St. John's: a wooden clapboard rowhouse from the 1920s, painted a bright yellow outside and small and cozy inside—thoroughly Canadian right down to the antique snowshoes on the wall and the wood stove in the corner. You could practically be living in a Canadian period TV drama when you're at Paul's place, complete with wartime yearning and hand-written love letters, if it weren't for Paul's extensive DVD collection of 1990s action-comedies.

The improv exercise we were practicing was simple: Paul and I were supposed to act as two characters with different goals, and we would be given a location and an object by the other members of the group.

"Okay, a location," Lisette said, pursing her fuchsia-tinted lips. Lisette is tiny and bleached blond, with a narrow face and pointed chin; she looks like a grubby Victorian street orphan who got dressed at a punk rock show. "How about a café?"

Paul nodded, and I smiled at him with the adrenaline rush that you get when you know you're about to embarrass yourself.

"What's their object, Mark?" Lisette asked.

Mark, the other member of the group, sat back and considered the question like he was a smug political commentator on a news show, sliding a thick hand across his five-o'clock-shadowed chin. "A cassette tape of Miles Davis."

"Great," I replied dryly. It was a very Mark choice: irritatingly specific and calculated to be nearly impossible to include in a café scene. Good luck with *that*, said his dry little smile.

We had to incorporate both elements into our scene, ideally with humor and surprise. Humor is one of the big goals of improv, but it's also the most elusive one, because you can never achieve it if you're trying to be funny. You know that feeling when you make a joke and the people around you fall silent, the room sinking into a painful mix of embarrassment and pity? Doing bad improv feels like that, distilled and bottled into an eau du parfum.

Kissing definitely wasn't on the list of scene requirements, so what happened next was probably my fault. I decided to pretend to be Paul's ex-girlfriend, trying to get back together with him. That would be easy enough for creating conflict, right?

That was my first mistake. Paul is handsome in a quirky way, tall and thin with an unruly cap of curly light brown hair. He has a lopsided smile and boundless energy, and it would have been safer for me to pretend I was his eye doctor, perhaps, or his disgruntled garage mechanic. I'd only known Paul for a few weeks, but I was pretty clear on who he was: one of those charming guys who totally wants to be friends with you and puts up sturdy fencing around the edge of that friendship. The polite heartbreaker. Mr. This-Is-Definitely-Not-A-Date.

Paul started the scene neutrally, sitting at his dining table a couple of feet from us, acting like he was silently meditating. I watched him for a moment and then made my approach.

"So you're back," I began. Not the strongest opening line, but that can be a good thing. It leaves the scene room to grow.

"From the monastery, yes," he said.

I was still pretty new to improv, but I knew enough to take whatever Paul said and run with it. 'Yes, and...' is the unofficial rule of improv. Don't argue with someone when they introduce an idea. Don't say that they weren't at a monastery. Say yes to the monastery and add more.

"Well, you look good," I said. "It looks like you lost weight there."

"We ate eight hundred calories a day. Near-starvation focuses the spirit."

"Is that why you ordered a hamburger?" That was my attempt to bring in the café location again. Well done, me.

"I'm not going to eat the bun," he replied defensively, and Lisette laughed.

I sat down across from him. "So have you been dating anyone since we split up?" There was a twinkle in Paul's eye as he realized which direction I was taking things.

"Did I meet a woman...at the monastery?" He cocked an eyebrow at me—an expression he makes in real life when I say something particularly 'American,' or worse yet, particularly 'New York.'

"Well, if you didn't," I went on, "I'm hoping maybe, now that you're back, we could get back together."

I waited for Paul to "yes and" back to me. He was supposed to say that we could get back together, but add some ridiculous stipulation, but Paul went the other way.

"I'm afraid I took a vow of chastity. It's part of purifying my spirit."

"I can think of other ways to purify your spirit."

The corners of Paul's mouth quirked upwards. "Kimberly," (that's not my real name), "I am trying to live a spiritual life now. If you want to meditate with me, that's fine."

"We can meditate in my bedroom. I have a Miles Davis cassette that's very spiritual." I mimed pulling out a cassette tape, and I could feel Mark nod, conceding my victory. You can't bring in the cassette tape right away, because that's too obvious, and when it shows up, it must feel organic to the scene.

"Seeing you here in a cafe is safer," he said. "So I won't be tempted to stray from my path."

Now I was supposed to commit to my objective. "If you insist," I said, sitting on his lap. "So how exactly do we start this meditation?"

That was my next big mistake. Don't escalate a situation physically when you are not supposed to kiss the person. There are rules for consent in improv, which Paul had outlined for all of us. *Don't grope, don't kiss, don't make unwanted advances.* No problem, I thought as I sat down. Paul would keep us on the straight and narrow.

"Are you going to sit on my lap the whole time?" he asked.

"That won't hurt your focus, will it?"

"My meditation requires a lack of distraction."

"Right." I looked him dead in the eyes, inches from his face. "No distraction."

"And to completely free my mind from any thoughts," he added.

"I don't have a single thought in my head." I could feel the others watching us, wondering where the scene would go.

"You're trying to tempt me."

"Only in a meditative way," I said.

"It won't work. I am completely focused on my inner peace."

"So am I. Completely focused on your inner peace."

Then we kissed, and my brain was tracking too many things at once: who had started the kiss, how his lips felt, and—very distantly—what I was supposed to be doing in the scene, and that two other people were watching us like we had turned into a bad reality TV show. Paul pulled away gently and shook his head.

"I felt nothing," he said. I could tell up close that this wasn't true. His eyes were wide, and his breathing sounded like he'd lifted something heavy and was refusing to admit that he should probably put it down.

"Well, I'll leave you with Miles, then," I said, standing up and patting the imaginary cassette flirtatiously. "When you're alone in your room, lying in bed, you can play this and call me, the next time you want to feel nothing again."

And scene. Lisette applauded, and I felt the way I always did after an improv: I wasn't sure whether it had been good, terrible, or completely silly, which is disorienting for me, since I usually have a pathological fetish about control.

I was feeling something else, too, and I needed to put some distance between Paul and me as quickly as I could. I crossed the room to slide into Paul's green leather armchair. No big deal, my body language said. Oh, look, a magazine on the table! With trout fishing on the cover!

I caught Mark eyeing the two of us. Mark's the cynic of the group—smart, dry, a few years older than the rest of us. He raised his eyebrows, and I gave a tight smile.

"Sorry," I said after a moment.

"Totally your fault," Paul said. "I blame you entirely." I realized he was blushing; he has the kind of complexion that makes for a handy barometer of his social angst.

"I could write you a formal letter of apology," I said.

He nodded, still not quite meeting my eyes. "I'm going to need an essay about consent in improv. Five paragraphs on my desk by morning." He is a middle school history teacher during the school year, so asking for essays is not completely out of character. He glanced around. "Mark and Lisette, you're up."

"I'm not going to make out with you," Lisette said as she stood up.

"We'll just see where the scene goes," Mark replied.

"No, that is actually a bad idea," Paul said. "I'm sorry about that, guys. That was setting a bad precedent. I'm sorry, Abby." That is my real name, though I noticed he still couldn't quite meet my eyes as he said it.

"I'm sorry, too," I repeated.

"Okay, okay, everyone is sorry," Lisette announced and stretched her arms over her head, hopping up and down a couple of times to get ready for her scene. It was a slightly sticky evening, the early August weather still thick with warmth in spite of the breeze from the open windows.

Mark glanced at me again. "That was a real kiss," Mark muttered as he walked to the middle of Paul's living room.

Those were the words that stuck with me, the ones that haunted me hours later. A real kiss according to who? A real kiss according to which one of us?

Then I reminded myself of the second rule of improv: don't take anything that happens too seriously.

Let me back up a few weeks, because I haven't always been an eager participant in the quirky world of improvisational theater. A few weeks ago, I was a normal, sane person who wouldn't have been caught dead at an improv show, let alone doing it myself in a rustic Canadian living room. I was cynical and pessimistic and sure that I'd die alone, like any sensible single person in their late thirties in New York. If you're going to enjoy the urban life in Brooklyn, you can't focus on all the lives you're not having: the house in the suburbs, the winsome children, the family-friendly SUV driven by a V-neck-sweater-wearing husband. Instead you have to focus on the parts of your life that make sense: the same-day Broadway tickets for half-price, the free mimosa refills at your brunch spot, the fact that you probably would have died alone even if you weren't living in the big city.

So how did I end up end up on one of Canada's island provinces, kissing a man who doesn't want to date me?

It started with my sister Laura's decision to move out of

New York a couple of months ago. Laura is three years older than me, and she and I have always been close, mostly because we survived the same childhood with its constant chaos and shifting father figures under the negligent eye of the world's funniest drunk, our mother. My mother is where I get my acidic sense of humor, but in every other way I try not to be like her: I pay my bills on time, I limit myself to two cocktails an evening, and I try not to pick up men in places like the cereal aisle of the grocery store or the line outside the theater for a kids' movie.

My sister Laura has always been prettier than me, with faraway eyes and a cupid's bow mouth. She looks like a young Linda Ronstadt, according to our mother, or like a young Linda Cardellini, according to my high school boyfriend. I have always had the role of her shorter, less enticing sidekick. I am pale, with dark hair, and if my sister looks like a goddess, then I look like an easily frightened librarian...or maybe one of those "relatable" ladies on television ads who pause my bike to talk about my endometriosis. I never much minded, growing up. It felt like the natural order of things to have my older sister getting all the attention while I entertained people by imitating characters from Saturday Night Live. Laura and I were a team when we were kids. We spent our formative years playing grown-up to each other when our mother couldn't quite manage it, asking each other whether homework needed doing or teeth needed brushing. My sister is the one who helped me apply for scholarships to college when our mother was too disorganized to fill out the financial aid forms. My sister is the one who told me whether a boy in theater class liked me or whether he was definitely gay. And when I graduated from college with a creative writing degree, my sister saw me through my first disastrous attempts to write comedy, and my less disastrous jobs in advertising and journalism. In exchange, I remained her biggest fan throughout her wild party-girl years and her transition to AA meetings and a stable career as an accountant. We were each other's most important person, and it stayed that way even when she got married.

It was Laura who let me stay on her sofa when my long-time boyfriend Farid left me for his future wife. And I helped her survive her rollercoaster marriage to the handsome rock musician Nick, who was out of town half the time and never did the dishes. She took care of me when my depression got so bad that I lost my job at a fancy magazine and had to switch to financial writing. And I helped watch her new baby Hannah whenever Nick was out of town for a gig, and then when she and Nick divorced a couple of years later after he moved to Los Angeles to pursue his dreams of musical stardom.

We were each other's solid foundation in a shifting world. And my niece Hannah was my surrogate daughter, whom I watched after school four days a week for the entirety of Covid. Their lives were as important to me as my own. I taught Hannah half of the letters in the alphabet, and I was the only one who watered Laura's houseplants.

So it came as a surprise when Laura announced to me, right at the end of Hannah's school year, that she was moving to Atlanta.

"The one in Georgia?"

"Nick got a steady job down there."

"Nick?" I waited as her expression shifted from nervy to embarrassed, like a teenage girl caught cheating on a test. She hadn't even told me her ex was back in the picture.

Laura took a breath. "He wants us to move there. He's rented a place that's big enough for Hannah to have her own room. He wants to work things out."

"You mean, get back together."

"He's in a very different place now, Abby. He's older. He's gotten over his obsession with becoming famous."

"And he has basically not seen his kid for two years."

Her eyes were wide with shock, like I'd said something deeply unfair. "He was here at Christmas. But that's why he wants us to move down there. He wants to try to be a family again."

"Why can't he move to New York?"

She rolled her eyes, like I was being utterly unreasonable. "Because he got a job there. The music industry is really good there, and the cost of living is way lower, and he got a steady gig at the same club four nights a week." I sighed. This sounded like Nick all over: the awesome gig, the big plans, the insistence that my sister fall in line to support him.

"And if he loses that gig?"

"Well, I'd also be working as an accountant."

"Your current job is letting you work remotely? I thought that was a strict rule for them."

"I gave them two weeks' notice."

"Laura." I knew I was taking the wrong tone. She hated being spoken to like she was the younger of us as surely as I hated being taken for granted, but I was angry enough that I couldn't seem to help it.

"I can get another job, okay? They need accountants everywhere. That's not going to be a problem."

I sighed. This plan had clearly been in the works for a while, which was the part that bothered me most. "Why didn't you tell me you were thinking about this?"

"I was worried you'd try to talk me out of it, and I had to figure out whether I even wanted it first. Can't you just be happy for me? You know I never really got over him. And we have a kid together, so I'd like to give it a shot. Come on, Abby. Please."

I saw in Laura's eyes that she meant it. She was happy and hopeful, and she wanted me to be happy and hopeful, too. So I told her I hoped it worked out, and that I was happy for her.

And I was happy, I guess, the way you're happy for a friend who announces they've sold all their possessions to embrace the 'freegan' lifestyle or that they've finally found true love with their surf instructor in Daytona Beach.

"You could move to Atlanta," Laura added. "It's a really cool town."

Something inside me hardened at the words. *Move to Atlanta?* Move away from my friends and my apartment and my very slow-paced yoga classes?

Laura pressed on. "You work from home, right? You said they never ask you to go into the office anymore."

This was technically true. My job in financial writing had gone through a weird transformation over the years. After my long-time boyfriend left me, I went through a depression that doomed me at my full-time job as a journalist, so I took a free-lance job I saw posted on craigslist. A business school graduate named Kedar was starting a small online magazine that was supposed to make financial writing fun and sassy. ("Those Horrible Warehouses Popping Up in Cute Rural Towns May Be Your Next Investment Opportunity!") He hired me despite my lack of business knowledge because I could deliver enough snarky articles to keep his readers amused, which he said was the 'special sauce' that was missing from other investment maga-zines. Kedar would pitch me article ideas and I would write them up like they were monologue material for a late-night show. It quickly turned into a steady gig—no healthcare or retirement plan, but I could live on what I made.

Then two years into the job, Kedar's magazine was purchased by a hedge fund, and we were incorporated into their larger business as a fun and sassy internal newsletter, and since then, my job has fallen under the umbrella of a big firm. We have office space on 47th Street, and I get regular paychecks and discounts on my gym membership. It's a reasonably cushy deal, except when the corporate execs look over our shoulders because we made the wrong investment recommendation or delivered a non-corporate dose of sarcasm about some environment-killing business. But the best part of the job is that after Covid started, I was allowed to do my writing full-time from home, and I could spend a lot of time watching my niece Hannah in the process. She's seven years old now, and very funny, with a smoky voice like a tiny Natasha Lyonne. Watching her after school Monday through Thursday was the best part of my week.

All the same, Laura's assumption that I would simply follow them to Atlanta rankled.

So Nick had screwed up his marriage, and now I was supposed to pick up my entire life and move to hot, sprawling Atlanta in the middle of summer to support his attempt to win back my sister, keeping my fingers crossed that he didn't blow it again? This after listening to her cry about him for the last five years?

Was I supposed to keep babysitting Hannah? Was that the plan? I wondered if Laura was ready to quit her job partly because of my assumed availability to continue providing free childcare if Nick decided to take a gig out of town.

"I am not moving to Atlanta," I snapped.

Laura looked startled, then annoyed. I wondered if some part of her, even after all these years, still assumed that her kid sister would follow her wherever she went. I was the gum-snapping sidekick on our sitcom, making smart remarks straight to camera, but I was not the lead.

"Okay, well..." Laura looked at the sky, as if asking for patience.

"I hate hot weather. I don't even like New York in summer. And if you and Nick don't work out…"

"Okay—"

"I mean it's possible you'll get there and after two days you'll realize it's a disaster."

"Maybe, but I don't think so, Abby. I invited you because I assumed you'd still want to see Hannah."

Ouch. She was going for the jugular, knowing how much I loved that kid, and it made me even angrier. "Or you assumed I'd provide free babysitting when Nick starts to flake out again."

Laura's eyes flashed with anger. "That is completely unfair."

Did I mention that we were having this whole conversation in Prospect Park, with children playing in the background? I was watching Hannah running around in an impromptu game of tag, like kids do in New York, making instant friends with strangers—and I thought about how I was probably never going to have kids of my own, and I wasn't sure whether to feel angry at Laura for using my love of Hannah against me or ashamed of myself for abandoning my favorite kid.

"Laur," I said, "I love Hannah. But watching her has kept me from doing other things, so if you're going to be leaving town, I may have other priorities."

"What priorities?" Laura looked skeptical. I felt like we were teenagers again, and she was asking me to do her chores while she went out because what else would I have to do on a Friday night?

"Well," I began, "I've always talked about moving overseas, and I never did it because you needed me."

"What, so you're going to *move to France?*"

"Maybe." My anger was gaining momentum, like it had reached the top of the roller coaster and was about to drop. "I could. I was helping you, okay, by watching Hannah, but now

Nick can do that, right? So there are other things I'd like to do. So yeah, maybe I will move to France." This was a bit of a test: if Laura needed me for babysitting, she was going to have to admit it.

Instead, she said with fake casualness, "Sure. If that's what you want."

I could tell from Laura's tone that she never thought I'd do it.

And that is how I ended up in Newfoundland, three weeks after Laura told me she was leaving, and a week after Laura packed her bags and moved a thousand miles south to try to build a life again with the world's least reliable rock guitarist. Laura may have expected me to drop everything and follow her, but I was placing my bets on a different outcome: that Nick was going to prove as unreliable as ever, and Laura would be back in New York by September.

In the meantime, I was going to see the world, my chin held high and suitcases swinging at my side, like a slutty, urban version of Maria from *The Sound of Music*.

The improv? That came later.

2

"YOU REALLY NEED TO HEAR ABOUT HIS MOTHER"

AT THE END of improv practice that night—the early August night that I'll call the 'kiss night'—Paul stood at his doorway like a good host to see us off. Paul speaks with a slight Newfoundland accent, which always sounds to me like friendly Midwestern with a dash of Swedish. I wasn't sure whether I should stay behind to talk to him in case there was any remaining awkwardness or hurry out with Mark and Lisette so that he wouldn't think that the kiss meant anything to me.

When I approached, he glanced down to avoid eye contact, like a man about to deliver bad news. I could feel myself tensing up: oh dear God, was he going to preemptively reject me? Or even worse, did he feel sorry for me? Then he glanced up and met my eyes with a half-hearted grin, and I had the same feeling I'd had since the first time I met him: this mix of complete familiarity, like I could understand every thought he had, every flicker of irony or self-doubt—and then seconds later, the certainty that I was getting him all wrong.

I let Lisette leave first. She leapt up to give Paul her usual giant hug—she's unreserved in a way that I could never be—and then skipped out the brightly-painted doorway. I figured I would leave before Mark, who was still shaking out his coat and examining the buttons. Mark is usually the last person to leave anywhere, even though he apparently lives the farthest away. Lisette thinks this is because his house is really dumpy, though she's never actually seen it.

"I'm betting it's a trailer," she said to me once. "He seems like the type to live alone in the woods."

"He works in advertising, so I kind of doubt it," I told her. Mark is divorced, like Paul, but he is close to fifty and has kids who are already out of the house, so he definitely seemed like he should have the money to live well. However, I could see Lisette's point: most of his energy was spent being pessimistic and asking people pointed questions, so I wouldn't put it past him to be living in a trailer out of spite.

As Lisette headed down the steps, her pale blonde hair bobbing in all directions under a handknit cap, I approached the front door and put out a hand to Paul awkwardly. It seemed like the safe choice. I could feel myself blushing a little and I wanted to project a carefully neutral attitude, like we were two colleagues at a business conference.

"Well," I said brightly.

"We're shaking hands, now?"

"You only get one kiss a night, buddy."

He opened his mouth and then seemed to change his mind about what he was planning to say. "Fair enough," he said, and shook my hand.

I almost apologized again but I knew I couldn't get through it without acting like a teenager, so I turned to go.

"Hey, I may call you," he said as I stepped away. I stopped, my heart lurching. Then he went on, "I have another improv book to recommend."

"I was that bad tonight, huh?" I was impressed with my own ability to sound jovial instead of desperately nervous.

"Or that good," he replied. "Good night."

Mark followed only a few steps behind me and caught up with me halfway down the block.

"Hey, you want to grab a drink around the corner?" Mark has one of those low, rumbling voices that suggests a one-sided love affair with cigarettes.

"Oh, umm..." It was a windy evening in St. John's, and I was calculating how late I wanted to get back to my sublet apartment. I had a meeting with my boss in the morning, even if I was planning on taking it on a laptop wearing fuzzy, mint-green slippers.

"I just want to chat. I'm not asking you out," Mark said testily.

"Um, sure, I can grab a drink," I said. "Where do you have in mind?"

"How about right there?" He pointed down the hill to a little pub in the basement of one of the old stone buildings from the late 1800s. It looked like the kind of place that had once advertised dry goods to women in wide brimmed hats. "They have some good beers on tap."

As we tramped down the hill together, I glanced back. I knew it was silly, but I wanted to see whether Paul was still at his door, watching us go. I could see his silhouette frozen in the doorway, but when he saw me looking, he turned and disappeared inside. When I turned back to Mark, he was watching me with a dry smile.

"There's something you really ought to know about Paul," he said.

So why Newfoundland? That will probably seem even more unlikely than my decision to pine after an improv comedy enthusiast who shows no apparent interest in dating me. The windy, foggy weather here was certainly a factor. I'm a hooded sweatshirt person at heart; I'm happiest when the weather is 62.5 degrees, with a light breeze, so I can enjoy a proper cup of hot coffee in the morning. Janeane Garofalo was my style icon growing up: casual, dryly funny, wearing shoes that could kick a door open.

Still, ending up on an island in the North Atlantic was more than just a pleasant way to avoid the smell of Brooklyn during July and August, when the city is most redolent with trash bags of stale pizza and spoiled milk. I was also thinking about leaving the U.S. for good.

Ever since I hit my thirties, I have had days when I start to feel like I've had it with the U.S.—that there are too many important things that we haven't gotten right. Still, until Covid and the 'work from home' policy that came with it, I never really thought seriously about the possibility of just picking up and going. For one thing, I don't have a particular claim to citizenship in a foreign country. I always envied friends who could skip around the world on multiple passports, whereas I was born in the exotic city of Troy, New York—a gritty, industrial back porch to our state capital of Albany. People didn't usually get out of Troy to see the world; they made a circular tour of the city's factories, pubs and pizza restaurants before winding up a block from where they were born, looking much the worse for wear. I had no 'in' that would allow me to duck away to Ireland or Portugal as a second-generation citizen.

All the same, for the last few years, on days when the news made me particularly anxious or the weather made me particularly sticky, I would daydream about the other places I could go. Maybe I would bring Laura and Hannah with me, I told myself. Maybe I would move once Hannah went off to college, and she could come live with me when she committed some minor crime and needed to flee the country. I had a secret folder on my web browser where I kept pictures of my dream locations: Stockholm, New Zealand, the beaches of Thailand, the shores of Baja, Mexico. I never looked up the immigration policies of these places. It was never supposed to be real.

Then Covid happened, and I got permission to work from anywhere, and suddenly my daydreams became a little more concrete. My tidy but not luxurious financial writing salary could set me up in places that were a lot more reasonable than Brooklyn. I could be one of those 'digital nomads' earning my salary from wherever I could find an internet connection. But where could I actually go? My international ex-pat daydreams began to take a realistic form, and they included a few requirements:

1. Somewhere not too hot in summer or too cold in winter. Newfoundland is pretty far north, and it definitely gets snow, but it's got the advantage of an island climate, so it's warmer in the winter than Ottawa or Toronto.

2. Somewhere that speaks English, because I'm not going to be picking up Romanian or Mandarin anytime soon. This is hard-won self-knowledge, for better or worse: no matter how many language apps I have downloaded on my phone, I will never be proficient enough to navigate Oslo or Majorca in their native tongues. I'm not built for knowing four different ways to ask where the nearest coffee shop is.

3. Somewhere that's walkable. As a long-time Brooklyn resident, if I can't walk to a laundromat, a movie theater, and a local pub, I feel like I'm in a backwater. (And more importantly, I'm a terrible driver. If I had to live somewhere that required a

car, I'd be caught up in an international sideswiping
incident within about two days.)

4. A functional government, without too much
political drama.

5. Reasonably affordable.

THAT LAST ONE is the trick, isn't it?

My research as a financial writer had taught me that the
London and Vancouver and Auckland real estate markets had
all been raked clean by fancy international investors and fierce
demand, rendering them nearly impossible for even the locals to
get a foot in the door. If cocky finance guys at my hedge fund
were placing bets on Edinburgh property values, then they were
already too pricey for people who lived there, let alone a
foreigner on a middle-class salary.

So that left me with the places that were a little undiscov-
ered, and after a bit of researching, I zeroed in on Newfoundland. It was a photo of St. John's that finally sold me on it. The
brightly colored row houses, the restaurant scene, the walkable
downtown...it reminded me of a smaller, cuter Brooklyn, somewhere that I could even settle eventually, assuming I could deal
with a lot more snow. Plus, I could buy a rowhouse for three
hundred grand. You know what three hundred grand gets you in
Brooklyn? A parking space.

I wasn't stupid. I knew perfectly well that my fantasy about
moving to Canada and writing in my pjs during long snowy
winters was probably just that—a fantasy that would have all
kinds of drawbacks if I tried it in reality. But when my sister
picked up and left me for the humid furnace of the American
South, I finally had a chance to try out the dream that I'd been
secretly nurturing for years. I decided I would rent a place for

two months in St. John's, and I would deal with the reality of living overseas in a windy, foggy city with an active port. It was probably not going to live up to any *Eat, Pray, Love* expectations, but this way I'd get them out of my system. And by the time I realized I hated living alone, far from my friends and favorite bagel spots, Laura would be back in Brooklyn again, because Nick was not going to be able to live up to whatever high expectations she had for him. I would fly back home as soon as I got her inevitable tearful phone call and she'd run into my arms and tell me how right I had been all along.

"I know," I'd say in my endless benevolence. "This is why I only signed a short-term lease."

My plan did not involve making new friends, let alone falling for anyone. The funny thing about improv is, you have to expect the unexpected.

So THERE I WAS, the night of the kiss, sitting across from Mark at a thick wooden table in the back of a cozy St. John's gastropub with a fire in the corner and a glass of wine in front of me. It would have been romantic...unless you know Mark.

Mark is dark. Mark is world-weary. Mark likes to talk about the pointlessness of existence, and more than one of his improvs has turned into an apocalyptic dystopia where zombie bankers are destroying the world. Mark is also exactly my type. Every guy I've had a crush on for the last few years has been like Mark —bitter and funny and a few years older than me. The problem is that most of them have been married, which hasn't always stopped them from hitting on me. Mark at least had the advantage of being divorced.

"Here's the thing you need to know about Paul," Mark began. "He is never going to get serious with anyone, romantically."

"It was just a kiss," I said.

"And who kissed who?" Mark asked.

I opened my mouth and then settle on a half-shrug.

"He kissed you as much as you kissed him. I think you know that. But it doesn't matter."

"You have a whole theory about this, don't you?"

"I have theories about everything." Mark grinned at me like a shark. "Do you want to hear how Paul's marriage ended?"

I hesitated. "Is this a story I should be hearing from Paul?"

"Meaning?"

"I mean, is it private? Would he not want you to tell me this?"

"He hasn't sworn me to secrecy. But I suspect the version he tells people is not exactly the way it happened, if he's told you anything at all." Mark's words hit me harder than I wanted to admit. I tried to keep my expression neutral.

"I'm not trying to date Paul. So I'm not sure why you think I need to hear this." That part was mostly true, but only because I was fairly certain he wasn't interested. We had been around each other a lot for the last few weeks. We were both single. He'd had plenty of time to ask me out, and the fact that he hadn't told me everything I needed to know. Didn't it?

"My point is you don't really know him."

"Okay."

"And you really need to hear about his mother."

"Is this some Freudian thing? Because I think that's largely been debunked."

"Paul's mother runs his life."

I glanced away, feeling caught out. "He doesn't talk about her very much."

"That's my point. His mother is a mess. Very dramatic, very involved. Probably has a personality disorder. Anytime something seems to be going right with any woman in Paul's life, his mother blows it up. That's what happened with his wife, you know. His wife left him for someone else, but they had problems before that because of the mother."

"So why doesn't Paul set some boundaries with her?"

"Guilt, I guess. Paul is all she has."

I thought of my own mother, who had nearly lost her housing a few times in the five years before she finally passed away. Laura and I had bailed her out with a few thousand dollars here and there until she stopped thanking us for it and started to expect it. "That's really hard for him."

"It is hard. I feel for Paul, but my guess is he doesn't plan on dating anyone seriously until his mother passes away. And that could be years, so I didn't want you to get your hopes up."

"Well, my hopes weren't up, but thanks for the warning. I didn't...Paul and I aren't..." I didn't know what to say, honestly. Mark's explanation made sense based on Paul's behavior over the last few weeks.

"So would you want to go out with me sometime?"

I looked up, startled. Mark was smiling again, with a little bit of an edge, his expression daring me to say yes.

"I uh...oh. I don't know if that's..." I trailed off.

"I think you're really something, Abby. And I never think that about anyone."

I smiled, but my heart was pounding from nerves. "From what Lisette has said, you date a lot."

"Yeah, but I don't like any of them." His feral grin was back.

I looked down. "I think it's probably good for me to...I'm only here for a few weeks..." I had no good excuse. Part of me wanted to go to bed with Mark just to forget what had happened with Paul. The other part of me knew he was dangerous.

"Fair enough." Mark took in my uncertainty with a shrug. "You can think about it. The offer stands."

3

"THANKS FOR TAKING IN THE STRAY"

MARK WAS RIGHT ABOUT one thing: I didn't actually know Paul that well. When Mark and I were talking in that tiny restaurant, I had only known Paul for four weeks, which is just slightly less time than I'd been in St. John's. The story of how we met begins with Lisette, and the story of Lisette begins with my rental apartment.

St. John's, the capital of Newfoundland, is not a good city for short-term rentals. That's the first thing I discovered when I started thinking about doing a stay there. There are some vacation rental options, but they're a bit pricey if you're planning on more than a couple of nights' visit, and most other rentals in the city tend to be found by word-of-mouth and Facebook postings, unless you contact a realtor, and realtors want you to sign a one-year lease. It's a city of a little over 100,000 but compared to New York, it operates like a small town. So it took some digging, even with my journalism skills, to find somewhere that I could live for just two months, which is the amount of time that I had calculated I could afford to explore my dreams without having to give up my place in Brooklyn. In the end, I negotiated a decent deal with a woman named Charlotte who had posted her place as a vacation rental and wasn't getting much interest. Ironically, Charlotte wanted to rent it out because she was moving in with her boyfriend and didn't want to give her place up until she decided whether she could make things work with him or not.

So while Laura was working things out with Nick, I was subletting this woman Charlotte's place while she tried things with Brett, her fisherman boyfriend who lived twenty minutes down the coast.

I would find out all these details later. When I flew into St. John's with my two pieces of luggage and laptop bag, all I knew was that I had found a decently priced rental on the second floor of a small two-family rowhouse right in the city center.

My first impression of Newfoundland was that I couldn't see much of Newfoundland. I arrived there by flying from Manhattan to Montreal and then switching to a smaller plane to make the second leg of the trip up along the Atlantic coastline. The first of July was a rainy day, and for most of the flight, I could see nothing but clouds, drifting in wayward columns like a goth metal album cover. Then suddenly we were dropping down through misty layers and emerging over a small city covered in fog and half-surrounded by water. St. John's is part of the Avalon peninsula, which is roughly the size of Connecticut and extends outward from the southeastern part of the much larger island of Newfoundland. It was the first region of Canada that was settled by Europeans, and the city remains the most populated part of the whole province. It has a protected port, and for centuries it has been a friendly stopping point for people braving the northern Atlantic on their way to North America from Europe.

Once we landed, I tottered along with my luggage through the small St. John's airport and managed to find myself a taxi. It all felt so cute that I was trying not to feel superior about it—the worst thing New Yorkers can do is point out how adorable things are compared to home. My taxi driver grabbed my luggage and immediately introduced himself as Rick. He turned out to be my second favorite kind of taxi driver—the tour guide—and he kept up a steady stream of conversation as he drove me through the unassuming suburban neighborhoods on the way downtown. (The *best* kind of taxi driver is the life advisor, but they've become increasingly rare in the era of Bluetooth headphones; why should a guy listen to your relationship problems and hand out free advice when he could be chatting with his cousin in Karachi?)

I soon learned about Rick's love of the *New York Times* crossword puzzle and his devotion to life on Newfoundland, where he had lived since he was born.

"This is the big city, here, St. John's," he said, as we pulled into the downtown and curved past a large Catholic church and down a steep hill, slipping along ribbons of rowhouses and grimy commercial buildings. The rainy day gave the city a dreary cast, in spite of the brightly painted colors of the houses, and I had a brief moment of wondering what the hell I was doing here. Then I looked out across the water and the fog parted to reveal a lonely green hillside across the bay, stark as the west coast of Ireland, laced with rocks. Gulls were wheeling, and mist brought in the scent of the sea. It was beautiful and lonely, and I remembered what I had fallen in love with: this ideal, remote city I had in my head, which was not completely different than the real place. But there was also a faint smell of…

"Cow manure," Rick informed me. "It blows in sometimes from the fields, depending on the direction of the wind. The rest of the time it smells like fish."

Excellent. Fish and cow manure. The taxi squeaked as it pulled to the side of the road.

"Here's the Fishing Net." I was supposed to stop by Charlotte's work to pick up the keys to my apartment.

"I'll just be a couple of minutes," I said. "Please wait. I'll pay for your time."

"You got it. Oh, can I ask you a question?"

"Of course."

"Ten Letters, Taylor Swift album."

"Reputation?"

"You're a genius. Guess that's why it's the *New York Times* crossword. All New Yorkers know this stuff."

"Every single one of us."

"There's a good bar scene here," Rick told me as I opened the taxi door. "Maybe too good. In the winter, people do a lot of…" and he gestured with his hand like he was chugging a bottle.

"I promise I'm not doing any of that now," I replied.

It's funny how when you visit a place that gets lots of snow in the winter, you can sense it even when the weather is warm. It's something about the low doorways, the compact windows, the sense of everything being ready to hunker down against bitter weather. I traveled to Quebec City once in summer, and I had the same feeling about it. It was a winter city, briefly enjoying the respite of flowers and sunshine before returning to its regularly scheduled programming of long nights filled with spiked coffee and wood-burning fires.

The Fishing Net had a slightly desperate, lonely air, like every bar does around three in the afternoon. The few patrons looked like they had been planted in their seats for hours already, blinking at the flash of sunlight as I swung open the door. I found Charlotte cleaning a table in the back with a rag. She was a tall brown-haired woman around my age who looked like she might be from one of Canada's First Nations tribes. I wondered if our similar age was why she trusted me with her apartment. She and I were both old enough that we'd been doing our own dishes for a long time; you don't make a mess in your late thirties and expect someone else to clean it up.

"The front door sticks," she said as she handed me the keys, "so just jiggle it a few times. And ignore Mrs. Mahoney on the first floor, she's a bitch."

"Got it."

"She'll give you a hard time about using the washer and dryer in the basement, but she doesn't own them, so there's nothing she can do about it. She just doesn't like the noise. I'm friends with the landlady, so don't let Mrs. Mahoney say she's going to complain about you. She can't do a damn thing."

"I'll try to use the washer and dryer at reasonable hours."

"Won't make a difference. She'll bother you about it anyway. But here are the keys," Charlotte said. "The apartment should be empty."

Those words—*should be empty*—could have been a red flag to me, but I didn't register them at the time. I was too busy trying to get out the door before I ran up the meter on Rick's taxi. I had decided to do without a rental car in Newfoundland, given my sordid history with rearview mirrors, so it was going to be taxis and walking for me. I decided to take Rick's card.

A few minutes later, Rick dropped me off with my bags in front of a small red two-family rowhouse, squeezed between taller ones on either side. I stood for a moment alone before trying my key. Maybe this was all a horrible mistake. The house had a slightly lopsided air, like it had suffered from a stroke, and one side had settled farther than the other. Trying the lock, I found that Charlotte was right: the front door keys did stick. I negotiated my bags into a narrow front hallway with two doorways and a set of stairs. I assumed one doorway led to the first-floor apartment and the other to the basement. I headed up the narrow wooden stairs, which definitely had a distinct lean to the left-hand side. This was an old house without a lot of what real estate agents call 'modern updates,' which was one of the reasons it was so affordable. I opened the apartment with my key, put my bags down, and discovered immediately that someone else was living there. There was a coffee mug on the table, 1980s New Wave music playing, and the distinct steamy smell of a recent shower.

"Hello?" I began without much hesitation, because I'm a longtime New Yorker and interacting with weird strangers is safely in my city living toolkit. "Hello? Is somebody..."

A tiny blonde woman emerged from the back of the house, towel-drying her hair. She was wearing a Sex Pistols t-shirt and long baggy pants, and her hair stuck out at weird angles like it had been cut at home with scissors.

She dropped the towel when she saw me. "Oh my God," she said. "What day is it?"

"It's Saturday."

"Oh, shoot. I was supposed to move out, then." She spoke with a very slight Quebecoise accent. I would later learn that she'd grown up in a small town in Quebec called Tadoussac and had spoken exclusively French until she started school at six years old.

"Yeah, I'm supposed to move in," I said, trying to sound polite and easygoing while actually feeling tired and annoyed.

"Oh no, I'm sorry. I totally lost track of what day it is."

"Okay..."

"I do that," she said. "Don't worry. I'll make this place clean, no problem."

I was trying hard not to look impatient, but the long travel day hadn't put me in a great mood. I just nodded and shuffled my bags down.

"You want an apple or anything? I'm Lisette. Charlie was letting me stay here for a few days, but I was supposed to get out once she rented the place. I'm sure she reminded me but my brain does this. It refuses to process dates and times."

"I'm sorry to kick you out, I don't have anywhere else to go..."

"I'm not sure I do either," said Lisette thoughtfully. "I was supposed to ask Paul but then I forgot. I have another friend Ray who I dog sit for when he's out on his boat, but I don't want to stay at his place when he's actually home. He keeps trying to hit on me, you know?"

I nodded warmly, pretending I had my own dog-sitting sexual harassment problems. This was my first introduction to Lisette's chaotic energy. She has a tendency to bound around the room like an untethered electron, but she is nearly impossible to dislike. I watched as she dragged a large Army/Navy style duffle bag out of the bedroom and plopped it into the middle of the living room floor.

"All my stuff fits in one sack, don't worry," she said, her slim neck hunched as she rolled up a pair of jeans. "I had to leave my boyfriend in a hurry a few years ago, and since then I've kept stuff really compact. Not that I had a lot to begin with. I had six older brothers and sisters. My whole childhood was hand-me-downs. Do you ever watch those shows where the lady has a walk-in closet just for her shoes? That's my dream."

I nodded. "I think I'd need a house first."

"You and me both. Once I pack, I'll call Paul. He'll let me stay with him. Unless his mother is staying with him, but I think she's gone home. She was there for a couple of weeks. Can you imagine your mother coming to stay and not leaving for weeks? Not that my mom would, my mom was great. Until she died."

"I know what you mean." I thought of my mother who had never showed up on my doorstep mostly because she couldn't be bothered to travel that far. Two hours on a bus to New York was two hours when she wouldn't be chatting up single men at her favorite bar.

"I'll pull the sheets in the bedroom and then you can settle in there and I'll take care of cleaning the rest of the apartment."

I looked around. "Actually, do you know where I could get a cup of coffee? I really just need a coffee. I can bring you back one if you like."

Lisette put down the pile of clothes she was carrying and looked straight at me. "I make the best coffee."

A few minutes later, I was seated at the dining table with a mug of coffee that said, 'I don't spit, I swallow' on it in a gleeful comic font. Lisette did not make the 'best coffee,' but it was very drinkable, and it put me in a much better mood. I finally had a chance to take in my new apartment as Lisette wandered around picking up random items. There was the living room with a distant view of the main harbor, a small comfy sofa and some hanging plants on what looked like fishing net baskets. The kitchen area formed the center of the apartment, with pale wood cabinets and a bright blue counter that opened up into the living room space. The bathroom was a tiny closet with a minia-ture shower, small enough to compete with some of my New York tenement apartments, tucked into the hallway near the front door, and the back of the house was made up of the large bedroom, which would be pleasant and bright once Lisette had finished her whirlwind of cleaning.

"So Paul is your...?" I asked politely.

"Paul's the best," Lisette replied as she walked by with a toothbrush. "And he has way more space now that his wife left him. He's in my improv group."

I said nothing. I knew from my college years that as soon as you inquired about somebody's improv group, you would imme-diately get invited to a show, so it was best to feign temporary hearing loss.

"You should come to one of our shows!" she cried, unprompted. "We're really good. We're called the Newfingers."

"That's fun."

"Paul's the best one of us, but Mark's pretty good, too." She rattled on about the strengths and weaknesses of these two men whom I had no intention of meeting, let alone watching on some tiny stage doing prop comedy about their sexual misadventures. I wasn't paying strict attention by this point. She had cleared out the bedroom, so I walked inside to start arranging my stuff.

"Those sheets come with the apartment!" she called, referencing the pile on the floor. "I'll wash them in the basement."

"I can get the wash started."

Lisette stuck her head in the bedroom. "Sure, that'd be great. Just don't let Mrs. Mahoney bother you."

"Charlotte told me."

"She acts like she owns the building, but the washer and dryer are for both apartments."

"I'll get these sheets going."

I walked downstairs with the sheets knotted up in one hand to find the basement doorway. Sure enough, the first-floor apartment door was cracked open, and a pair of blue eyes peered out at me with the flat stare of a hired assassin. When I turned to say hello, the door shut again. That must be Mrs. Mahoney, destined to be my nemesis. I'd had neighbors like that in New York, so I wasn't too intimidated; I could probably turn on my Brooklyn charm and bring her around to tolerating me. It was a skill I had learned from years of apartment living: the key was to ignore any hostile behavior directed toward you and ask them for advice about the neighborhood food.

When I arrived back at the top of the stairs, I could hear Lisette on her phone, and I paused to listen through the door.

"No, I understand. I—Paul, I totally understand. I'll find something. It's no big deal." I waited for her to end the call before coming inside. Lisette turned to me, a forced smile on her face.

"Paul can't take me for a couple of days," Lisette said. "I can call my church, though. There's lots of old ladies there with empty rooms, and they're bored now that their Haitian refugee family moved to Gander. Someone should be able to take me in. I'll be this week's arts and crafts project in the basement."

"Okay," I said, then added impulsively, "or you could stay. On the sofa, I mean. If you need to. If it's really just for a couple of days."

"Not really?" Lisette gaped at me.

"I mean, if you don't mind me having the bedroom…"

"No, of course. That would be incredible. Paul can take me, just not until Tuesday. And I work in a coffee shop. I can bring you really good muffins at the end of the day."

"I love muffins. I think we have a deal," I said.

"That will give me time to talk to the women at the church, too."

Later that night, sitting in the bedroom without a functioning lock, I wondered if I was insane to let a stranger stay with me whom I had only just met. I was probably lonely, with Laura away. But I also liked Lisette. I sensed in her stories something like the chaos from my own childhood, the quick moves where your stuff went into a duffel bag, the inability to keep track of times and dates. It sounded more familiar than I wanted it to be.

THE NEXT MORNING, I woke up to light pouring into my eyes and reminded myself that this far north the sunrise would be insultingly early. I stumbled up out of Charlotte's comfortable bed and wandered over to the back window. As soon as I opened it, there was the faint smell of fish and cow manure. I tried to tell myself it was romantic, that it meant I was in some remote, lonely corner of the world where my horizons would be broadened and my soul renewed. This was likely to be more convincing once I'd had my first cup of coffee.

I shuffled into the living room, where I saw that Lisette had rolled herself into a perfect cocoon on the sofa.

"Sorry," I whispered, as I began to putter around the kitchen looking for coffee-making ingredients. She sat up almost immediately and gave me a tired smile.

"Let me!" she cried. "I don't mind at all. I'll show you how it's done."

"In the meantime, I'm going to stumble over to the eastern windows and glare at the sun for a bit. It rose at least half an hour earlier than in Brooklyn and I'm feeling resentful."

Lisette laughed. "You can scold it for me, too," she said. "It's like that friend who always tries to convince you to go running."

LISETTE and I made a good couple of days of it, as it turned out. She was away most of the time at the café where she worked, but when she was home, she was careful about being quiet when she came in, especially if she saw that I was on a video call for work.

"Did he just say, 'Good-bye, rock star'?" she asked me after I got off a work call with Kedar.

"That's my boss. Corporate people talk like that."

"They call each other rock stars?"

I laughed. "Kedar is very, very positive. Everyone he works with is the best. Everything we're doing is amazing. Every article I write is a home run. It lets us both pretend we're not working in finance, which is an incredibly boring industry."

"I want someone to call me a rock star."

"First you have to hit some home runs," I said.

"Maybe that's my problem. No home runs."

"Are you kidding?" I said. "You just worked a full day at a café. Did anyone spit out their coffee in front of you?"

"No."

"Did customers complain to your manager?"

"Nobody does that here."

"Did you get into a fistfight with the guy delivering the milk?"

"No."

"You just hit a home run, Lisette. Gold star."

She laughed. "Americans are crazy."

"I am not arguing with that, but corporate people are especially crazy."

Later, as she headed to bed, I said, "Good night, rock star."

"Good night, rock star," she called back, laughing. It already felt like we were better friends than we were. I suspected Lisette had that effect on people.

THE NEXT DAY, my best friend Jasmine called me up. Jasmine, Lucas and I had been brunch buddies for over a decade. We were all in our late thirties, all perpetually single, and we managed to have a good time pretending to be fabulous while debating the life choices of characters on TV shows.

"Hey, Chica," she sang out. Jasmine has one of those voices that can turn a two-syllable word into a Mariah Carey song. "How is the 'New Found Land'? Are they having a lot of July 4th festivities?"

"Shockingly, no, given that it's not their Independence Day. I guess July 1st is Canada day, but I arrived late enough that I missed any parades."

"That seems unfair."

"Somehow, I'll pull through without an evening spent

wondering whether that's fireworks or gunshots for six hours straight."

"But you like it there? Lucas said he thinks you're doing some kind of cleanse."

Lucas, Jasmine and I had gone out for drinks together when I told them I was leaving, and he had stared at me in silence for a few moments when I mentioned Newfoundland and then immediately pulled out his Google maps app to remind himself where it was.

"What am I supposed to be cleansing in this scenario?" I asked.

"Urban life," she replied.

"I'm literally in a city."

"Not a real city. St. John's is the size of Hartford, Connecticut, isn't it? No one ever says, *I'm going into the city* and means Hartford."

"Well, tell Lucas I am cleansing all my negativity and I'll come back in a Live Laugh Love t-shirt, carrying a golden retriever puppy that I've named Chastity."

"We can't be friends anymore if you do that, you know that, right?" I laughed, but there was some truth to it. We spent an awful lot of our time together venting. "So," she went on, "is it like Prince Edward Island? That's my one reference. I'm picturing you in a white farmhouse, wearing a wicker hat and reciting poetry."

"Just add tanker ships and a lively bar scene and you've nailed it."

"Have you met Gilbert Blythe?"

"Definitely not."

"Justin Trudeau is hot," Jasmine said thoughtfully. "And Ryan Reynolds and Ryan Gosling. That's it. That's my entire knowledge of Canadian men. I know nothing about Newfoundland."

"It's an island."

"See, the only islands I know are in the Caribbean."

"Well, the food is expensive here. So I guess that's one thing all islands have in common."

"Tell me when you're home so we can start planning things again."

One of the things I liked about Jasmine was that our primary relationship was in person. She wasn't one of those people who stayed in touch via Facebook or Instagram. She actually wanted to see people and give them hugs and get meals together. The flip side was that she didn't quite know what to do with our relationship now that I couldn't meet up.

"I'll let you know," I said. "And I'll let you know if I sleep with Justin Trudeau."

"I would fly up to meet him. That's something I would do for you, so let me know if you need that from me. Gotta go, I'm trying this new artisanal yogurt place with Lucas."

"Artisanal yogurt?"

"It's going to be so disgusting, but I have to prove that to Lucas because he's convinced that probiotics will turn his life around. When did gut flora become our new excuse for depression? I thought we were still blaming it on our parents. Okay, he's calling me from downstairs, love you, bye…" And her voice trailed away again.

I ACTUALLY GOT a fair amount of work done, sitting curled up by the window with my wi-fi and my laptop, watching the container ships moving in and out of the harbor. It was fun when Lisette came home and we ordered dinner together, and she made good on her promise of day-old muffins from the café where she worked.

It was on our final morning together that she told me the

story of her duffel bag break-up. He had been her first serious boyfriend, and she was with him from the time she was sixteen to the time she was twenty-five. He didn't start out violent, she said, but things escalated when they moved in together after she graduated from high school. First, he separated her from her family to run a Christmas tree farm way up on a logging road in Quebec. Then he started to get abusive, and her family tried to get her away, and in response, he moved them both to Newfoundland—to a small town up the coast—where he thought he could completely isolate her since her English wasn't very good.

"Little did he know I was picking up tons of good English from watching *Orange is the New Black*."

By the end, she wasn't allowed to leave the house or speak to anyone or use the phone, until one day, when he was at work, she packed up her only bag and hitched a ride from a trucker heading to St. John's. She had been living out of a suitcase ever since, afraid to establish a permanent address in case he was able to use the internet to track her down.

"Lisette. That's awful."

"Well, you know, I learned a lot about Christmas trees, anyway." She grinned brightly. "So I ended up at the Catholic church here because I'm Catholic, you know, so I figured they had to take me, and they got me to a shelter, and they've looked after me since. And the old ladies at the church like to feed me, which is nice. And then Paul helped, once I met him. He and I worked together at a summer restaurant job for a little bit, until I got fired, but then we started the improv group together."

"Did you ever think about going home to your family?"

"My ex would look for me there. I email pretty often with one of my sisters and she says he has come by a couple of times asking about me. But eventually I think I just have to legally change my name and start living like a grown-up again. Rent an apartment and all that. I was never really on my own, so it's been a lot to figure out. Credit cards and bank accounts and all these things. This is why I'm bad with dates and times. I spent a long time where it didn't matter what day of the week it was. Anyway. Enough about him, eh?"

"Well, I'm glad I got to meet you. And I'm going to miss having you around here," I said. "If you need to stay another day or two—"

"No, no," Lisette said. "Paul is happy to take me in now that he has the space. He's been all alone since his divorce. And he doesn't hit on me, which is nice. He's one of the good ones, you know?"

"Maybe I will come to your next improv show."

It popped out of my mouth before I could stop myself. Lisette has that effect on people.

"Paul's coming by tonight," Lisette said. "So you'll get to meet him. He's the best."

BEFORE I MET PAUL, I had a very specific image in my head of what he would be like: some goofy improv guy in a band t-shirt who precisely matched Lisette's wild energy, the kind of guy who made dick jokes on stage and hadn't been able to hold a steady job because of his weed habit. As soon as Paul knocked on our door that night, I realized I'd gotten him very wrong.

Paul was tall, thin, and clean-shaven, and he wore a navy wool peacoat that made him look like an 1850s sea captain, or just like someone who might actually read books that weren't sports biographies. He smiled politely at me as he stepped in the open door, looking around as Lisette ushered him inside. She had been sitting by the window for half an hour waiting for him, and then she had rushed downstairs to let him in as soon as she saw his car.

Now she introduced us. "Abigail, this is Paul. Paul, Abby is the angel from Brooklyn who let me sleep on her sofa the last couple of days."

"It's what we do in Brooklyn," I said.

He looked me over with a smile, then walked up and shook my hand. "Thanks for taking in the stray."

"It was an extortion racket to get free muffins."

"Abby is going to come to one of our shows!" Lisette cried.

Paul looked at me, seeming to read my real thoughts about improv comedy in spite of what I thought was a convincing smile.

He chuckled and leaned over to say into my ear, "It won't be as bad as you think, I promise."

Was he flirting with me? No. He liked Lisette, surely.

"I'm sure it'll be great," I said.

"No, you're not. But we'll convince you." My heart sped up from how near he was standing, which felt ridiculous because Paul was so emphatically not my type. He didn't look cynical or world-weary. He looked cheerful and organized and polite. If Lisette hadn't mentioned his divorce, I would have assumed he had a wife at home, holding a beautiful baby in one arm and a charcuterie board in the other.

Lisette walked up to us. "I'm going to miss you. We have to hang out, yeah?"

"I'd love to. We'll meet up for sure."

"Okay. You have my cell number, right?"

"You keep texting me memes, so I must." Lisette sometimes got bored at work and had been sending me gratitude memes that started out earnest and quickly turned extremely silly.

"And now I'll get out of here and you can finally have some peace and quiet," she said.

Paul was picking up Lisette's massive duffel bag. He walked

over to the door. "Anything else, Lisette? Anything you may have forgotten?"

"That's it," said Lisette. "My whole life is in that bag."

Paul nodded, a quick flash of grimness on his face revealing that he knew Lisette's history too.

Lisette gave me a massive hug, then turned to Paul. "We have to show her around. She's only here for two months and she doesn't have a car. So you'll have to drive her around and show her the whole province."

Paul caught my eye. "Sounds like I'll have to."

"Alright," Lisette said to me, "I'm finally out of your hair, as promised, and you can have the whole apartment all to yourself!"

"You can stay for a cup of tea or—"

"Nope, I'm going! It's American Independence Day, and you're finally freeeeee!" Lisette turned and dashed down the stairs.

"Bye, rock star!" I called after her.

"Bye, rock star!" she called up at me.

I turned to see Paul smiling at me, a funny expression on his face.

"Well..." he began. I felt it, right then, the sense that he definitely found me attractive. It was something in his eyes— amused, wary.

"It was nice to meet you," I said, trying to sound bright and cheerful instead of like a city-dweller who was terrified of being alone.

"It was great of you to do this for her."

"My pleasure. She's lovely."

"Yeah." He smiled ruefully and I felt suddenly afraid that I was misreading him. Was he secretly in love with Lisette, and that was the source of his half-hopeful, half-wary expression?

Then he nodded and took the door handle. "See you soon, Abigail." And he turned and left.

THAT NIGHT, I had a video call with Laura, who had begun to unpack as soon as her moving van finally arrived from New York. She seemed cheerful as she held up her camera and walked around the small house that Nick had rented for them in Atlanta. She showed me where Hannah was reading on a little twin bed, all curled up in pajamas after a bath. Hannah waved to me and blew lots of kisses, and we promised to video chat for longer when Hannah was not supposed to be going to sleep. Then Laura showed me where Nick was working in his 'recording studio'—a small, repurposed office downstairs. Nick turned and gave me a half-hearted wave before going back to restringing a guitar. I knew I couldn't manage much more than a half-smile, but I gave it with as much warmth as I could manage.

Then Laura walked back upstairs, entered her bedroom and closed the door.

"So, how are things really going?" I asked her.

"Fine!" Her brightness seemed to require some effort, but maybe that was my wishful thinking. "Just fine. We're still getting used to everything. Hannah is taking swim lessons because there are so many pools down here. Her doggy-paddling won't quite do it anymore."

"And how are you?"

"Good, good. Just started looking for work down here."

"And Nick?"

"We're easing into it. But it's going well. Things are fine, Abs. Why don't you tell me about Newfoundland?"

"Well, this is my apartment," I said, waving the phone in a slow circle. I had decided not to tell her about my decision to take in a tiny blonde woman for a couple of days. "Here, look at the view. I can see the waterfront."

It was sunset, and a vibrant pink ray of light shot out below the clouds.

"That's beautiful, Abs."

"Yeah, well, Canada's got a lot of the natural beauty. That's what they say in the brochures."

"You're not actually going to move there, though, right?"

I hesitated, swinging the phone back toward my face. "I would have to look into visas and everything, but I could."

Laura said nothing. Then she said, "I just think it would be lonely."

"I've made a few friends already. They're in an improv comedy troupe."

"Good God."

"I know." I laughed. "These are the kinds of things that happen to me when I leave the borders of Brooklyn. I may even go to one of their shows."

"Are you okay? No one has indoctrinated you, right? Blink twice if someone's forcing you to learn to unicycle and start wearing pageboy caps."

"This is just an experiment," I said, feeling tempted to add, 'like your life is right now,' but I didn't. No point in starting a fight.

"We miss you," said Laura.

"I miss you, too."

After we got off the phone, I had a horrible thought. What if everything worked out perfectly with Nick? Would I move to Atlanta? Or lose them forever?

4

"IT'S A TRICK WE
PLAY ON TOURISTS"

AFTER LISETTE LEFT to go stay with her handsome friend Paul, I spent the next couple of days entertaining myself by trying to figure things out about Charlotte, the woman I was subletting from, based strictly on her apartment.

Number one: she had a series of artsy photos of boats from somewhere called Makkovik, which I looked up. It's an Inuit town, so I'm guessing that's where she's from. Makkovik is on the coast of Labrador, which is a spectacularly beautiful part of the Canadian mainland that is part of the same governmental province as Newfoundland. My guess is that she came to St. John's for work or college or a crush on a fisherman and decided to stay.

Number two: she really likes Ben Affleck. Her movie collection is eight DVDs shoved in a drawer, and three of them are Ben Affleck movies: *Good Will Hunting*, *Argo*, and *The Town*. I would not be surprised if her fisherman boyfriend ends up being a dark-haired guy who looks like he could use a second shave by 9:30 in the morning.

Number three: she kills houseplants. She has a small collection of succulents that are barely hanging onto life, and a big pile of empty flowerpots under the kitchen sink that hint at previous losses, like she's some kind of horticultural Bluebeard. I don't think all that carnage could have happened under Lisette's watch, either. My guess is that Charlotte wants to be the kind of person who keeps plants healthy, but can't quite manage it, which I definitely relate to; I went through a decade trying to keep various plants alive through the dry, overheated winter in my New York apartments before I discovered the power of humidifiers. So I felt a wave of fellow feeling for Charlotte when I discovered her hidden graveyard.

Number four: she has a disproportionate amount of obscene, punny mugs. A 'Tits and Boobies' mug with various birds on it. (Get it, a tufted titmouse?) An 'I Spread for Nutella' mug with a drawing of Nutella on toast that manages to feel lascivious. A soap dispenser that says, 'Clean Hands, Dirty Mind.' I wonder how many of them are gifts. My bet is all of them, recalling my own birthdays in my twenties.

Number five: she is not a book reader, except for a couple of thriller novels in her bedroom: *The Pelican Brief*, Cormac McCarthy's *The Road*, *Gone Girl*. Wait a minute, didn't the *Gone Girl* movie have Ben Affleck?

I guess none of that really mattered, but it made me feel less lonely while I passed the time waiting for an improv show and an actual face-to-face conversation with other human beings. I was so lonely that I even thought about texting Lisette so I could stop by the coffee shop where she worked, but that seemed a little needy. This trip was supposed to be about figuring out who I was without my sister Laura, not seizing the first Laura-replacement that I found and hanging on for dear life.

I also did my second load of laundry and finally encountered Mrs. Mahoney in the flesh.

A few moments after I started the washer and was on my way upstairs, a wiry woman with short iron-grey hair opened her door on the first floor and said, without introduction, "You know that's very loud."

"Oh, I'm sorry." I gave my best good-neighbor smile. "If you let me know a convenient time for you when it won't be disturbing, I'll do it then."

"It's always too loud."

"Well, I'm sorry about that. Hey, do you know of any nice restaurants near here? I'm looking for a good place to order dinner."

"You're allowed to do laundry once a week, that's it."

"That's probably how often I'll do it."

"That's how often you're allowed to do it."

"Okay. Thanks for the help."

Mrs. Mahoney gave me a look. She hadn't offered me any help, so she wasn't sure how to respond. I smiled and headed upstairs. Take that, Mrs. Mahoney. I have dealt with too many New York neighbors with social anxiety or rage issues to be intimidated by one grumpy Canadian. I would woo and win her affection eventually; it was just a matter of time.

By the time Thursday rolled around, I was more excited than I should have been to be going to an improv show. The show was being held in a small music venue called the Puffin Hut down by the waterfront. I recognized the kind of place immediately when I walked in the door: the walls painted black, the small rack of ceiling pipes holding scant theatrical lighting pointed at a stage just large enough for a five-person garage band, the cafe tables with wobbly legs, easy enough to move aside for dance space, easy to slide back for a poetry reading. There were about thirty people in the crowd—not enough to fill the room, but not empty, either. I saw on the small hand-written poster for the evening that the Newfingers were wedged between a few other acts: someone named Lachlan Allen, someone named Raahid, and then someone I guessed was a singer named Amber Sorelli.

I was about to take my seat at one of the precarious little tables about ten feet from the stage, when Lisette spied me from where she'd been sitting in the corner and bounced over.

"You're here!" She made it sound like she'd spotted a celebrity.

"Yes, I made it!"

"Come sit with us!"

"Don't you have to get ready?"

"No. There's a folk musician up first. And anyway, the whole idea with improv is that you don't get ready. If you're thinking ahead, you're terrible."

A folk musician? Of course. Suffering through improv would not be enough to fill an evening; I was getting a full, multi-course meal of cringing in my chair. Lisette dragged me over to where she was sitting with Paul and introduced me to Mark, who was wearing an oversized checked shirt and holding a pint of beer. Mark looked me up and down once and raised his eyebrows.

"Where are you from?" he asked brusquely.

"Brooklyn."

"Brooklyn!" he replied. "What the hell are you doing all the way up here?"

"Plotting against the locals," I replied. Mark gave me a half-smile, but I got the sense that it slipped out of him unwillingly.

"Of course," he muttered.

Paul's eyes were on me when I sat down. "The plan is to be our nemesis, then?" he asked. I had that same odd feeling, like I could read him perfectly, like he was an old friend.

"You'll never be sure. That's half the fun."

"It's all fun and games until we're going over Reichenbach Falls together," he replied.

"Whichever one of us crawls back from certain death is the winner."

"Sounds like your marriage, Paul," Mark drawled.

Just then, a young man tapped the mic from the stage. He strummed his acoustic guitar and then adjusted the microphone height.

"Here we go," Paul said drily. "Good old Lachlan."

I turned to Paul. "You own all his albums, then?"

Paul chuckled. "Just my workout playlist."

The handsome young singer began speaking. "This is a story about a massacre of miners in 1931 by the Canadian government."

I met Paul's eyes, and he grinned again as the earnest young man began to sing about the union-busting Canadian Mounties. "Bodies falling one by one, Tumbling with the setting sun," the young man sang, emphasizing the tragedy with each chord. Poor Newfingers, having to leap to the stage after the world's most mournful history lesson.

"So that's a metaphor for getting laid, right?" I whispered.

Mark leaned over. "You think you're kidding, but he brings down the room and then manages to take home the hottest woman in the room, every time."

"I'll get my coat," I joked.

"Good God," Mark said to Paul. "Abigail here has a sense of humor. We usually don't get that in our audience members."

"It's a poor performer who blames their audience," Lisette chided.

"That applies in the bedroom, too, Mark," Paul added.

"Alright, alright." Mark waved his hand wearily.

"Excuse me, I'm a tough New York critic," I replied. "You guys better be good because my standards are extremely high."

"We're not afraid," Paul replied. "Bring on your judgment,

Moriarity." He grinned again as the next song began, and I felt my stomach drop.

Oh, no, I thought to myself. *I like him, and I'm about to watch him do improv. At least my crush will die a quick death.*

I was probably more nervous than anyone else in the room as Lachlan ended his set. Paul got up, hopped on stage, clapped his hands together, and thanked Lachlan for making everyone cry, which got a few chuckles from the room. He quickly introduced their group of three as Lisette bounded onstage and Mark stomped after her. Then Paul asked for stories from the audience.

"Can someone tell us how you met your best friend?" Paul began.

"Middle school," someone shouted.

"We were in jail together," somebody else said.

Paul paused. "What was your crime?"

"Drunk driving."

"Hmm, what else?"

"We worked together," someone cried.

"Where'd you work?" Paul asked the last person.

"Tim Horton's."

"Tim Horton's," Paul said. He glanced at the group. "We're doing it. Okay, and now we need a movie genre."

"Action!"

"Romantic comedy."

"Science fiction."

"Heist," I called out.

Paul smiled at me. "Heist movie. I met my best friend at Tim Hortons, the heist movie."

Lisette jumped onto stage and began to act out that she was making fries.

"We need more fries," she began, calling out behind her. "We're running low, and the lunch rush is coming."

Mark walked onto stage. "There are no fries," he said. "We're out."

It would be impossible to sum up the freeform ridiculousness of the next few minutes: how Lisette and Mark planned a heist together to steal potatoes from the local supermarket, how Paul stepped in as the detective on their trail, complete with some 1940s-style film noir narration, how Lisette imitated a scene from *Mission Impossible* in her theft, arms swinging out wildly as she leaned her whole body over a stool, how at the end, in jail, Mark and Lisette agreed that they were now best friends. They might be in prison forever, but the important thing was the journey. Even the audience member who had met their best friend in jail got a little callback.

I had been worried that I would be embarrassed the whole time, but I wasn't, because it turned out that Lisette is very, very funny. Watching her up there, I thought about how she'd spent ten years living with an abusive guy, suppressing everything about herself, and now she was being completely silly, open, willing to commit to everything with absolute dedication. It was impossible to be embarrassed for someone with that level of commitment. Everyone was laughing when she pulled her Tom-Cruise-on-a-wire impersonation, or when she tried to sweet-talk the detective by offering him free poutine for life. Paul was also funny, but in a more cerebral way, with the eye of a storyteller shaping the direction of the tale. He was the one who threw in movie references, literary jokes, committed reactions to whatever Lisette was doing. And Mark was the deadpan pessimist, ready to go dark whenever required.

After about twenty-five minutes and three sketches, they came back to the table and sat down. Paul caught my eye as he took a seat. He could tell I was impressed, so I tried to look grumpy but couldn't quite manage it.

"So what's the New York critic say?" he asked.

"You'll know when I write about it in the *Times* tomorrow."

"Better than you feared?"

I laughed. "Okay, the only improv I've seen was in college. Lots of cunnilingus jokes and Britney Spears references."

"Oh, we do those, too. If you'd just put in a request…"

"Next time," I said.

"So you're coming back, then?" he asked, grinning.

We quieted down as the next person got up, a Black stand-up comedian who gave a very funny set based on moving to Newfoundland from Uganda as a child. When he was done, he came and joined the table. Clearly, he and Paul knew each other, and Paul introduced him to me as Raahid while the final woman got up, another earnest folk singer named Amber.

"You were killing it, man," Paul quietly told Raahid as the singer tuned her guitar.

"Thank God for you guys…every time I go after Lachlan…" Raahid began.

"Oh, we're aware," Paul agreed.

"Look at that asshole," Mark muttered. We all glanced over and saw the folk singer seated at a table with three young women leaning in closely as he gave each of them looks full of world-weary longing.

"Unbelievable," Raahid agreed. "That mournful son of a bitch does better than anyone except you, Mark."

Mark shrugged. "I do alright."

"Are you kidding me? You get more girls than me and Lachlan put together."

I gave Mark a glance and then looked away, listening to Amber Sorelli's throaty alto singing. She wasn't bad. In fact she wrote the kind of music I liked best, filled with complex lyrics and catchy melodies. The only issue was that her songs had precisely one topic: she had clearly had the world's worst ex-boyfriend. Her ex sounded like a cross between singer-songwriter Ryan Adams and Charles Manson. Between songs, I whispered to Lisette, "If you tell me her ex-boyfriend is Lachlan, this will be so much better," and Lisette laughed so hard she snorted.

The show wrapped up a little after 9:30 p.m. because the space had to clear out for a band coming on at ten, and I found myself tumbling out onto the street with Raahid and the Newfingers, wandering up the hill to find another bar where we could drink and chat. It was a warm evening broken up by great gusts of wind, and Paul walked next to me, blocking the worst of it, though I couldn't be sure if he was doing it on purpose.

"So..." he began. "Why Newfoundland?"

"They told me there was good improv comedy here."

"Better than New York?"

"I was told the New Yorkers are all sellouts and this was the purest form of the craft."

"Oh, we're nothing if not pure," Paul said. "On stage at least."

That was flirting, I realized. He was definitely flirting with me.

Lisette ran up behind me and threw her arms around me. "Paul," she said, "where are we taking her this weekend? I have off on Sunday. We have to show her around."

"I guess we do," Paul agreed. "What do you want to see?"

"Anything," I said. "I'm a Newfoundland virgin."

Paul looked away, amused; it was fun to watch him deliberately not make a dirty joke. "Have you been down the coast at all?" he asked. "Witless Bay?"

"I have been to the Coleman's Market half a mile from my house, which is the extent of my travels."

"Well, it's a plan, then," Paul said. "We'll show you puffins. Newfoundland is famous for them."

"Brooklyn is famous for rats," I replied. "Your puffins better steal pizza and get into fist fights or they can't measure up."

Paul smiled. "I'll have to tell my students to get more of our puffins on TikTok."

"You teach?"

"I'm off for the summer, but yes, middle school history. How about you? Lisette said you're a writer."

"That's a nice way to put it. I write for a financial magazine. I used to be a journalist."

"And then you went for the big money?"

"Then I went for getting fired. But my current job does let me work from anywhere."

"And you picked here. Of all the places in the entire world."

"I threw a dart at a world map and then went with the place I could afford."

"See," Lisette said to Paul. "Didn't I tell you she was funny? We should ask her to come to improv practice sometime."

"Oh..." I began.

Paul smiled patiently at Lisette. "She doesn't want to join our improv group."

Lisette shook her head. "She'd be really good, though. I mean it, Abby. I'm totally serious."

"But she doesn't want to," Paul said.

Lisette pouted. "But the people who do want to are never, ever funny."

Paul gave me the wry smile I was starting to get to know well. He was waiting for me to make an excuse. He knew I'd say no, and he was waiting for me to let down Lisette. It reminded me of the way Laura had been certain I would never leave the country.

I met his eyes. "I mean, I could come to a practice."

Take that, Paul.

He nodded and looked away, his expression unreadable.

Was he upset? Why did I keep thinking I could read his thoughts?

"Unless you don't want me to," I said. "I was mostly kidding."

He looked at me, serious. "Of course we want you. Don't we, Mark?"

"What?"

"Can the tourist from Brooklyn come to improv practice sometime?"

"Of course!" Mark gave me a sharp glance.

"I talked her into it!" Lisette said.

"We need more women. I've got a very specific sketch in mind," Mark said.

"Oh, gross, Mark."

"That was your dirty mind," Mark said to her. "I just wanted to pass the Bechdel test for once. Or is that not important to you?"

Later that evening, I would wonder what I had been thinking. It wasn't just that I was starting to get a crush on Paul. It wasn't even that his doubts had annoyed me enough to say yes, or that I liked Lisette and had trouble letting her down. It was also that the very thought of doing improv comedy terrified me. It was silly, and I was starting to feel too old to be silly. It was also probably the only time in my life that anyone was ever going to invite me to do something like that again. Nobody in New York asked you to join anything after you turned thirty, aside from a book club where you brought expensive snacks and talked about a bestseller. Everything felt different up here. Nobody knew who I really was. Maybe I didn't have to know either.

When I said goodbye that evening a little after midnight, Lisette got up to give me a hug, and when I waved goodbye to the rest of the table, I could see Paul watching me with that same slightly rueful expression, like he already regretted something. I just wasn't sure what it was.

Tʜᴀᴛ Sᴜɴᴅᴀʏ, I saw the same expression when I opened the door for him at ten in the morning. He was in jeans and a grey t-shirt with a light windbreaker, looking slightly too put-together for a puffin sightseeing mission.

"So," he said, already apologetic. "Lisette just texted me. She has a church thing today."

"Oh no, all day?"

"Sounds like. I guess she forgot it was this particular Sunday."

"She does that. Forgets what day it is."

"Yeah." He rubbed a hand through his hair. "I think she's hoping one of the families will rent her a spare room. Not that it's a problem for me if she stays in my spare room for a while, but she doesn't want to do that indefinitely."

"I get it. That's not a great dynamic between friends." *Are you just friends?* I wondered.

"Yes, so anyway...It would just be you and me today. If that's okay with you." He gave me a little smile.

"I mean if you don't mind. If you have other things to do—"

"Well, I do mind, actually, as I have a lot of childhood trauma from puffins, but I'm willing to suffer."

"That's very noble of you."

"A noble sacrifice," he agreed. "Please take note of any particularly heroic things I might do along the way, like stopping for donuts."

He gestured to his car, which was a small green Mini Cooper. I started laughing as I got inside.

"Of course you'd have a Mini Cooper."

"What's wrong with a Mini?"

"You're too tall for a Mini. It's a short person car."

"That is not a short person car." Paul smirked. "If Jason Statham can drive one in *The Italian Job*..."

"That was Mark Wahlberg."

"It was Statham and Wahlberg and Charlize Theron. You do not want to go up against me on the Mini question."

I settled into the front seat.

"The Mini question?"

"The films. You've got *The Bourne* films, *Austin Powers*...the original *Italian Job* from 1969."

"I will admit that Michael Caine is tall."

"The other reason I have this is that my house relies on street parking, and it can be helpful to have something that can squeeze between the two incompetent neighbors who take up half the street."

"Say no more. I have vicarious trauma from watching my sister once try to fit a full-sized car into a space big enough for a motorcycle in Brooklyn."

Paul took off down the road with surprising speed, as if to make his point that his car was flashy and cool. Once we'd driven a few blocks and were emerging from the downtown area onto the highway, he glanced at me.

"So..."

"Why Newfoundland?" I guessed.

"You never actually answered. Unless you want me to believe there is no good improv in New York City."

"I hate hot weather," I said. "And honestly, I was thinking of maybe leaving the United States for good, so I did this as a...a dare to myself. My sister moved to Atlanta, and I'd been watching her daughter four days a week, so suddenly I was free to go anywhere."

"That was nice of you. To watch your niece."

"I didn't mind. Hannah's a great kid. But it was a shock

when they left because I guess my life revolved around them. I got used to having no kids because Hannah was like my kid, and then suddenly they just..." I hesitated, wondering if I was admitting too much. "Though I don't know if they'll stay in Atlanta. She's trying to work things out with her ex, and he's not reliable. I may have to dash back home and take care of her unexpectedly when it all falls apart."

"So why did you leave the States? Why not just move to a different city?"

"I'm running from the law." I grinned.

"Murder I assume?"

"Murder, armed robbery, credit card fraud..."

"So a typical weekend in Brooklyn."

"Well, we do get brunch first."

He continued to look at me, and I knew he was waiting for a real answer.

"I guess...I mean...it just seemed like I needed a change. Not that everything isn't perfect at home. You Canadians can tell that by watching our news."

"Of course." He nodded. "Honestly, I thought about moving to the States from time to time. I used to love Westerns as a kid. That's what I'm hoping to do later this summer, maybe. Go there for a trip. Arizona, Wyoming..."

"You're going to go to Arizona in August?"

"I know it'll be hot."

"And full of rich retirees and golf courses."

"Well, don't ruin the surprise."

"Some of it is pretty," I said. "But in August?"

"I'm tougher than I look."

I swallowed a joke about how he looked, because I couldn't think of one that didn't reveal anything. We stopped for donuts and then drove down the coast to Witless Bay, which was a spectacular stretch of the coastline with an ecological reserve that was mostly accessible by boat.

"The best views can be seen by boat," Paul said. "So I hope you're ready for a boat trip."

"I get kind of queasy on boats."

"Oh, no, really? You should have said something."

"I'm a terrible traveler. Carsickness, too. But I'll give it a try. I should be alright if it's not too choppy."

Half an hour later, Paul and I were on a two-hour boat trip around the bay on a small tourist boat with about twenty other puffin enthusiasts. He insisted on buying the tickets, and I tried hard to studiously ignore that I was effectively on a date with an attractive man who was recently divorced, according to Lisette's intel.

"So you're not married or anything, I take it?" I finally asked as we were leaning over the railing together.

"No," Paul said to the horizon. "Divorced. Six months ago. I'm surprised Lisette didn't tell you."

"Why does that surprise you?"

"Because Lisette likes to celebrate the demise of my marriage. They weren't close. My wife left me for a TV producer who came through town."

"Oh, no."

Paul shrugged. "He was in town for two months doing a show for the CBC, and she was working on it as a freelance editor and uh...fell for him. Picked up and moved to Vancouver. So..."

"So you can't watch the CBC with quite as much enthusiasm."

He laughed a little. "And how about you? No husband either?"

"No husband, no boyfriend."

"That's who you murdered, presumably, before fleeing the States."

"My last boyfriend? I wish." I thought of Farid, and then I thought of Colin, who was technically my last boyfriend. Farid had made me miserable, and Colin had made me so ashamed that I didn't even talk about him. Not to Laura. Not to anyone.

"Murder would have been a much more satisfying end to things," I went on. "No, Farid left me for the person he'd been cheating on me with. And then married her, after years of telling me he didn't believe in marriage, philosophically. He was against the whole concept of marriage until he met someone he actually wanted to marry."

"We'll have to get him together with my ex. Sounds like they would click." Paul smiled.

"What happened with her? If you don't mind talking about it."

He shrugged. "When we met, we were both actors in Toronto. And then I moved here to take care of my father, and eventually got a teaching job, and she came out here to help start a small advertising firm her friend was running, so it seemed to make sense to get back together. And then I guess our lives got really boring."

"What? In cool, happening St. John's?"

"The guy she left me for travels around Canada doing documentary-style stuff. He's in Vancouver one week and Banff the next. And they apparently vacation in Spain and St. Barts."

"He sounds insufferable."

He laughed. "I was thinking that would sound normal to someone from New York. Jet setting around."

"I do jet-set around the F train a bit." I considered. "But New York is actually really hard in that way," I said.

"What way?"

I blushed. I realized I was thinking of dating, and that probably wasn't where Paul's mind was. Would he think I was hitting on him? I tried to sound casual. "Well, for dating. It's hard to find people."

"I would think it would be the opposite," Paul offered.

"There are dating apps, and bars, and so on, but by the time you're in your thirties... It's like with the dating apps," I said. "Everyone you go on a date with knows that there are hundreds of other options aside from you, so if things aren't working out, everyone can cut their losses without putting any effort in. And eventually it starts to be like no one is really trying to get to know anyone. I went on a date with a guy, and ten minutes into it, he said, 'Well, I'm not feeling this, are you?' And I said, 'Uh...' And he said, 'Let's cut this short, then.' And he got up and left."

"What? He left?"

I shrugged. "No point in wasting time."

Paul looked outraged on my behalf. "I can't believe that. And with you?" Now I definitely felt myself flushing, so I looked out over the water.

I shrugged. "And if I am what somebody wants, he's bitter and damaged by his horrible divorce."

Paul looked down.

"I didn't mean you!" I cried. "Not at all, honestly. You don't seem bitter at all."

He shrugged. "I have moments."

"Well, you are a million times more pleasant than the guys I've been meeting in New York."

"Pleasant," he said. "Excellent."

I opened my mouth. "No, I..." I trailed off. I wasn't sure this was a date. It wasn't a date, was it? He hadn't asked me on one.

He looked down, a ghost of an ironic smile crossing his lips. "Speaking of pleasant," Paul said, "time to scour the puffin population for viral video material."

I turned to look over the side of the boat where the tourists were gathering. Ahead of us was a hillside with literally hundreds of puffins. They were individually very cute, but the effect of so many was a bit stunning, especially after the nature deficit of New York City. I had expected I might see ten or twenty birds, but this was a giant colony, fluttering wings and calling out and jumping into the water.

"They are so ridiculously cute," I said.

"Are they giving the Brooklyn rats a run for their money?"

"Not in sheer numbers. But they may have the edge because they aren't trying to run across my sandals."

"Whale!" came a cry from the other side of the boat. And the crowd of tourists rushed over just in time to see a large whale breaching from the water and then returning with a splash.

The boat ride turned into a whale watch, as the captain turned the boat to get us closer to a small pod of humpback whales. It was dazzling to watch the giant, beautiful creatures. It also took all of five minutes for me to feel ill as we crossed into the choppier water further out in the bay.

"I may need to sit down," I said, and found a space on a bench inside the boat.

Paul came and sat next to me.

"No, no, no," I told him. "There are whales. Go watch them. They're frolicking."

"I've seen whales," he said. "I haven't seen nearly as many seasick tourists."

I laughed and then felt worse.

He looked me over. "Do you know all the tricks for seasick-ness? Look at the horizon. Don't look inside the boat. Deep breaths. Don't go into small, enclosed spaces. Do you want me to find a wristband?"

"A wristband?"

"You put pressure on your pulse point on your wrist." He

put his hand around my wrist. "Some people think it relieves seasickness, but it may just be the placebo effect." He looked at his hand on my wrist and held it firmly. I looked up at him, thinking that he had very lovely brown eyes, and that I wished I didn't want to die quite so much because I could enjoy this more. He met my eyes, and his expression went very still. There was a moment when I was sure he wanted to kiss me, and then he gave a quick, internal smile and an almost imperceptible shake of his head, like he was dismissing me or his feelings. It killed me that I didn't know which one it was, that I couldn't tell whether he was thinking, 'Abby will never like me,' or 'I will never like Abby.' It made me want to kiss him, just to settle the issue one way or the other, but he was already back to his polite cheer.

"I'll look around for a wristband," he said briskly, standing up. I gazed at the place where he'd put his hand on my wrist. It still felt warm. He must be one of those people who still had warm hands even after clutching the sides of a boat for an hour.

He came back with a small rubber bracelet from the boat crew. "Put this on."

I looked at the bracelet and rolled it onto my wrist. "I feel like I'm in an aerobics video from 1985."

"That's good," Paul said. "Nobody ever gets sick in aerobics videos."

I smiled and then felt queasy again, so I did my very best to focus on the horizon and not get sick off the side of the boat. A few minutes later, though, it was too much, and I rushed to the very tiny boat toilet while Paul stood outside it, waiting for me.

"That is a tiny toilet."

"It's called the head."

"What now?"

"The toilet in a boat."

"What I just did gives the phrase giving head new meaning."

He opened his mouth to reply, didn't.

"You do this thing," I said. "You look like you're going to make the world's dirtiest joke, and then you stop yourself."

"I'm trying to be a nice, well-behaved Canadian."

"Is that why you took me on a boat tour? Because I'm pretty sure this was a torture technique."

He looked apologetic as he led me back to a seat outside in the back of the boat. "I'm genuinely sorry."

"Not at all. I'm having fun, in between the vomiting. I promise."

By the time I stepped off the boat, I was a bit unsteady, and Paul gently held my elbow to make sure I didn't fall.

"I'm feeling very guilty. How do I make it up to you?"

"I'm easygoing. I just need your firstborn child and access to your bank account."

He grinned. "You could do better than either of those things. I don't know when a firstborn child will be on the offer. How about a classroom full of restless thirteen-year-olds? I don't think their parents would miss them."

"That's another torture technique, isn't it."

"You caught me."

He looked ready to apologize again, so I cut him off. "You know I'm teasing, right? I had a great time. I saw puffins and whales. I'm just a little disappointed that neither one was eating pizza."

"I guess it may not be the right time to ask if you want lunch."

"I will want lunch, sometime in the future. I can conceive of wanting lunch at some point before I die."

. . .

I BOUGHT Paul a thank you lunch at a little local seafood restaurant. Over lunch, he told me about his love for school teaching, which he'd been doing for four years, and how he originally studied acting in college and had tried his hand as an actor for a few years in Toronto before returning to Newfoundland to help care for his father, who was dying of cancer. Since then, he'd been helping his mother to navigate life on her own.

"It seemed like the right thing to do, but I also started building a life here. Trish was…my ex… I felt bad, because I was half the reason she came to St. John's in the first place. It's not glamorous, compared to some other places."

"I know people who lead glamorous lives," I said. "They spend half their mornings with their head in a toilet and the other half asking their therapists whether anyone *really* likes them or just their Bombardier jet."

Paul shrugged. "Anyway. My wife found it boring."

"Or she found herself boring," I said, "and went off looking to escape herself."

Something flickered in Paul's eyes, but I couldn't read it. The same look. "So tell me about your work," he said after a moment.

"Speaking of boring," I said. And I told him about my financial writing job, and about my previous job as a journalist working for a fancy magazine.

"For a while, I specialized in interviewing very wealthy people about how they were getting their kids into college, or how they paid their nannies under the table. Illicit stuff, the rule-bending that goes into fancy people getting their way. It was morally abhorrent but really fun to read about. And for some reason I could get people to confess to all sorts of things, off the record. They liked talking to me. But then my love life went downhill, and I stopped being able to get people to share with me. I guess I sounded too cynical on the phone, which was a vicious cycle, because the closer I came to being fired, the more grumpy I got, and the fewer people I could convince to share their dirty secrets."

Paul smiled. "I bet you were a formidable interviewer."

"Want me to grill you about your darkest secrets and you can find out?"

"I'm an open book."

"Not with that many dirty jokes floating around your brain." I smiled at him, and he looked out the window again, holding something back. "What was the dirty joke you were going to say on the boat?"

He flushed a little, embarrassed. "I was just going to say I was sure you gave excellent head."

"There," I said. "Was that so hard?"

He laughed. "Technically, being hard would be the point, there."

Neither of us looked at each other for the next minute or two, but I was flushed and grinning and I had a feeling he was, too.

PAUL DROVE us slightly too fast up the coast on the way back north. I had heard once that people's real personality came out when they were driving, and Paul seemed more assertive, more confident behind the wheel of a car than he was the rest of the time. He told me we were going to make one more stop at Cape Spear National Lighthouse, the easternmost point in North America.

"If that's okay," he added.

"Of course. As long as this is another noble sacrifice."

"Always. I'm having a terrible time." He gave me a warm look and then glanced back at the road.

We found a place in the small parking lot, which was mostly

empty. At the end of a grassy bluff was a beautiful white light-house, set high up on cliffs. We had to shout at each other as we walked toward it, buffeted by the wind.

"Please don't fall off!" Paul cried. "Lots of paperwork I'd have to fill out."

"No promises. I sometimes get sudden whims to run off cliffs. Did I forget to tell you that?"

"It slipped your mind."

"Well, you'll just have to hope for the best! Oh wait…the impulse is coming upon me…"

"Right now?"

"I want to fly, Paul! I think I can fly!"

I dashed a few steps forward, and he raced to catch up with me and grabbed at my arm, swinging me around.

"Please don't," he said. "My heart can't take it. I'm a schoolteacher. I spend too much time around kids who might actually do it."

"What about following your impulses? Isn't that big in improv comedy?"

"This is why we don't do improv next to a cliff. Lisette would go right over, but it would get a big laugh."

"Audience engagement would reach an all-time high."

"This is the New York cynicism I was expecting."

"I'm always New York cynical," I replied. "It's why I'm thirty-seven and alone."

He raised his eyebrows and said nothing. Now he knew my age, so that should put some distance between us. Thirty-seven was the age at which you really did start to wonder if you were broken, and if you didn't wonder, the men around you did, pointing it out to you on first dates. I looked away from his gaze and toward the water, thinking that this was where the first ships would have come across the ocean from Europe. The day was clear, and the ocean was frilled with white-capped waves that crashed onto some unseen shore below us. When the wind died down for a moment, we could hear seagulls in the distance. I caught his eye, feeling briefly like we were in a movie together.

"So, Newfoundland," I said. "You do a nice job hiding this place."

"Wait until winter. That's when you'll find out what it's really like here."

"If I stay that long."

He nodded to himself.

On the drive back, I was silent for a long time, waiting for him to say something, watching the flicker of thoughts crossing his face. I kept making the same mistake, I thought. I kept thinking I could read him.

"So why improv comedy?" I said at last, managing to make my voice sound more cheerful than I felt.

He glanced at me and shrugged. "I did improv a bit in college, a couple of classes," he said. "And then when I met Lisette...she came to work in this restaurant I was working at over the summer. I usually work a summer job, but this year I've been dealing with some divorce stuff, but anyway. Lisette worked with me for a few weeks, and we really clicked, but she had trouble keeping track of her schedule and the manager eventually fired her. But we stayed in touch, and I thought—I guess I thought it would be good for her. And me. I missed acting. I was afraid I would turn into one of those middle school teachers who acts out historical events for their students just so I can have an audience."

"Your students would love it if you brought in a sword."

"They do enough damage to each other with pencils. Anyway, I hoped it would give Lisette somewhere to channel her energy, and it seems to have worked. She hasn't lost another job since we started the Newfingers."

"You really care about her."

He nodded slowly. "Yeah, I do."

"So the two of you…if you hadn't been married at the time, would you have…"

"Oh, no. I couldn't date Lisette. I don't think that's what she needs right now, anyway. I think she needs people who want her to be healthy and safe."

"You're a really good person," I said.

"Oh, no," he said, grimacing. "The death sentence."

"I'm saying you're amazing and you're turning it into an insult?"

He shrugged. "I'm just like everybody else, only secretly much, much better." He was smiling.

"I think you may be, though. You took me on a boat trip, and you definitely didn't have to do that."

"That's a prank we play on visitors to see if we can make them sick."

"To keep them from falling in love with this place?"

"Exactly right. Have to keep those property values low." He looked out of the car window and didn't say anything for a moment.

He pulled up his car in front of my rental apartment and got out to walk me to the door. We stood there for a moment. It felt like we had just been on a seven-hour date, and I didn't want it to end yet. Except that it probably wasn't a date, and he wasn't going to kiss me.

"Serious question," I said, "do you really not want me to come to improv practice? I won't mind if you don't."

"Do you seriously want to come?"

"I kind of do."

"Then I want you to be there." He took a small step closer to me.

"Because I don't have to come if you were just being polite," I added.

"Thursday night, then. My place. 7:30 p.m."

"Okay. Text me the address."

"Give me your phone number."

I did, and then on impulse I hugged him good-bye. He gave me a quick, surprised look and then wrapped his arms around me. He smelled like sea air and warmth, and I felt his thumb run across the top of my neck with one hand before he let me go.

"Hey, Abby?" His face looked surprisingly serious. "How long exactly are you planning to stay?"

Oh no. Did he think I was expecting to join his improv group forever? Did he think my intention was to weasel my way in?

"Don't worry. I promise I won't pull an *All About Eve* thing and try to steal the group from under you."

He frowned, not taking the bait. "But do you have a timeline of when you're going back?"

I shrugged, forcing a little laugh. "Probably a month or two. At some point, my sister's going to break up with her ex-husband and I'll have to fly back home to deal with that drama, so don't even worry. I'll be out of your lives by the fall, for sure."

For some reason, he didn't look relieved.

"Sure," he agreed. "I'll see you Thursday." He turned to go. Whatever was bothering him didn't seem to have gone away.

That night, as I ate dinner alone, I fixated on certain details—his hand on my wrist, certain expressions he had when he looked at me, the feel of his thumb running across the back of my neck as we hugged. He'd had an opening to kiss me. Surely he knew that? It felt even more embarrassing because I'd expressly told him I was leaving, so this wasn't going to be a long-term thing where I'd come into it with high expectations. I wasn't even desirable enough for a quick fling, apparently. Maybe he was still too hung up on his ex-wife?

Then I went back to a piece of advice that my sister Laura

had told me when I was overanalyzing the behavior of a high school crush.

It was my sophomore year, and we were sitting in my bedroom late one night when she was home from her freshman year at college. "I think this boy likes me," I told Laura, "because he keeps walking really close to me, but he also walks close to Lily, so maybe he likes her, but then sometimes he talks to me about what he's done over the weekend..." I went on like that for several minutes before Laura finally stopped me with five words.

"Has...he...asked...you...out?"

"No."

"Are you going to ask him out?"

"Not if he likes Lily."

"Then don't spend any more time thinking about it."

She was right about that guy (who did indeed end up asking out my best friend), and she had been right several times since then. Paul was a grown-up. If he was interested, he could ask me out. If he wasn't interested, he would see me only when we were part of a group. Things would sort themselves out soon, I told myself.

The problem was that they didn't.

5

"NO PRESSURE"

LISETTE and I had dinner together at my apartment on Tuesday night, exactly one week after she'd moved out of my place. I had managed a little food shopping over the weekend and managed to pull together a chicken tikka masala from one of those tasty but inauthentic jarred sauces that would make an actual chef weep into his apron.

"Isn't Paul the best?" she said as she set the table; she still knew more about where to find the various forks and glasses than I did.

"He's really nice."

"You should marry Paul," she said, "and get your Canadian green card, and stay here forever."

"So the two of you never dated?"

"Oh, no. He's like a brother to me. Except my actual brothers would knock out Paul in a fistfight. Two of them are wrestlers, and Paul's not really a fighter. Not that I've seen Paul fight, but I can't see him breaking a beer bottle against a brick wall, you know?"

"Have you seen someone do that often?"

"At least twice." Something in her tone made me leave the comment without pursuing it.

"Paul's lovely," I said. "But it seems like he's still getting over his divorce so maybe no green card weddings yet."

"Trish was awful to him," Lisette said. "The worst part about her was that she seemed so nice. But you could tell she wasn't. She was one of those people who has a soft, gentle voice," Lisette adopted a breathy, kindergarten teacher tone as she spoke, "and *everyone* likes her but she's not *actually* going to do anything that will be *difficult* for her. Because she doesn't *like* things that are *hard*." Lisette rolled her eyes, dropping the voice. "She wouldn't go out of her way for anyone, you know what I mean? And Paul's so nice that he's easy to take advantage of. When he falls for someone, he goes full on, head-over-heels, you know?" My breath caught painfully at the words as I imagined what Paul would look like if he were head-over-heels in love with someone. "So he let her push him around. And then she announced she was leaving him one day. Without warning. He was completely shattered."

"Has he dated since then?"

Lisette leaned forward. "I knew it. You like him!"

"No, I just wondered." Was I blushing? I hoped not. I shrugged one shoulder lightly, doing my best casual, *Sex and the City* romantic sangfroid.

Lisette considered the question. "He hasn't dated that I know of. One time he took a woman to dinner, and afterwards he told me he wasn't ready. But you may be right. He may be obsessed with Trish. I think for a while he was hoping she'd come crawling back. But that's why I want him to date you. Have a fling with the lady from Brooklyn who's only here for a couple of months."

"*The Lady from Brooklyn* sounds like the name of a scandalous 1940s movie."

"That would be a good comedy sketch. *The Lady from Brooklyn*. A musical."

"With songs like Pizza Rat and Rent Control and Fear of Intimacy," I offered.

"See," Lisette said with a knowing grin, "that was improv. You're one of us already."

I grinned, wishing it was true, wishing I could be a carefree improv comedy person. What would that be like? Dashing up on stage in overalls and shouting, 'Who here has had an embarrassing sexual experience they want to share?'

"So what's the status with your housing?" I asked her, carefully steering the subject away from romance.

"Oh, good news! I successfully did the church rounds with my sad story and one of the families is letting me rent out their basement, so I will be out of Paul's by the weekend!"

"That's wonderful!"

"It's such a good deal," she said. "They're only charging me two hundred dollars' rent, and all I have to do is watch their kids once in a while so they can go to dinner and a movie. It's in their basement, and the ceiling isn't finished, but there is a toilet in the corner and a shower. It's gonna be perfect. I can save up for my own place."

It sounded appalling, even by my own low standards from the cheap-rent trenches of the outer boroughs, but I could tell she was relieved not to be relying on Paul or me anymore. I had a sense of fellow feeling with her desire to be independent. I remembered once at my liberal arts college—I had gone to Bard on scholarship and spent four years in rolling green fields among wealthy animation and social justice majors—a much wealthier classmate found out about my neglectful upbringing. I considered her a friend and had been telling an amusing anecdote about my mother forgetting our existence for a weekend and Laura and I surviving on three different brands of sugary cereal.

Suddenly, her eyes welled with tears, and she clutched my hand with blue-painted nails and said that she was *so sorry* that happened to me, and if I *ever* needed anything, I could come to her. I extracted myself from the room and her friendship as fast as I could. Nothing makes you feel worse about your life than genuine pity.

"Well, it may not be perfect, but I'm glad you found somewhere," I said briskly.

"So are you excited about improv practice on Thursday?" Lisette asked.

"I have no idea what I'm walking into, to be honest."

"Okay, perfect." Lisette folded her knees up in her dining chair and set both elbows on the table. "Let me give you the basics."

While we finished dinner, Lisette gave me a quick talk about improv. It was the first time I'd seen her get deadly serious, even including when she told me about escaping her abusive boyfriend.

"Improv," Lisette said, "is not just comedy. It's not—you know—a means to an end. It's the end. It's a way of thinking. You have to observe and connect and return back to things and see them in a new way. Those are all the things that are required to live a good life, yeah?"

She told me that the key to improv was to listen to your impulses, to trust your inner gut, and not to push things.

"Don't try to be clever. Definitely don't try to be the funniest person up there."

"There is no risk of me trying to be the funniest person there," I said. "I've seen you guys."

"And don't push an idea."

"That's going to be harder. I try to push things all the time. I tried to push someone to marry me for years." I was only half-kidding, and I saw that Lisette could tell.

"When you're doing improv," Lisette said, "you listen to the scene. It's okay if it goes nowhere. Let it go nowhere, and trust something will come. And listen to your partner. Listen to what they're giving you, because they're channeling their own life and creativity. And using that to build something new is one of the best feelings in the world."

Lisette walked me through some of the sketches we might do in practice.

"Here's the key," she said. "Between now and then, you're going to want to come up with funny ideas. Don't."

"Okay."

"Just listen and respond honestly, and trust that the funny stuff will come. Because it will. Because you're funny."

"No pressure," I said, drily.

"Exactly!" Lisette cried. "No pressure. Just be in the moment. It'll come to you."

"Can I tell you a deep, dark secret?" I said to Lisette. "In college, I wanted to write for Saturday Night Live, and I put together a packet and applied when I was twenty-three."

"That's great!"

"No, it's not, because they rejected me. But you know the worst part? I didn't realize that I could apply again. I didn't know that sometimes writers applied for several years before they got the job. I thought that meant that I officially had been found to be not funny, like a stamp on my forehead, so I gave up and chose another career. I didn't find out until years later that I was wrong. So this is bringing up a lot of repressed trauma."

"Repressed trauma is *perfect* for improv."

I laughed.

I ARRIVED at Paul's house right at 7:30 that Thursday for my very first improv practice. Lisette had explained to me that they practiced every Thursday for a few weeks in a row and then had a show about once every six weeks. It was July 13th, and their next big performance would be late in August. She said I was welcome to come to any of the practices, as long as I was on time.

"Paul takes it pretty seriously. But don't be scared, though. Everyone will be nice. Except Mark, he'll be mean, but that's his way of being nice."

I stood outside and took in Paul's cute little house—much less ramshackle than the one I was staying in, neatly painted yellow with lights shining from the windows. Paul's Mini Cooper was parked out front. The sight of the house made me happy and nervous, which I knew was another warning sign that I was feeling too much already. I reminded myself that it was probably Paul's wife who had picked out this quaint little two-story building with the stained glass over the front door— the wife that Paul was hoping would return to him.

Paul opened the door and smiled when he saw me. "You came!" He seemed so genuinely surprised that I felt foolish, like I was a freshman in college who'd accidentally crashed an upperclassman's party after mistaking a mention for an invite. I followed him into the house, peeling away my jacket. "Lisette's made cookies," he said, taking my coat, "as you can probably tell from the faint smell of burning."

"Hey!" came Lisette's angry voice from deep within the house. "Fifty percent of them are fine!"

Beneath the charred scent of oatmeal cookies was a hint of woodsmoke that suggested occasional use of the shiny black wood stove gleaming in one corner. Paul had a large wall of books and DVDs in his living room, an acoustic guitar on a stand, and a deep sofa flanked by two leather armchairs. The open floorplan included a dining area that led back toward an aluminum-and-black modern kitchen. It felt somewhere between a marital home and a nice bachelor pad: sparse, warm, with the appropriate allotment of leather furnishings and a screen big enough to capture every detail of a movie star's steely glare when he faced off with terrorists.

"It smells amazing, Lisette!" I called.

"I know!" Lisette replied as she spun toward the dining table with a plate of cookies. "I think I got it right, unless I messed up the salt and sugar. Who wants to test one?"

Lisette's oatmeal walnut chocolate chip cookies were very good, in spite of a few burned corners. Paul opened up a bottle of wine and banged around with his expensive coffee machine while we waited for Mark, who turned up twenty minutes late, grumbling about a road closure. By eight p.m., everyone was settled into the living room, and I realized I had grown more and more terrified during the last half hour without noticing it.

It was bad enough to stand on a stage and act goofy—not that I'd done that much since high school—but it was entirely another thing to do it in someone's living room after eating cookies and chatting about the weather. It felt like you were walking into humiliation in cold blood. Sure, in ordinary life, you might embarrass yourself accidentally, but this was making an evening of it.

I felt certain that I couldn't go through with it at the exact moment Paul said, "All right!" He stood and clapped his hands together, the way he had done at the start of his show. "Let's get to it. Abigail, you're going to sit out the first one so you can get the idea, but this is a classic tap in and tap out game. All we're doing is keeping the scene going. Lisette, you want to start us off?"

Lisette nodded and jumped up. I admired her fearlessness. She didn't even hesitate. She walked up, sat in an armchair, and began digging through an imaginary bag.

Mark walked up, joining in the scene. "What are you looking for?"

"My shirt. I think it got mixed up with your laundry."

"What color is it?"

"Blue. I need to wear it to work today. We have to wear corporate colors."

"Well, how did it get in my laundry?" Mark asked.

"I don't know, but it wouldn't be the first time. You do seem to like women's clothes." I watched as they built a scene out of nothing, taking little cues from each other.

"Come on," Mark asked. "Do I look like I could fit in one of your shirts?"

"All I'm saying is that my shirts are very stretched out sometimes."

"It could have been the dog."

"Our dog is a dachshund."

"That's a very smart breed. And known for tunneling. Maybe he went into the shirt like…"

Mark gestured at a dog digging into a shirt and I laughed.

"Wait a minute," Lisette said. "What are you wearing under your sweater right now?"

"It's not what you think!" Mark cried. Lisette pointed to him, and he pretended to lift his sweater.

"My blue shirt!" Lisette cried.

Paul hopped up and tapped Mark and replaced him in the scene.

"It's not what you think!" Paul cried.

"Oh really? Then what is it?" Lisette asked her new scene partner.

"I'm experimenting with a new identity."

"As a woman?"

"As a superhero." Paul took a superhero pose.

"Well, that does explain the underwear that's gone missing."

I laughed.

"What's that?" Paul cried. "I think I hear a shout for help. I'm sorry, but I need to save the city." He pretended to tear open his sweater to reveal the blue shirt underneath.

Lisette gasped. "Why is there a letter D painted on my shirt?"

"That's my superhero symbol. A big D."

Mark chuckled quietly.

"For dachshund," Paul added. He turned, as if to an imaginary dog. "Let's go save the day, Milo!"

"Wait a minute! What am I wearing to work?" Lisette was good at playing her objectives.

"Fine. You can have it. I'll just have to be a shirtless superhero." Paul paused, sighed, and pretended to take the shirt off. "I'll be cold, but the women of the city will thank you."

Paul flew away. Lisette held up the imaginary shirt and examined it. "Well, I guess the baggy look is in," she said with a sigh.

I applauded at the end, but Paul just shrugged. "That was a warm-up. This time, I'll start, Lisette will come in, and then Abby, you have to jump into it in place of one of us."

The terror came back as Paul smiled at me. He knew that I was nervous, and he was enjoying it.

"I'm uh..." Scared, I thought.

"Scared?" Paul finished for me. "A New Yorker is scared?"

"I have no training in this, you know that."

"You'll be great," Paul said.

"Or completely terrible, which is even better," Mark added.

"Much funnier," Lisette agreed. "Let's start the scene, Paul."

Paul stood up and began the next improv by walking to the shelf and looking at the books. Lisette walked up to him.

"I see you're in our self-help section," she said. "Looking for anything in particular?"

"I'm having trouble believing in myself. My friends really cut me down." Again, it amused me how quickly they ran with whatever the other person gave them.

"Oh," said Lisette, taking a book off the shelf. "Have you considered this one, *All My Friends Hate Me, and I Probably Deserve It?*"

"I read that one. It didn't help."

"How about, *I Suck at Everything and My Friends Agree.* It's a new release."

"I tried that one, too, but it was a little prescriptive," Paul said.

"What about, *Find Your Confidence through Crying Alone in Your Room.*"

I stood up. I had an idea, out of nowhere.

"Maybe," Paul replied to Lisette. "I do like to cry."

I stepped forward and tapped Lisette on the shoulder and took her place, taking over her role in the scene. "That book worked wonders for me. I read it a couple of years ago and it changed my life. If you'd like me to show you some of the techniques..."

Paul grinned at me. "Please."

"Step over to our seating area," I said, noticing Lisette smiling at me from the corner of my eye. "Now I need some full-on body sobbing. We're talking Matthew McConaughey in *Interstellar* weeping. I did this for two whole years after my last break-up and look at me now. Perfectly happy."

"You do look happy."

Paul took a seat and smiled at me.

"The key is to sob loudly enough that the neighbors complain."

Paul sat in a corner and gave a good wail. I had a strange sense of elation.

"Louder!"

I didn't know what was coming next, though, so I began to panic, but Paul caught my eye and smiled. "And if this doesn't help?"

"You'll get a partial refund on the book."

Mark jumped into the scene as a new character. "Hey, this book about *Finding Confidence through Crying Alone in Your Room* didn't work for me at all. I tried it, and I still have absolutely no faith in myself. I'd like my refund."

I glared at him. "You were confident enough to ask for the refund, so it actually did work, didn't it?"

"You're right, I'm so sorry. What was I thinking?" Mark said, walking out of the scene.

"That will be eight-two ninety-five," I said to Paul. "Any interest in our customer loyalty plan?"

Paul laughed, then stood up and grinned. "Look at Abigail," he said, gesturing to me.

Mark and Lisette applauded.

"Look at her," Mark said. "How many times have you done improv before?"

"Never."

"Never ever?" Mark shook his head.

Paul looked delighted with me.

"I told you!" Lisette cried. "She's Saturday Night Live good," Lisette added, giving me a meaningful glance.

"You mean Second City, I hope," Paul replied. "The Canadian sketch comedy tradition takes a back seat to none."

"I said about four things."

"That in itself is an accomplishment," Paul said. "Just following the scene takes most people a long time."

"Well, the truth is I was just pulling from my own life of crying alone in my room, so..."

"Use what you've got," Paul agreed. He looked at the others. "Mark and Lisette. You're up."

I sat down, focused but amazed. It had been fun. There was something about it that reminded me of being a very little kid, playing pretend with my sister. It was silly, of course, but a wonderful silly. I knew what Lisette meant by the end of the night. It felt like I had connected with a part of my brain that I didn't even know was there—the part that was open to anything, the part that could take something and run with it.

"I have some books for you," Paul said, when the evening began to wrap up at around 11 p.m. "Stick around a minute."

Lisette made Paul promise that on the upcoming weekend, all three of us would go to Bell Island together, which is the next place she had decided I needed to see. Then she made her good-byes and I gave her a hug on the way out. Mark grumbled as he put on his coat and then told me I wasn't terrible before he gave me a kiss on the cheek. He glanced between me and Paul's retreating figure before nodding and closing the door.

I waited for Paul to come back, standing dutifully in his hallway like a good student.

A part of me wondered if something was going to happen. Paul had been flirting with me all day on Saturday, hadn't he? Were we going to talk more? Kiss? Had I ruined things with that comment about bitter men and their divorces? Were the books an excuse to be alone?

I wanted them to be an excuse, and the thought mortified me, my sheer desperation to have a nice guy want to date me, just once.

As I waited for him to return, I sat on his sofa and pondered the wood stove, wondering when he used it. It was mid-July, and he probably saved it for winter, curling up with a movie after an early sunset, grading papers. The image was so vivid that it made my chest ache. I glanced through his DVDs—lots of westerns, action, Edgar Wright films. Every single Humphrey Bogart. *Blackadder*. *Dr. Who*. It was a portrait of what he cared about, and I realized how much I already knew about him, the way his mind worked when he built a joke. He returned a couple of minutes later with three books on improv.

Because he had been serious. And this wasn't a seduction.

"Sorry about that. I wanted to give you these. Keith Johnstone, *Impro*, is the best of the lot, I'd really love it if you checked it out. And this one is all about Del Close, who was the leader of the Chicago school." He handed me the pile. "You don't have to read them, but I think you're really good, for your first time. If you want to keep coming to practices, I thought you might like to be inspired." He looked a little shy as he said it, like he was expecting me to laugh at him, which surprised me after his total willingness to be goofy all night.

I took the books, wondering if I was taking his most prized possessions. I tried to handle them with appropriate respect. "I would like to come again. But just to be clear, I mean, I'm only here for a few weeks." I was still nervous that he would think he had to let me down easy when it came to joining the Newfingers.

"Well, yes…I hope…" He trailed off, then regrouped and continued. "But even if this is just for when you go back to New York, you should consider sticking with improv."

"You're being so kind."

He looked wary. "Is that what I'm doing?"

"I feel like you're about to ask me to buy into your multi-level marketing scheme. Tell me it's not crypto."

"I do have a lot of NFTs to unload."

"Ah, makes sense."

Then his eyes got a twinkle in them. "You don't like compliments."

"I don't?"

"You get uncomfortable when someone says you're good at something."

"Doesn't everyone?"

Paul shrugged. "Yeah, but it's different. You deflect the compliments completely. Watch. You ready?"

"For what?" I looked up into his eyes again, and there was a flash of something again.

"For a compliment."

I searched his expression. "You better not be about to say something horrible."

"See? So here goes. Abigail? I wish you weren't leaving the country so soon."

He waited, while my face flushed pink. "Now what?"

"Now you have to accept the compliment."

"How does that work exactly? They don't teach us this back home."

"You say 'Thank you, Paul.'"

"Ah. Well, fine, okay. Thank you, Paul," I forced out at last.

"Like pulling teeth," he said.

"Now your turn, because I bet you're no better," I said.

"I'm great with compliments. I'm an actor. I insist upon them or I storm back to my trailer."

"Paul. You are very nice..." He rolled his eyes. "Don't look skeptical," I said. "And you spent a whole day showing me around even though I'm basically a stranger."

"We have to do that, it's Canadian law."

"Let me finish. And I know you think being nice makes you boring, but I think it makes you kind of sexy."

His eyes widened. I could see his lips part. "Right," he said slowly. The air felt thick, like it was growing harder to breathe.

"Just say thank you," I said. "Easy enough, right?"

"Easy." He took a half step forward, his eyes darting to my lips and then away again. "Thank you, Abigail."

I took another step forward. This really was a dare. I watched him take another breath, then release it. Another charged moment came, then went, as I watched him visibly shake off whatever was going through his mind. His polite smile was back in place. It was maddening.

"Well," he said, his voice a little less steady than usual. "Bell Island has excellent seabirds. So. It should be interesting. Lisette is working on Saturday, so she wanted to do something Sunday. If that works."

"Sure. I mean, unless something better comes up. Can I confirm at 2 a.m. the night before?"

He flashed a smile. "Anytime. But you should know there's a boat trip involved. Not as shaky, I promise."

"I'll stare at the horizon and breathe slowly."

He raised a hand like he was going to touch my arm, but I watched as he dropped it. He walked me to the door, head tilted, wearing a faint smile.

"Goodnight, Abigail."

"Goodnight, Paul."

I gave him one more look at the door and then turned and walked down his stairs as quickly as I could.

What had just happened?

6

SHE COMES FROM DILDO

THE NEXT DAY, late on a Friday night, I had a video call with Laura that somehow turned into a fight. It started out with Laura sending me a text saying Hannah wanted to talk, and I quickly jumped on a video call, carefully putting on my jovial aunt voice so that I wouldn't say anything negative about her father. Everything was great, and I loved Nick, and wasn't this whole thing a bucket of fun?

"How're you doing, Hannah Banana? Everything okay?"

She shrugged, which looked like an earthquake on the tiny phone screen. "It's too hot here."

"Well, that's why we have the miracle of air conditioning."

"I don't like the kids in Georgia, Tabby."

"Why not?"

"One of them said I needed a manicure."

"A manicure?" At seven years old? I tried to keep calm.

"Yeah. She said my nails were gross."

"Oh, sweetie." I gritted my teeth at this classic mean girl behavior in its infant form, maddening in its inevitability. "Your nails are fine."

"Hers were pink, and she said I needed a manicure because

mine were gross. Can I come stay with you? Mommy says it's not as hot where you are."

"It is cooler here, but you can't come stay yet. It's a very long trip."

"Please Tabby?" That is Hannah's nickname for me, especially when she wants something. "You could pick me up from the airplane if Mommy doesn't want to come. I could fly by myself."

"Oh, honey, I miss you, too. But you're going to be starting school, and you need time to get used to Atlanta. I promise that if I end up settling up here for good, I'll fly you up lots of times. You'll become an international travel expert. But not just yet. You're still getting settled."

"I don't want to live in Georgia. I want to live in New York. I hate it here." It was the first time she had openly admitted to being homesick, and I felt it like a horse hoof to the chest.

"I'll come see you before you know it!" My voice was thin from desperation, the kind adults always have when they can't tell a child the whole truth. "As soon as I can. And Atlanta is so cool. Lots of new things to do and people to meet. I heard you're getting good at swimming."

"Yeah," Hannah agreed proudly. The change of topics seemed effective. She started telling me all the different strokes she was learning, and how she was better than some of the kids who were nine years old. Eventually, Laura appeared and sent Hannah to get in her pajamas so Nick could read to her before bedtime. The image of Nick reading to her gave me an embarrassing flash of jealousy. How dare he act like Hannah's parent and Laura's emotional support when that had been *my* job for the last few years?

"So how's it going for you?" Laura's tone was polite, even a little reserved.

"Good. I went to improv comedy practice."

Laura blinked for a moment, taking in my words. "Well, that's sounds fun and cool."

"Definitely fun. Definitely not cool."

"So…how did you get into that? Like an improv troupe?"

"I'm not into it. It just seemed like something different to try. I made a friend here and she asked me."

"That's neat."

"Yeah." My heart was speeding up and I realized I was furious with Laura's patronizing tone. I consciously took a breath to calm down.

"You know you could have done improv comedy in New York, right?"

"Well, no one ever invited me."

"Okay. Well, sure." A long moment passed. "Listen, Hannah's really missing you."

I took another breath. In-and-out, Abigail. Slow and steady breathing. "Yeah, I'm going to come see you guys whenever I get back from Newfoundland."

"So you're not moving there permanently." Emphasis on the *permanently*. Emphasis on the fact that Laura had never taken this seriously.

"I might be." I said it just to bait her, to see if I could get a reaction, but she didn't give me one. I pressed on. "But in any case, I would have to come back to Brooklyn to organize the move and clear out my apartment. Assuming I can figure out a green card and stuff. I have to see a lawyer. I'm still deciding."

"I guess I don't understand why you had to move halfway around the world in the opposite direction from us to make some kind of a statement."

"I'm worried about climate change."

"Climate change." Her video image was perfectly placed for me to see her entire eyeroll.

Sister fights are always particularly nasty because they're about everything and nothing.

"Abs, I know you're just doing this to try to prove a point," Laura said.

"What point?"

"That you can survive without us."

"You're the one who told me to leave."

"I didn't say go to Newfoundland. I said if you had something you wanted to try, you should go ahead. But I didn't think you were moving to the Arctic Circle."

"I'm not in the Arctic Circle."

"Well, it seems like a deliberate way to make it impossible for us to see you. You could have stayed in New York where you could actually fly down to see us for like three hundred dollars instead of thousands of dollars from Newfoundland..."

"Okay, well if you guys decide to stay there..."

"We are staying here." Now Laura looked angry.

"Okay, well, *if* you do, I will come and visit," I went on. "And you know, maybe I'll just buy a place up here and then I can come stay with you guys for a couple of weeks every winter when it's really snowy up here."

"You're serious about moving to Newfoundland? Newfoundland. New...found...land."

"Why is that so hard to believe?"

"Because your niece misses you and you are choosing to never see her."

"If you stay in Atlanta."

"We are staying in Atlanta. Nick wants to buy a place here, before the market goes up anymore, because if we wait another year, we may not be able to afford it."

This was news. "But you're still figuring out if this is going to work."

"Abby, we were married for years. I know him."

"And things are going well?"

"Why is that so hard for you to believe?"

"Okay, so what do you want me to do, Laur? Move there?"

"Well, yeah, I want you to be closer to your family." I don't know why Laura and I always managed to go full *Desperate Housewives* when we disagreed about something. It was probably because we agreed often enough so that every disagreement seemed like betrayal.

"How about this?" I began. "*If* you and Nick can make it a year together..."

"Oh, stop."

"If you do, I'll think about moving closer, but right now, I'm pretty serious about Canada."

"Because you're that sure Nick and I will break up."

"Why couldn't he come to New York? And why doesn't he pay the child support he owes you before he started talking about buying a home? Isn't it up to like four thousand dollars?"

"This is none of your—"

"And I assume he wants you to put in some money for this home he wants to buy."

"Enough, okay." Which meant yes, of course.

"What?" My attempts at calm were fully out the window. "You guys left me, okay. You moved away from me, and I'm supposed to follow you at the snap of your fingers?"

"So Newfoundland is your life now? And improv comedy?"

"As much as Georgia is yours."

"And your new improv friends are more important to you than your niece?"

"It's not me who moved away, Laura. You left."

"You know what? I'm going to go."

"Fine. Bye."

"Bye."

I regretted my tone as soon as I hung up. Okay, I regretted it an hour or two after I hung up. I knew I'd been sarcastic and unsupportive, but the fight had made one thing clear: deep down, Laura really had been expecting me to follow her down there. She still was. If she and Nick worked it out, then I was going to have a decision to make. I missed Hannah, but I wasn't sure I wanted Laura's life to be my entire life. Not anymore.

PAUL WAS right about the improv books. They were surprisingly good. I spent my Saturday wandering the city while reading most of *Impro*. I had a good reading system that I'd developed for my literature courses in college: read one chapter and then change your locale. Coffee shop, hillside park, brick wall with a decent view, different coffee shop, living room, bed. You could get a lot of pages covered that way and flatter yourself that you were getting exercise in the process—a form of interval training where the intervals were croissants.

The author of the first book seemed to have been raised in a really repressed British education system, and it made him want to explode all the little boxes that people put themselves in. For him, improvisation was about reconnecting with the rule-breaker within. One of the improvisational exercises he used to do was having people imagine that they had taken a book off a shelf, and then they opened it to a page, and he would tell them to pretend to 'read aloud' what they saw there. He had examples in his book where people had come up with whole poems, beautiful stories, just by pretending that somebody else had written them.

That struck me, the idea that we can be more creative and imaginative when we pretend we are reading from someone else's work. I wondered if I could believe I was more capable if I was channeling someone else.

Lying in bed that night, I had a distinct memory of Laura

and me putting on a play for our mother as children. It was one of those recollections that came back to me in pieces, jigsaw memories that didn't quite fit into a whole picture. I remembered that we wore costume dresses from a past Halloween that were way too small for us, and that we were acting a scene where we were princesses, and that our mother spilled her wine midway through, and we stopped whatever we were doing to help clean up the mess. We were so happy to have the chance to help her. It made us feel useful and important, and we pretended we were princesses scrubbing the floors, and she said, "Oh, thank you, princesses, your fairy godmother needed help," and I remember feeling panicked that she was pretending to be my godmother instead my mother.

"You're the Queen!" I said. "You're the Queen!"

Then Laura took over the play and insisted on putting Mom to bed on the sofa with a blanket while our mother told us how pretty we looked.

"This is a high-class establishment," our mother drawled as we pulled the cover up to her neck. "I'm getting the fancy treatment!"

"Because you're the Queen!" I cried once again.

When our mother was asleep, I told Laura that I still wanted to do our play for nobody, and Laura flatly refused. I was heartbroken, but I could see that the moment was gone for Laura. I was young—maybe seven—but intuitively I realized that Laura had concocted this whole play as a gambit to win our mother's attention, to be the center of the room for once, instead of all the attention being on our mother, and perhaps on me as the baby of the family. Maybe that's why Laura turned into a drinker during college: because in our house, the drinker always got to be the one everything revolved around. It had been different for me. I hadn't done the play for attention. I had actually wanted to be a princess—safe, loved, well cared for.

I never wanted to be the person spilling my drink, the messy one who took attention away from others. Instead, I wanted to be the one in control, the one to make the rules. I stopped playing dress-up around that time.

Doing improv brought me back to the seven-year-old kid who liked to pretend things. I hadn't been—and wasn't now—someone who wanted to bask in the heat of stage lights, absorbing the anonymous applause of a huge audience. I just wanted to get back the part of me that knew how to play, the part that wasn't already a responsible adult by the age of fourteen, spouting my bitter wisdom at the freshman lunch table.

That night I wrote silly nonsense in a journal—poems, daydreams, word associations—just to practice what it felt like. I was in such a good mood that I made a renewed effort to connect with Mrs. Mahoney downstairs as well, bringing her cookies that Lisette had given me as extras.

"I don't eat stuff like that," she said. "Sugary stuff."

"Well, let me know if there's anything you'd like. Or if you need anything from the store."

"I don't need anything. Are you doing laundry again?"

I told her that I would have to do so eventually, and she gave me an encore lecture about intolerable sound levels, as if I was planning on practicing Rage Against the Machine guitar solos instead of running a dryer. Then she sent me on my way. I hadn't broken her icy façade yet, but I wasn't giving up, either. New Yorkers aren't known for being nice, but we know how to break people down over time. It's not the theme of every Scorsese movie for nothing.

By the next day, when Lisette rang my doorbell to pick me up, I was feeling strangely elated, even before she greeted me with one of her massive hugs.

"Bell Island is gorgeous," she said. "You're giving us an excuse to go visit all the best spots. And the ferry is very steady."

"If I feel ill, it's okay to jump overboard, right?"

"You won't. Much bigger boat. Almost Staten Island Ferry big."

"How do you know about the Staten Island Ferry?"

"I watch rom-com movies. That's the ferry where you all run toward each other just as it's leaving the dock, announcing you're in love, right?"

"It's a standard part of the morning commute."

She considered this. "I suppose there are fewer movies set on the Bell Island Ferry. We should make one up! We can do an improv called Love on the Bell Island Ferry."

Paul smiled in greeting as I reached for the doorhandle of the back seat of his car, but Lisette slid by me and insisting on taking the back.

"You both have at least six inches on me. You should have the front. I'll just pretend you're my parents and demand that we go to McDonalds."

"Only if you're very, very good," Paul replied.

"It's not really a tall person car, is it," I said to Lisette as I buckled the front seatbelt.

"No, not at all," Lisette agreed.

Paul gave me an amused glance and muttered something under his breath that may have been "Michael Caine."

Lisette talked through her romantic-comedy idea on the drive across the peninsula to the ferry, and we filled it in with little details that would make our hypothetical movie feel especially Newfoundland. I learned a lot about the local culture from that conversation—the fishing traditions, the phrases, the nightlife.

"Newfoundlanders are really funny," Paul said. "But in a deadpan way. So for example we have a town named Dildo.

And the claim is that it's a reference to a part of a boat, but people know what it also refers to. You'll never get them to admit it, though. That's part of the joke. They'll look you straight in the eye and claim they have no idea what you're talking about while they sell you an 'I Love Dildo' t-shirt. It's island humor. Putting one over on the outsiders."

"Maybe our rom-com should be called *She Comes from Dildo*," I suggested, and that's what we stuck with. By the time Paul had pulled his car onto the Bell Island ferry, Lisette was insisting on filming some scenes on her cell phone.

"You two can be the leads in the movie," she said. "We need clips where you're falling in love on the ferry." Paul and I looked at each other, then looked away.

"I don't know," Paul said. "I don't have leading man potential. We need to send the script to Ryan Reynolds."

"He would do a film called *She Comes from Dildo*," I agreed, "as long as you pitch it as a *Deadpool* sequel."

"This can be our trailer when we send the script to him," Lisette began, waving her phone.

"Proof of concept?" I asked, remembering my days in advertising.

"Exactly," Lisette said. "Whatever that is."

We all knew that we weren't going to write the script, but it was fun to speculate about it for the day, coming up with new ideas. Eventually, Lisette left to wander the ferry and Paul and I ended up standing on the deck together, looking out at the waves. The Bell Island dock was already approaching.

"I've told Lisette that she should actually write down some of her ideas, but she never follows through."

"Maybe you two can write a screenplay together," I said.

"No." He looked down. "I don't think I'd have the heart to write an actual screenplay. I might get my hopes up about getting it made. That's the kind of thing I did when I was younger. I have a huge folder of broken dreams on my laptop."

"Well, you could act in it yourself. Pull an Ed Burns or Mark Duplass and write your way to stardom."

"That time has definitely passed."

"Not entirely," I said. "I saw your Tim Horton heist film, and there may have been some buzz in the audience about securing rights. By the way, *Impro* is fascinating. I finished it."

Paul lit up, his eyes filled with enthusiasm, which didn't feel entirely flattering. He always seemed careful to stay calm with me, to put just a little distance between us, just enough so I wouldn't think anything was going on. *We're not dating. You do know that, right?* But on the topic of improv books, he was like an eager teenager. "It is so cool, isn't it? He's a smart guy. Very of his time. Of course, some of that stuff you could never get away with today."

"Thanks for lending it to me."

He shrugged, looking away again. "Well, I wanted you to read it. You really do have a talent for it. So if—I mean when— you go home…"

"I don't think it would be as much fun doing improv at home. In New York, the improv scene involves lots of acting school grads in competition with each other to launch their comedy writing jobs. It's like an alt comedy fraternity rush system."

"I'm glad Lisette brought you along to practice, at any rate."

"She's the best. I know she's had a hard time, too."

"You letting her stay at your place like that was really amazing."

"It was nothing."

"It was incredible."

"I don't feel incredible." I considered the waves. The island was growing closer to us. "My sister thinks I'm selfish for not moving down to Atlanta with her. So I guess I'm not feeling like a good person right now."

"This is the sister who had you babysit her child four days a week? For what, a year?"

"Two years."

"And you were paid?" He raised his eyebrows, knowing the answer.

"No. But that's not even..." I trailed off. It had been so long since I'd heard anyone defend me that I didn't know how to react. "The thing is, Hannah misses me."

"I'm sure she does, but you have a right to your own life."

"It's hard to set limits with people you love."

"Yeah." Paul grimaced and looked away.

"I like it here, you know," I said. "Don't start making your good-byes now. I've got a few more weeks to decide. I could stay, if I can get a work visa or something."

He glanced at me. "It's not much compared to New York City."

"Well, Bell Island better impress me. I'm expecting at least a Disney Store and Hard Rock Café."

He laughed.

"And I'm told it has excellent seabirds."

Paul looked away, embarrassed.

We got back in Paul's car to wait to unload onto the island, and then Paul drove us off the ferry and up through the ring of cheerful houses that tumbled around the terminal like nesting gulls. Before long, Paul's car was wandering through a stark and beautiful green landscape with empty stretches of scratchy fields and tiny houses tucked low against the wind. It reminded me of photos I'd seen of places like Ireland or Maine, those northern stretches of the Atlantic where the light seemed to hit the world sideways. Eventually, Paul found a place to pull over, and we all climbed down a rocky cliff staircase to get down to a beach together. It was low tide; everyone on the coast of Newfoundland seemed aware of things like tides and sea levels, and I realized I had never, not once, clocked a high or low tide in New York. Here, though, there were treasures to be found when the sea drew back: starfish and sea anemones and a rocky cave that we wandered into together, still occasionally planning out our Newfoundland love story.

"It starts raining," Lisette said, "and they get stuck in a cave together."

"Like Dido and Aeneas," I offered, "but with access to condoms."

Paul shot me an impressed glance. "Classical references."

"I only remember the things I read in college that felt like porn. Ask me about Samuel Richardson's *Pamela* sometime."

"The two leads should make love in a tidal pool," Lisette suggested.

"No," I said, "they should be arguing the whole time, and then they suddenly kiss, and a big wave crashes in the background."

"And they get soaked," Lisette said, "and get hypothermia on the way back to the car."

"They get caught in a cave by high tide," Paul suggests, "and have to cling to each other all night to stay warm."

"One bed," Lisette cried. "Only it's a mussel bed!"

One thing that became clear was that Lisette, Paul, and I worked well as a little group. It was fun to be with the two of them, keeping the game going.

"Too bad Mark is missing this," Lisette said. "He never comes out to play."

"Should we go find him?" Paul offered. "He lives up in Torbay. We could drive there and ask around."

"He would hate that. I don't even want to know what he does all weekend," Lisette said.

"Probably works on an old car, or an old house, or an old girlfriend," I offered.

"Right? You've seen him put the moves on girls at the Puffin?" Lisette asked. "He's shameless."

"He does okay for himself," Paul said. "Not quite sure why."

"He keeps asking everyone until he gets a yes. That's what you need to do, Paul." Lisette turned her blinding enthusiasm toward him again, and he turned away as if to shield his eyes. "Throw yourself at women constantly!"

"Don't I get another few months of being a sad sack?"

"Just promise you aren't lying awake at night waiting for Trish to return."

"I promise you I'm not." Paul's gaze on the horizon seemed a little too careful, too emphatically not in my direction. It felt a little insulting, somehow, the constant care about not giving me any ideas, like he was a movie star, and I was his eager intern whose expectations needed to be kept in check.

When I finally did catch his gaze, I smiled. "So what's our ending for the movie? A big church wedding? What do you think, Paul?"

He looked a little wary at my tone and didn't answer.

"Nah," Lisette said. "Twist ending. They're both spies and now they have to kill each other."

When we got back to St. John's, Paul dropped off Lisette at her new place and then drove me home. We sat together in the car for a moment.

"Well, thank you. Today was lovely," I said. "All that island needs are a few more chain restaurants and it could really be something special."

"You're going to keep coming to improv practice, right? This Thursday?" Paul asked.

"Do you really want me to?"

"Of course." He looked serious.

"Okay, then."

He spoke again just as I reached for the door handle. "Wait a second. There's something I wanted to tell you." He took a breath. "My ex-wife..." The words came out of nowhere. I waited for Paul to finish the blow. *...is the love of my life? ...may be coming back any day now, which I'm desperately hoping for?*

"...messed me up a bit."

I nodded cautiously. "Divorces will do that."

He shook his head as if I wasn't quite understanding him. "So I'm trying to be really careful about..."

I waited. His eyes were full of something that I couldn't read. He took another breath. "What Lisette said about me dating again, I'm not sure if—"

"We can just be friends." I cut him off as quickly as I could. I didn't need him to let me down easy, if that's how this was going to go.

"Okay." He smiled, the rueful look appearing just for a moment. "Okay, sure."

There. That had saved us both from a lot of suffering. I got out of the car and walked to the door, telling myself I was happy that things were settled.

Good for him, to be that healthy. Good for him to be able to set boundaries that a therapist would approve of. Good for him that he knew he needed more time to process his divorce. Good for him that as soon as he met a woman he actually liked, all of that would go out the window.

7

"WILD ENTHUSIASM"

A COUPLE of days after that, at the next improv practice, I learned that I clicked surprisingly with Mark when we did improv together. Paul had set up a simple game based on one of his improv books. The goal was for us to do a scene in which one of us acted high status (and belittled the other person) and the other acted low status (and belittled themselves)...and then over the course of the scene, things slowly switched, so that both people were acting high status, and then eventually the person who started out 'high status' turned into the 'low status' person. Paul pointed to Mark and me and said, with his schoolteacher's authority: "Are you two ready to give it a go?"

Mark began the scene in full high-status mode. "So," he said, "you're back again. I'm impressed you had the courage to show your face."

"You're right," I agreed, in low-status mode. "I probably shouldn't be here. Everyone is much more talented than I am. I can't believe I even got into college."

"I could help you to study," Mark said, "but I'm not sure you'd be able to follow what I'm saying."

"You're probably right," I said. "My mother used to say I was the stupidest of all her children."

"Well, I'm sure she was just being honest."

Then our status was supposed to start to shift. "I imagine your mother must have said something similar to you," I said.

"Not really," he replied. "She was too busy driving me to all the schools that were begging me to attend."

"That's nice of them," I said, "given that you weren't taking the most difficult classes."

"Nothing is really difficult for me," he replied.

"I imagine it feels like that to everyone sometimes, when they are new to a subject." Being passive-aggressive was surprisingly cathartic.

We went on like that for a while, cutting each other down until finally Mark switched to treating himself as low status. When we were done, Mark leaned back, looking amused as Paul and Lisette applauded.

"She's brutal," he said. "That was fun."

"I think we were both a little too good at that one," I said. "I don't know what that says about us."

"It says that I am witty and sophisticated," Mark replied. "And you are from New York."

"I'm terrified of both of you now," Paul said.

"My mother was the queen of passive-aggressiveness growing up," I said. "I learned from the best."

"My mother was just aggressive," Paul replied.

At the end of the practice, Lisette waved everyone to silence. "I have a suggestion. Abigail here doesn't know if she's staying here past the summer, but we have that show on August 17th. What do you say we let her join in until then?"

"And be in a show?" Paul asked, considering.

I was already frantically waving away the idea. "I'm definitely not ready."

"No one," Lisette said, "is ever ready. Mark, Paul, what do you say? It'll either be her going away gift, or the way we convince her to stay in the country."

"Sure," Paul said, giving me a little smile.

"Why not," Mark said with a shrug.

I glanced between them.

"Don't worry," Lisette said. "That's Mark's version of wild enthusiasm."

BUOYED by the elation of being invited into the Newfingers on a temporary basis, I found myself setting up a meeting with an immigration lawyer the next day. It wasn't so much that I wanted to do improv; it was that Lisette had signaled that I actually belonged in their strange little group. I had people here, now.

The immigration attorney, Dave Bui, had a shabby little office in a converted storage building near the main port, but he was friendly and efficient when he waved me inside. He was in his fifties and wore a dark, tweedy suit, and he offered me a lollypop like I was a kid at the bank before sitting me down to give me a frank take on my situation. Unsurprisingly, he informed me that there was a lot to arrange if I actually wanted to move to Canada and work from home, even if I was still working for an American company. I might have to set up my U.S. address with my sister, for example, assuming she didn't hate me. Or I might have to find a job with a company here.

I asked him whether I had any chance of moving here permanently, getting a job, and becoming a permanent resident.

Dave considered this as he leaned back in his squeaky office degree. "You have a degree and some useful skills, but they're not in high demand. So you would need to apply for a work visa," he said. "And if they decide you have skills they need, you may be able to stay up here. But in the meantime, if I can put this as bluntly as possible, don't quit your day job in the U.S., know what I mean?"

This made sense, of course. A final answer from the Canadian government could take months. It also meant that I had absolutely no way of planning my future. I was going to have to wing it.

"So how can I start the application?"

When I walked out of the building, I felt brave. Free. Excited. What if I was the kind of person who moved to another country? What if I was the kind of person who followed their dreams, skipping with joy through the endless bureaucracy of a visa process, to end up a sexy ex-patriate in another country, offering respite to my friends and family when they needed a place to escape? It seemed pretty unlikely, but then again, being in this entire city seemed pretty unlikely. That's what I loved about it.

I texted Lucas and Jasmine and told them that my negativity cleanse might be extended indefinitely. Lucas replied that if I had decided to become an organic farmer, there were certain crops that were in high demand in his social circle.

LISETTE INSISTED that I hang out again the next Sunday, when she had the day off from the café. I was happy to do it, since I had started feeling pretty lonely. Laura and I weren't ready to stop fighting yet. It felt strange not to have seen my sister in person in a month, and to know that things weren't settled between us.

At the last minute, Paul announced that he could join us, this time for a hike into the woods. It was a sticky day, away from the breezy coastline, and the air felt thick and unusually still. We were soon batting away tiny flies and peeling off sweatshirts. It was during this hike that Lisette filled me in about Charlotte and her fisherman boyfriend, and the whole story of my rental apartment.

"If it all works out for Charlie," Lisette said, "maybe you can move into her place permanently, I mean if you want to stay here. But I don't know if they're headed for a big church wedding. Brett, the boyfriend, is one of those guys who talks in grunts. You say, 'Hello,' and he says, 'Mmph. Hmm.'"

"Hey, can I ask a question?" I asked Lisette. "Is her boyfriend dark-haired, kind of scruffy?"

"Yeah, why?"

I did a happy little dance in the middle of the trail, while Paul watched with raised eyebrows. "No, no, no, I'm proud of myself! I'm a great detective!" I cried. I explained how I'd worked that out from the Ben Affleck DVDs. "She definitely has a type."

"Ooo," Lisette considered. "I think my type is those nature documentary fellows who are always trying to get you to warm up to deadly snakes." Lisette adopted a Steve-Irwin-style Australian accent. "And this little fella has a lot of teeth but 'e's actually 'armless. See how 'e's giving my arm a little cuddle." Lisette spun toward Paul. "Do you have a celebrity crush, Paul?"

"Me? Geena Davis. One hundred percent. *Cutthroat Island.* I always wanted to date a pirate."

Lisette snorted a little laugh. "Trish looked literally nothing like Geena Davis."

"That must be why it didn't work out." He glanced at me and smiled. "And you, Abby?"

"I had a horrible crush on Mike Myers in *Austin Powers.* I always liked the witty, clever ones. Then I realized in college that guys who were sarcastic and funny and into comedy did not like girls who were sarcastic and funny and into comedy."

"That is absolutely not true," said Paul. "As someone who was into all those things."

"Trish wasn't funny, either," Lisette said.

"Oh," Paul replied, "she managed some dark humor right at the end."

"I honestly think you were only with her because she—" Lisette's eyes widened, and she staggered backwards and screamed. Paul and I glanced at each other for a second before he rushed forward to help her.

"What is it?"

"A porcupine. In a tree."

Paul glanced up. "Didn't you grow up in Quebec? They can climb trees."

"That's how I know it's after us!" Lisette hissed, half-joking, half-gripped with a sincere terror.

Paul grinned. "Come on, let's give it some space."

We moved a few feet off the trail to make a wide circumference around the porcupine, which was watching us with a blank look.

"It looks angry," Lisette whispered. "This is the moment in the horror film where it all seems quiet before it leaps into action."

Paul glanced between us. "I can't believe the girl from Brooklyn is less scared right now than you are."

"Technically I'm from Troy, New York," I offered. "It's about half the size of St. John's."

Lisette glared at me. "You've been lying to us this whole time? I thought you were cool."

"Will it ruin your opinion of me if I tell you that as a girl, I had to chase off feral raccoons in my backyard with my sister's hairspray bottle?"

"We can never be friends again," Lisette replied.

There was a noise in the branches. "Paul! It's moving!"

Lisette ducked behind him, leaving Paul as a buffer against the dreaded assassin who was gently chewing on a branch fifteen feet up a conifer tree.

"Pathetic," Paul said. "That was pathetic of both of you."

I laughed and ran ahead with Lisette. "We don't have to outrun the porcupine!" I called. "We just have to outrun you!" Lisette and I began to dash down the trail.

A few moments later we stopped for breath.

"He really likes you," she said.

"Paul? He is carefully avoiding me," I responded. "He didn't even seem to want to come today, right? You had to talk him into it."

"He's avoiding you because he likes you."

"He told me he just wants to be friends."

Lisette gave me a funny look. "That's what he said about you."

Paul appeared around a turn of the road, grinning when he spotted us.

"I killed it!" Paul called to us. "I wrestled the porcupine to the ground for you, put it down like John Wick. No big deal. Chivalry and all that. Barely broke a sweat. Just don't look up in the trees when we're walking back."

"Well done, Paul!" Lisette called.

"Look, a moose!" Paul pointed off the trail where a view had opened up, and for a moment we thought he was kidding. Then we walked to where he stood, and through a break in the trees we could see a distant lake where a tiny, antlered creature was visible as a dot.

"They're real," I whispered.

"It's not the Loch Ness Monster, Abby," Paul said, grinning.

"Let's do a photo with it!" Lisette posed us in a selfie, with the brown dot barely visible behind us. Paul was pressed to my side. I felt a little giddy as I looked at him. This was even weirder than a crush, I realized. Walking through the woods with Paul and Lisette was strange precisely because of how normal it felt. After three weeks, it felt like we had known each other forever already. We already had our inside jokes. We had a rhythm and rapport. That never happened back home; my New York friends were all people I had known since we were in our twenties, back when we were malleable and optimistic and still thought fruit-flavored vodka was a sign of sophistication. You didn't just pick up random strangers in your late thirties and go hiking with them. You could get killed that way, or forced to appear in TikTok videos.

I wondered if my Canadian friendships felt so effortless because they knew I was going to leave. Lisette had joked about being a stray dog, but I felt like the real rescue. Maybe it wasn't a big deal that I was broken and cynical because they weren't making a long-term commitment to me. They could ferry me around and listen to my snarky American humor, knowing that in another few weeks they would be free of me for good. My rental was up at the end of August; I was temporary.

Then Lisette threw her arms around my neck and said, "If you want to stay in Canada, I'll marry you," and my heart warmed. I watched Paul glance at us and then turn away to reorganize his hiking backpack.

After the hike, the three of us went home to shower and then met up again at Lisette's place because she wanted to get a ride from Paul to do some shopping for items for her new apartment. Calling it an apartment was a bit of a stretch, because it was clearly a very illegal sublet in someone's basement with a couple of wobbly temporary walls and a thin rug rolled atop a poured concrete basement floor. In one corner was a small refrigerator and hot plate, and behind a half-wall was a toilet and sink. The shower was a hose adjacent to the sink that ran straight into a drain in the floor.

"My beautiful sanctuary," she said to us when we came in. "Gives that Count of Monte Cristo vibe."

"Does that mean someone will scratch through your wall and start giving life advice?" I ask.

"As long as it comes with a huge pile of money, I'll take it."

Paul looked around. "You know you don't have to stay here."

"I love it," said Lisette. "No, seriously. It's perfect because I can afford it, and it means I can actually save for a security deposit on a real apartment."

"Do you want to stay with me in Charlotte's apartment? I really wouldn't mind."

"Nah," Lisette said. "Charity wears me down. It's boring."

"I understand," I replied. "If it helps any, my first studio apartment had a bathroom so cramped that they had to cut a notch into the door to get it to close around the toilet lid." She snorted with laughter while I drew her a diagram in the air.

We headed to a shop called HomeSense, which had the blank white cheerfulness of the furniture section at Target, and wandered the aisles pondering painted bits of wood with cozy statements on them.

"When archeologists dig up our homes someday," I told Lisette, "they will date our sites to the early third millennium A.D. by the swirly script on cocktail glasses saying Wine Mom."

"I must have it!" Lisette cried, placing the ironic glassware in her shopping cart. "For my dungeon lair."

"You know," I told her, "a lot of my childhood, we lived in terrible places. My mother wouldn't pay the bills, and the electricity would go out. She would find a man and he'd pay the utilities for a few months and then he'd be gone again and so would the heat."

Lisette nodded. "We were also dirt poor."

"We were dirt and poor," I replied. "So whatever else you

worry about, don't worry that I'm looking down on you. You got yourself out of a bad situation. You're my hero."

"I mean, yeah. Obviously."

Lisette glanced behind me, and I saw Paul listening to us, slightly embarrassed.

"I'm sorry," he said. "I didn't mean to interrupt. I just found this pillow with a porcupine on it, and I thought of you."

"You asshole!" Lisette cried. "Of course I want the porcupine pillow."

"I'm buying it for you," he said. "Housewarming gift."

When Paul dropped me off at the end of the day, he looked serious for a moment. "That stuff about your mother, I'm sorry to hear that."

"Well, my mother is dead, now. It's a bit of a relief, which is horrible to say, but...growing up, she was *so funny*. She was this force of nature, and I wanted to be exactly like her. The sarcasm, the wit, the way she could hold your attention. But by the time she died, she was so bitter and angry, and I was terrified I would become exactly like her."

"You're not. A bitter person wouldn't have become friends with Lisette."

"She picked me up like a penny on the sidewalk. I got lucky."

Paul looked at me, seriously. "You really don't see yourself very well, do you?"

No, he didn't get to do that. He didn't get to be kind and sweet and confusing. I looked away. "So improv practice again on Thursday?"

He hesitated, looking like he wanted to say more. "Sure, Abby."

. . .

MY NEXT IMPROV practice was the one—and Lisette had warned me ahead of time this might happen—where I was really bad. I went in a little more confident, and then I had no good ideas. I found it hard to focus. Everything I did felt forced and stupid.

Our scene assignment was supposed to take place in a high school, and Lisette decided to act like a teacher, while I was her student.

"I am very disappointed in you," she said.

"Sorry," I said.

"How could you have thought that bringing a live goat to school was a good idea?"

There were any number of things I could have said at that point. I could have suggested that the goat was intended for a ritual sacrifice. I could have said he was my new boyfriend. I could have explained that I had to give a talk about goat cheese. But no.

What I went with was, "I'm really sorry."

Lisette was undeterred. (She's always undeterred.)

"Cindy," she said, "you're my best student. And the worst part was that you let the goat eat your friend's clothing."

I could have explained that my friends wanted their jeans to look distressed. I could have explained that my goat had a learning disability. I could have explained that my goat was on a gluten free diet. Instead I said, "Well, it was hungry."

Yes, I went for the most obvious, pedestrian answer every time. I was being safe, and I didn't even know why. And on and on it went, the scene getting worse each minute. I could feel all the life draining out of it slowly, as Lisette gave me a detention, and my character said, "Okay, fine."

Paul applauded when we were done, but it was polite applause. Mark said nothing.

"That was horrible," I said. *You see, I knew it*, I thought. *I knew I'd be bad at this. I knew my previous couple of times doing well were a fluke.*

"You were trying to be logical," Paul said. "When are human beings ever logical?"

I smiled. "I get it," I said.

But I didn't get it. Because then I went the other way. The next time I was up, I was playing a scene against Mark, and our location was a police station.

"Sit down, detective," Mark said to me. "Tell me about the case."

"Well, there were some clowns committing a murder," I said.

"Literal clowns?"

"French mime clowns."

Now I was determined not to be boring, so I was going to be wacky. I started acting out what the French mime clowns were doing as they murdered someone...only they murdered them with daggers shaped like bananas...

Hilarious, right?

No. Not hilarious.

Mark's sheer deadpan managed to carry us through the muddle I was making, and at the end I sat down and looked at Paul for a long moment.

"Sorry. I know."

He smiled affectionately at me.

"I'm deeply offended that you mocked French mimes," Lisette said. "That is a part of my culture."

Lisette was so endlessly encouraging that she barely seemed to notice how horrible I was. Mark knew and was saying nothing. Paul gave me a little smile, like he was charmed by how bad I was, which was annoying in its own way.

You've gotten the first great disaster out of your system," said Paul. "And we're all proud of you, Abby."

I stood up and took a bow. "Now I'll commit ritual suicide in Paul's kitchen," I added.

He gave me that little smile again. "Don't use the good knife. I only really have the one that I like."

At the end of the night, I was the first out the door. Paul came to see me off.

"You were hard on yourself," he said.

"Only because I was terrible."

"Being hard on yourself puts you in your head and then you can't improve. You know that, right?"

"Thanks Mr. Stewart," I said, pretending I was one of his students.

He laughed. "You'll be better next time. Were you distracted about something?"

"Anniversary of my mother's death."

"That would do it." He looked serious. "I can't see you and Lisette this weekend," he said. "I have a history teacher conference in Montreal. But next week? Same time, same place?"

"Okay."

He pointed over his shoulder. "We're gonna talk about the show in August, too."

I took a breath. "If you don't want me doing the show, I won't take it personally. Honestly, I'd be pretty happy not to ever do a show in front of other people."

"That's a reason you should do it, though, isn't it?"

He reached up and absentmindedly pushed a hair out of my eyes, tucking it behind my ear. I tried to meet his eyes, but he dodged my gaze and gave me a very quick hug good-bye, and then turned to talk to Mark, who was putting on his coat.

I stood outside his door for a moment, looking out at the night, the stars, the cars hurling headlong through the city to bars and restaurants and then home again. Everything still felt new here. I had been a disaster, and that was okay.

. . .

THAT SUNDAY, while Paul was away in Montreal, Lisette turned up at my front door after church wearing a hiking back-pack that she promised me was stuffed with Canadian snacks.

"Where are we going?" I asked. "Are we taking a taxi, or..."

"Taxi! To go hiking?" She looked scandalized. "Not when we can take advantage of the rolling hills of the great city of St. John's. You're okay with ten-kilometer hikes?"

I did the mental math. That was about six miles, so between Lincoln Center and Battery Park. I could handle that.

"Good, then we're off to see the coast." It was a spectacu-larly beautiful day, and Lisette and I posed in front of my house for a picture that we texted to Paul: our thumbs up, giant grins, water bottles raised proudly like we were eager young tourists in front of our first youth hostel. *Ready for a 10 km hike!* Lisette texted to Paul and me. Paul gave the picture a thumbs up.

Entering the conference, he wrote back.

Twenty minutes later, as we were meandering toward the downtown waterfront on our winding route, Lisette stopped me.

"Wait, wait, I have an idea. What if this is a death march? What if it's hell for us?"

"Because this is the most gorgeous day ever?"

"No, what if we convinced Paul that it's hell? Come on, here. Let's pose looking tired. And we're going to look worse and worse as the day goes on."

We took photos of ourselves looking weary and exhausted. *After half a km!* Lisette texted. He didn't respond, so he was probably in a lecture at his conference, which somehow only increased our hilarity.

We posted a series of increasingly more sad and depleted pictures as we walked along. In reality, we were having an absolutely lovely time, stopping at a little ice cream stand and pausing to eat our lunch on a rock overlooking the harbor.

4 km, so tired we have forgotten what country we're in. Lisette texted. *Abby thinks she's back in nyc and keeps swearing like a sailor*

That's a fucking lie, I added to the text chain.

If she kills me it's your fault because you aren't driving us paul, Lisette added. *she is delirious with exhaustion now. possibly delusional. keeps mentioning the movie 127 hours and talking about how I'm her rock.*

Eventually, Paul must have stepped out of a conference lecture, because he reacted to them all at once.

This is what happens without my car? I could have lent it to you.

too late, Lisette wrote. *Much too late.* She sent him a photo of herself looking dead, her eyes glazed, by the side of the road.

Paul responded to both of us. *Abby I told you if you were going to kill her you had to do it in a place where you can easily hide the body.*

I took a photo of a small waterfront shack.

No worries. I texted. *Just need to break open the window with my fist.*

Too visible, he replied. *You're gonna have to weight her down with stones and dump her in the ocean.*

"How did this get so dark?" I asked Lisette.

"We kept yes, and-ing each other. This is the world's most long-distance improv practice," said Lisette, grinning as she read Paul's response. "Hold on, we need to pose like you're about to dump me in the water."

"I can do a selfie of that," I offered. I held the phone up while Lisette sagged in my arms.

A man paused nearby to watch. He had been walking a tiny dog and looked a little horrified. "Sir?" Lisette said. "Can you take a photo of us and make it look like I'm a murder victim?"

Late on Sunday night, my doorbell rang. I ran down the stairs, assuming that it was Lisette there to grab something from my backpack that she'd forgotten, but it was Paul, standing in front of me looking amused and tired. He seemed like he had come straight here from the airport.

"Hey," he said softly. "I just wanted to make sure that the two of you actually made it through today alive." I noticed he was checking on me and not with Lisette.

"Well, Lisette didn't make it, but I had a lovely day."

"You got some sun," he said.

He gave a sleepy, remote smile, leaning against the door frame, and I had the same feeling again. This is it, I thought. He's finally going to kiss me. I waited. Neither of us moved for a moment.

Then I looked away to cover my nerves. "Conference was okay?"

He nodded. "Yeah, it was good. It's for educators. Professional development. I learned a lot about teaching twentieth-century political history, which would be more useful if I end up teaching high school. I'm sure it sounds really boring, but just the way people approach introducing things like fascism, it was amazing."

"I don't find you boring, Paul."

He looked serious again, and I took a tiny half-step forward. He looked down at my shoes.

"So when do you go home?" he said quietly.

"To New York?"

He nodded. I met his gaze.

"I'm staying as long as I can, but realistically, August 31st. Unless the Canadian government steps in and hands me a visa, but that's hard to predict. I'm still paying for my apartment in

Brooklyn, so I would eventually have to give that up, or at least sublet it, and I can't really do that without having a way to work here, which I'm not sure I'm allowed to do."

"Right," he said. "Right. Well, I um...here." He took out a greeting card from his pocket and handed it to me. It was blank inside, but it had Mike Myers as Austin Powers on the front, with the words, "Oh, behave."

I smiled, feeling a little confused. "Thanks."

"That was your first crush, wasn't it? I saw it and thought of you."

"True." I examined the card. "A Canadian who did sketch comedy. I had terrible taste in men."

"Clearly," he agreed. His eyes were warm again. I waited, but he didn't move.

"I hope they had a Geena Davis one for you," I added lightly.

"Dark-haired sassy American."

I waited. We were flirting, weren't we?

"So Thursday night. Improv practice. My place," he said at last, as if collecting himself. "I'm looking forward to it."

"I'll work on that French mime bit, see if it could be a longer sketch." My heart was pounding. "That one was really working."

"Can't wait." He turned to go.

Well, that's it, I figured. I've been giving him openings, and he hasn't been taking them. He just wants to flirt. Maybe it's some kind of protective field while he's still getting over his ex. Heck, maybe this is why his ex-wife left, for all I know. Because he was flirting with everyone, and she couldn't take it anymore.

Whatever I was expecting when I came to improv practice that Thursday, it wasn't that we were going to kiss each other.

8

"THAT COUNTS AS
TAKING IT SLOW, RIGHT?"

THE FRIDAY MORNING after the kiss during improv practice, Paul called and asked if he could come to my place.

"I have a few more improv books for you," he said. "If you're still willing to read them. I told you last night that I would bring them."

"Of course," I said. "I really liked the other ones."

"Can I come by now?" he asked. "I know you're at work right now."

"Of course. Anytime. I just have a meeting at 2 p.m."

It was a Friday and Paul was still off work for the summer, so I knew he would probably be over soon. I also knew Paul was probably using the books as an excuse to talk about what had happened, and I began to get nervous as I waited for him to arrive. I was supposed to be researching the impact of a change in interest rates on rental markets. Instead I walked back and forth around the living room practicing alternate versions of the upcoming conversation, varying between readying polite responses to his lack of interest and throwing his obvious interest in his face. Then I imagined us admitting that we were madly in love, which gave me the push I needed to open my work laptop to distract myself.

When he arrived, he had several improv books in hand, and he waved off an offer of coffee or tea and sat down at the table and spent a few minutes walking me through each of the books. I could sense that he was nervous, too.

"So last night..." he began at last. We were now seated an arms-length away from each other on Charlotte's sofa.

"I'm sorry about that," I said.

"You? No. Why are you sorry, I was the one who..." He trailed off.

"My essay on consent in improv isn't finished yet."

"Ah, right." He smiled at his hands. "I kissed you," he said firmly. I could feel my face warming.

"I'm pretty sure I kissed you back," I offered, and watched his expression for any indicator of what was coming next. He was giving me nothing. I felt like he was a clever murder suspect on a police procedural, and I was the cop examining his face for clues.

I waited as he stood up and walked to the window, then started to pace around the apartment looking at Charlotte's fishing boat photos. None of that seemed good.

"The thing is...I uh...finalized my divorce six months ago..."

"I know." I tried to sound gentle.

"It had been a long time coming. She left me almost a year before that. And the whole thing was really messy. It messed with my head."

I put up my hand. "Okay. I'm going to stop you right there. We don't have to do this."

"Don't have to—"

"If you have some long speech about how you can't date anyone right now, because you're emotionally fragile, but then as soon as you meet someone you actually like...I don't need to hear about why you haven't asked me out. It's okay if you just like me as a friend."

"Hmmm." Paul's face was unreadable.

"No, I'm sorry, I guess I've heard some version of this enough times in my life that I don't want to put either of us through it. Because I really like you, and I'm having fun spending time with you and I didn't demand that you to explain yourself to me."

He came closer, sitting opposite me. "What if that wasn't what I was going to say?"

A moment passed. I took a breath and then laughed. "Fine. Go on."

He leaned forward. "Okay, well, I was going to say something more like, I just got divorced and you are the first person I've really liked since then, but I have a feeling that if I let myself get close to you, and then you leave in a few weeks, it's pretty likely that I'll get my heart broken."

"Oh." My voice sounded small in my own ears.

"Not exactly what you expected me to say?"

"Not precisely," I said quietly. "Well, you don't have to worry about that because no one ever falls in love with me."

"Abby, I'm being serious. You're not the kind of person I'm going to be able to date casually and then watch you leave."

"Most guys think casual is the only way to date me, so..."

"That's not what I think."

"Oh," I said again. A moment passed.

"So I do want to kiss you. I want to do all of this. I was just hoping to find out whether you're leaving the country before I do."

"I don't know if I'm leaving." My voice sounded a little wobbly. "I applied for...I mean, I sent in stuff to the Canadian government, for a work visa, but the lawyer wasn't optimistic, and if something comes up with Laura, or work...I don't know, Paul. I wish I could say for sure."

"You met with a lawyer?"

I nodded. "An immigration lawyer. He wasn't sure how it would go. I started the paperwork, but I can't promise anything."

He nodded thoughtfully. "That's okay. I don't—it doesn't necessarily sound to me like you'll stay, honestly."

"But I want to." As soon as the words were out, I knew that I meant them. It was a strange feeling to know that I wanted to stay.

"My mother," Paul began, "I take care of her. It's not always easy. But she's the only family I have, and she needs me, so if your sister needs you, I understand. If things don't work out for your sister in Atlanta, and you have to go be with her, I mean, even if...you may just want to see your niece more. I wouldn't want to stop you from the thing that would make you happy."

I looked at the floor, trying to find the words. "Our mother was an alcoholic, so Laura and I always relied on each other. And now she doesn't need me, and I don't know what to do with myself. I keep assuming she'll need me, but it may be wishful thinking."

"You want her to need you." He looked like he was trying to puzzle out something.

"I want to be there if she needs me," I said. "But I really like it here. And I like you. Kissing you was nice." I felt like an idiot, confessing to that.

"Nice."

"Wonderful." I hated myself for saying the words. I couldn't pretend it meant nothing, now.

"I just don't think I can do it anymore," he said softly.

"Okay." I tried not to look disappointed.

"I mean, I don't think I can stay friends." He came closer. "I just can't anymore." He put one hand against my cheek, and then he leaned over, his lips brushing mine, then deepening into a real kiss, pushing me backwards. We were sliding together onto the sofa, my back scattering the pile of Charlotte's nautical pillows. Now that I finally had him in my arms, I wanted to kiss all of him. His neck, his cheeks, his shoulders. One of his hands slipped behind my head, cradling me as he kissed me again.

Then he paused and breathed out a little laugh against my neck.

"What's funny?"

He pulled back a few inches to meet my eyes. "You really thought I was going to come in here and give you a story about why I couldn't date anyone right now?"

I looked up at him. "I assumed."

"That's what you were assuming the other night?"

I nodded. "Yeah."

"Because your ex-boyfriend gave you a line about why he couldn't get married, and then changed his mind?"

"I was trying to be logical."

"Logical." He kissed me again. "Abby," he whispered. One of his hands slid under my shirt, gently gliding along my ribcage. I could feel him against me, my body aching to get closer. He released me gently, resting his lips against my neck, breathing in and out.

"You're going to break my heart," he whispered. "But okay."

"Okay?" I wasn't sure what he meant.

"Okay." He gently slid away from me. "Maybe we can take it slow."

"Slow," I repeated. That hadn't felt slow.

"A contained explosion."

"How do those work?"

"The hell if I know. It sounds good in theory, though, right?"

I understood him too well, for the first time. The problem

had never been whether he liked me. It had been that this was inevitably going to end.

"We can take it slow." My voice sounded faint. He reached over and laced his fingers through mine, then squeezed my hand. I leaned toward him to take another kiss, this time because I wanted one, and it caused a chain reaction to another, and another, and another...

He finally caught his breath, head against my shoulder, and then stood up, running a hand through his hair and facing away from me. "Okay, well I brought you the improv books..."

"You did."

"I did," he repeated. "And you have work today."

"I appreciate your respect for the demands of capitalism."

He gave a little laugh and then headed toward the door. I walked after him. He put one hand on the handle and then took it off and put it around my waist and kissed me again. His whole body was flush against mine, glowing with heat. One hand traced down my arm like a slow-moving electric current. When the kiss finally tapered off, he smiled a little.

"That counts as taking it slow, right?"

"Snail's pace."

"Perfect."

He gave me a warm look and then slipped outside, and I stood there, trying to breathe normally, one hand pressed against the closed door for support. My legs were about to collapse beneath me.

Paul was absolutely right. That was not how I had expected that conversation to go.

He called me that evening a little a little after 7:30.

"Hey, it's Paul."

"I know." My voice sounded higher pitched than normal,

like I was sixteen again, twisting my fingers through the phone cord in my mother's kitchen.

"I wanted to call you after work, but it turns out that I'm dealing with some stuff for my mother tonight. She started some trouble with the neighbors and I'm trying to diffuse it, but do you have any time this weekend?"

"Yeah, I think so. I can probably squeeze you in between the goat yoga and laser tag."

I heard him laugh. "Great. Shuffle around the schedule and see what you can do."

"Or you could come over tonight, after you finish the stuff with your mother."

"Yeah, no, I'm thinking a proper date might actually be nice. So." There was a brief pause. "I'm thinking we hang out, we take things slow. And hopefully that means if you end up having to ditch me the next day to head back to the States, it'll be easier. Because I'm not very good at..." He muttered something.

"Was that casual texts? I'm sorry, I didn't hear that, Paul, if you could just repeat..."

"Ha ha, very funny."

"I didn't know nice Canadian boys had casual sex. I thought you hooked up one time and then asked her to marry you and live on the maple sugar ranch."

"Did you say maple sugar ranch? A ranch?"

"You know. A big open space with trees."

"An open space, with trees. Do you know what the defining quality of open spaces is?"

"Okay, okay."

"So does that sound okay? Not that we couldn't...I don't even mean we couldn't go to bed. I just want to be cautious. I'm not sure how else to do this."

I took a breath. "We can try."

"Okay, then if you're free tomorrow…"

I glanced out the window. "The weather is supposed to be terrible, right?"

"Yeah, but we could go to a museum, maybe? There's a place called The Rooms. Lots of interesting stuff, usually. Art gallery, archives…"

I could suddenly picture it: Paul wandering around an archive talking about history trivia, and I loved it. I wanted every minute I could get, especially if we got to hold hands for some of it. Maybe this was just like a high school romance, in the worst possible way.

"Archives?" I said.

"I know it doesn't sound—"

"I want to visit the archives with a history teacher."

"You're being sarcastic."

"No, I'm completely serious. Because you're going to have a lot of deep feelings about fishing licenses in the 1800s."

"I actually do have strong feelings about the history of fishing licenses."

I grinned. "Is this where you take your students?"

"Every year. I can give you my whole lecture if you like."

"I'll insist."

PAUL PICKED me up and drove me through the rain to The Rooms, a museum and cultural center up the hill near the center of town. We spent half the day there, wandering around, having lunch, and looking at exhibits on indigenous culture and local art. I coaxed Paul until he went into teacher mode, which involved providing neat mental lists of facts interrupted by bouts of boyish enthusiasm.

"I mean, St. John's is the oldest English-speaking city in

North America. Discovered in the 1490s, founded in 1583. The pilgrims were twenty-five years later than that."

"What's the oldest non-English-speaking city?"

"If you mean continuously inhabited, I believe that is Cholula, Mexico, which is twenty-five hundred years old. Showoffs."

Teacher Paul was different than Improv Paul. In improv, he was free, occasionally cocky, a bit sexual, and very witty. As a teacher, he bounced between funny and intellectually serious. He could quote a movie or dive into an analysis of the province's poverty levels and supply chain problems. I liked both versions of him: the one who could go into film noir detective voice and the one who could explain why bottom trawling was harming coastal communities. And then there was the one who had kissed me like he wanted to keep doing it forever.

"So why did you decide on teaching?" I asked.

"That took some time." Paul told me he had grown up in a little town where his father had become a mechanic after he was injured in a fishing accident.

"We had four generations of fishing, mining, and logging," he said.

"Newfoundland's greatest hits."

"And I was sure I was going to do the same myself until my dad got injured on his boat. Kind of took the shine off it when you realized you could lose the use of your left arm."

"So you decided to become an actor?"

"No. First I discovered the video rental shop."

"They still have those?"

"Where I lived? It was the most exciting place in town." Paul grinned. "I took out every single video until I had to get a job there to cover the costs."

"What was the movie that really hooked you?" I asked.

"It's cliché, but I was a huge James Cameron fan for a few years," he said. "So it was the first *Terminator*."

"I knew you were a romantic."

He laughed. "That is a very romantic movie. He traveled through time because he fell in love with her photograph."

"Oh, a lot of men have fallen in love with women through photographs."

"I can't believe you're implying that Kyle's love for Sarah Connor wasn't pure. I mean, you have seen it, right?"

"Oh, I've seen it. 'In the few hours we had together, we loved a lifetime's worth,'" I said, quoting the film.

Paul looked at me, surprised, for a long moment. "Anyway," he went on quickly, "I convinced myself that I wanted to be a movie star, but looking back on it, my favorite films were always historical. And *Indiana Jones*. So it makes sense I circled back to history teaching once I grew out of thinking I was going to be an actor."

"You're a good actor, though," I said. "I've seen you on stage."

"Not good enough. In four years in Toronto, I booked three whole commercials and two whole plays. And I spent one memorable summer playing a talking lobster at a children's amusement park."

"There better be video evidence."

"There was, but I had the people who took it eliminated. A tragedy for their families, but it had to be done."

"Then I'll expect a live performance."

"Only during sex."

I cackled, and he grinned.

"I got my teaching license while taking care of my father after he got sick. I could do some of the coursework remotely, which helped. And then I finished the licensing and got a job." He shrugged. "There need to be more male teachers. The boys especially need it. So I feel like I'm part of the solution to a problem."

"Indiana Jones is your role model, huh? Do your female students ever write *I love you* on their eyelids?"

He smiled. "If so, I politely ignore it."

"I would have been completely in love with you if you were my teacher," I said.

He looked away again for a moment. "So can I make you dinner? My place?"

I nodded. He leaned over and kissed me, lightly, and then immediately swore.

"What's wrong?"

"I just spotted a student. Aidan Johnson, the little bastard."

"They can't fire you for kissing someone, right?"

"No. I am just about to get non-stop questions about you through at least November."

"Just tell them I was a hooker. That'll settle them down."

As soon as we were inside his apartment, I wrapped my arms around his shoulders, and he leaned me against the doorway, hips against mine.

"So taking it slow means..." I asked quietly.

"Making out. Definitely. Come here." He pulled me toward the sofa where we'd had improv practice. "It'll be like high school."

"This is hotter than anything that happened to me in high school," I whispered.

He crawled over me, knee on one side of me, leaning over to kiss my collarbone. "I can't believe the boys weren't all over you."

"You haven't seen my sister. My first boyfriend only asked

me out because she said no. Of course, he didn't tell me this until after we'd been dating for three months."

"Unacceptable. I'll have him assassinated."

Paul was kissing down the front of my shirt, now, and both my hands were on his shoulders. I was afraid to talk again, afraid to stop the path that we finally seemed to be on. It was so easy to kiss him.

He leaned back a moment later, his eyes dark rings of brown. The look in his eyes was too much for me. I looked away.

"So did you do a lot of this in high school, then?" I asked.

He shook his head. "I was terrified of girls, so I put a lot of effort into being polite."

"A good Canadian boy."

He nodded, smiling a little.

"And what would happen if I asked you to be very, very impolite?"

He groaned and pushed me back against the sofa cushions. I hadn't expected him to be like this: intense, utterly focused. I found that my hands were gripping his shirt, wanting to pull him closer. I could smell his faint scent of soap and pine trees, his body against mine, our breaths starting to sync up faster and faster. I could hear him muttering my name into the shell of my ear, one of his hands tracing along my side. I could hear the sound of the doorbell.

We both sat up. Our breathing was too fast, too messy.

"One second," he said lightly, running a hand through his hair. "Don't move."

He walked to the door and looked out through the peep hole. He glanced at me, his expression shifting.

"I'm sorry. Hold on a minute."

It was in his face. I knew something was wrong as he stepped outside, and I tiptoed toward the window. His mother again? I wanted to see what she looked like. The rain had turned into a blustering sideways wind, and when I leaned forward to look outside, I could just see a blonde woman standing at his door in a billowing trench coat with a plaid lining. She looked beautiful and wind-tossed, like she was in an advertisement for a high-end British clothing line.

I could see that Paul was talking to her, though only his shoulder was visible. She was nodding, speaking earnestly, nodding again. Then she ran a hand through her hair and laughed.

I leaned out of sight behind a curtain.

It was his ex-wife. I knew it, somehow. It was something about her expression, and everything Lisette had said about her. I didn't want her to see me here, in case Paul decided to get back together with her. It was like I had already cast myself as the Other Woman.

I had to remind myself that Paul was not married. I was not doing anything wrong.

They only talked for a few moments, but I sat very still, waiting for it to be over. I listen to the opening and closing of his front door, a wrestling against the wind. I turned around. At least he was alone, I thought. At least he hadn't decided to introduce her to me. That would have been more than I could handle. "And this is my friend Abby, up from New York. Lisette's friend, really."

"Sorry," he said.

"Who was it?" I asked, like I didn't know.

"Patricia," he said quietly. "Trish."

"Ah, okay." I sounded casual, didn't I?

"I'm sorry," he added, a strange expression on his face. "I didn't know she was back in town."

Of course she just got back to town, I thought. It felt faithful to the narrative of my life that I had foolishly tried to deviate from. "Is she back permanently or...?"

"It sounds like she's not sure. But probably. I should..." He shook his head.

I nodded. "So it didn't work out with the other guy?"

"I don't think so. I need to talk to her more. I'm sorry, Abby. This doesn't..."

He trailed off. He leaned against the wall for a moment.

"I'll go," I said, quietly, rising. "It's okay. You want to go talk to her more. It's okay."

"No, no," he said. "Not right now. I can do that later."

I remembered what he'd said about trying to be polite with girls in high school. That's what he was doing now. He paced back and forth and then moved toward the kitchen.

"Tea? Coffee?" he said.

"Tea would be nice."

Paul nodded. He looked toward the window, his mind elsewhere.

"Do you want to talk about it?" I asked gently.

"No. There's nothing to say."

I watched as he walked around the kitchen making the tea. This was a test. If we were friends, he would talk about it, but after what had just happened between us, he wasn't sure how to find his footing again.

"I'm being quiet, aren't I?" he said after a minute.

"Understandable. I can go. I actually just ordered a Lyft, and it will be here soon."

"Are you sure? No. Abby. I can drive you."

"I'm sure. I think you need a moment to yourself."

He walked over, put his arms around me and squeezed once. "I'm just distracted. You deserve better than this."

"Paul, it's okay. Whatever is going on with us, I'm your friend, too."

"I know." He gently kissed me on the lips. An apology kiss. It was the first one I'd received from Paul, but I knew what apologies tasted like; I'd gotten enough of those. Then he walked to the door and grabbed his coat. He looked back. "I really like you, Abby."

Oh, *no*.

"I like you, too," I said flatly. He had been worried about his own heartbreak, but it would be mine that got smashed up, in the end. Today, tonight, tomorrow. Soon.

"Right, then...I need to—I'll call you soon. I promise." He smiled once more.

Promise? Oh, double no. He was promising to call? Soon? I'd be lucky if I ever heard from him again.

"Well, my Lyft is almost here, so..." I waved my cell phone. I hadn't ordered a Lyft, but he wouldn't know that.

He nodded once, then opened the door for me to go, and shut it slowly behind me.

At that moment, racing downhill through the gusts of wind among the sloping streets, it hit me again how much the city of St. John's looked like parts of Brooklyn. At the moment, they felt like exactly the same place.

9

"A WELCOME DISTRACTION"

NEVER HAD I missed my conversations with Laura more than I did right then. She would be able to talk me through this. She always did. She would tell me to ditch any guy who shut down a first date because his ex-wife showed up, and that was probably exactly what I needed to hear.

I texted her, trying for a sly approach that conceded everything and admitted nothing. *Hey, I miss talking to you. can we just talk?* I texted, *I feel like we're fighting, but I'm still here for you.*

I didn't say, *I need you.* I wasn't sure if I was allowed to say that to Laura, not when she might be having troubles with Nick, too. Her life could come first if we had a discussion; her problems would be the headliners. I was happy to slip mine in at the end of the conversation as a post-script.

She called me fifteen minutes later. Her voice sounded scratchy. "Abs?"

"Yeah, hon?"

"This is a mess." Laura's tone was flat.

"What's wrong, babe?" I found a comfortable seat, clicking back into supportive sister mode and mentally pouring myself a

139

cup of tea. She was dealing with Nick, after all. This would take a while.

"This whole thing about buying a house," Laura began.

"He's still pushing that?"

"He wants me to take money out of my retirement account. He says we have to do it right away before the market goes up, and he only leased this place until September, so he wants us to find something so Hannah can stay in the same school that she's starting."

"Whoa, what? So she started school already, but you can't keep renting the same place?"

"Soon. Georgia schools start really early. But I think Nick thinks that if we buy a house together, it's a way for Hannah and me to have to stay. But I'm not ready to make that kind of a commitment. I mean, I haven't even found a job here yet. I'm interviewing, but..."

"It's too soon for you guys to buy a house together."

I heard her sigh. "I know, but he makes a really good point about getting settled. That way Hannah could be in one school all the way through high school, you know? I mean, in New York, the kids keep changing schools, and they have to apply to middle schools and the magnet schools..."

"Laura. You're not ready to buy a house with him yet. End of story. Nothing to stop you guys from renting another place in the same school district together."

"I know, and that's what I told him. But I understand why he keeps pushing it—he's trying to make up for lost time."

"But you aren't ready for that, and he has to prove himself to you. And one month isn't going to cut it."

Laura went silent for a long moment. "Yeah. I just don't know how to tell him 'no' without making him feel like I'm rejecting him. And I want him to know that I really want to work this out."

"Tell him 'I'm not ready.' That's it. That's what you say."

"I've missed talking to you." Something rose inside me when she said it. A tidal wave of relief.

"I've missed talking to you, too," I said.

"So how are things going with the improv group?"

"Okay."

"You okay?" But after letting Laura pour her heart out, I suddenly didn't want her to feel like the only reason I'd called was so that I could do the same. "I'm okay. Just lonely. How's Hannah doing?"

Laura and I talked for a few minutes until she said she heard Nick's car pulling up and had to go.

I could tell her about Paul another time. The important thing was that it felt like we were sisters again.

My phone rang again a few minutes later. A Newfoundland phone number.

"Hello?"

"Hey, Abigail. It's Mark. I was unexpectedly in the city tonight and I'm in your neighborhood. I wondered if I could stop by."

"Oh, um…"

"Just to check in on you. Assuming you're just sitting there by yourself on a Saturday night." I wondered how pointed the remark was.

"I am just sitting here, but it's okay. I wanted a quiet evening."

"Let me come by. Just for a quick chat?"

"Okay, sure."

Mark arrived a few minutes later. I felt nervous waiting for him, though I wasn't sure why. When I opened the door and saw him standing there, rubbing the back of his neck, I realized the problem: I found him attractive, though in a very different way than Paul. Paul was funny, clever, polite. Mark was a misplaced New Yorker, all cynicism and dark humor. He felt familiar in a way that Paul never had.

He stepped inside and deposited a box of pastries on the table.

"These are for you. Had to get some business done in town today," he said. "It's gotten nasty out there. Figured I'd stop in and check on you after our chat the other night."

"Check on me?"

"See if you changed your mind about a date."

"Oh." His reckless confidence was charming, in a way. I let myself wonder if I was making a mistake, picking the wrong guy, but it didn't matter. I had fallen for Paul whether I wanted to or not.

I opened my mouth to say that Paul and I were dating but then wondered if that was still true. Paul and I had been together for a Friday and a Saturday afternoon; we weren't exactly a twenty-episode K-drama miniseries. If Paul broke up with me after one date, I would be allowed to grieve for twenty-four hours and then move on, according to my friend Jasmine. It might be better not to say anything to Mark.

"That seems like a no," Mark said ruefully. "Fair enough. Chocolate éclair? They're from a bakery across the street from my house called the Chocolate Fair. I have to buy some every week or the smell torments me. I feel like a priest living next to a whorehouse."

"I wouldn't peg you as a man of the cloth."

"A fallen priest. Like that fellow in *Fleabag*."

"Or Dimmesdale in *The Scarlet Letter*."

"Exactly. Self-flagellating about my éclair addiction."

I made him a cup of coffee, and we sat at my table eating pastries. They were slender, rich, and lighter than air, and did a nice job of earning their sinful reputation.

"So I know this may not matter to you," Mark said slowly,

"but Paul's ex-wife is back in town." I froze at Mark's malice, then wondered if it was indeed malice or indirect kindness.

"Oh, yeah. She stopped by."

He raised his eyebrows. "Paul told you?"

"I was with him. At his house."

"You were with Paul? On a date?"

"Sort of." I didn't want to admit to Mark that it was our first one, officially.

"Sort of." Mark chuckled. "Paul is something, isn't he. So how did that go? When she stopped by, I mean?"

"He spoke to her for a few minutes outside. He seemed surprised."

"I'll bet." Mark leaned back, looking delighted. He could lounge in the stories of other people's misery like a cat on a sunny windowsill.

"So how did you hear about it?" I asked. "Did Paul tell you?"

"Trish called me. She and I used to work together. She was putting out feelers for jobs and wanted to know if I hated her."

"And what did you say?"

"I said I hated everyone, but I didn't have it in for her in particular."

I took this in, trying for Mark's casual irony. "So it sounds like she has fallen out of love with documentary filmmaking."

Mark snorted, then looked into his coffee mug. "If you want my opinion, it sounds like she wants to get back together with Paul. That was another thing she wanted to talk about. How he was doing."

I tried not to look like any of this was affecting me. "Well, it's up to Paul what he wants to do. If he still loves her, he should be with her."

"Sure." Mark sighed. He looked tired. I felt like I was seeing the real person, suddenly, under the sarcastic façade, and I felt a wave of affection for Mark. He took a breath. "You know, I feel for Paul but I'm also jealous of him. I got married way too young, and I feel like I missed out on playing the field, on dating. I don't think anyone should stay with the person they met when they were fifteen. You miss out on too much of life. So the last couple of years, I've been making up for lost time. But...with you, I feel like I actually connect. I actually want to date you, not have a one-night thing. So I guess I'm being persistent, because I think you're a tiny bit attracted to me. And if you could be leaving soon, I have to make a move. Am I completely off-base?"

"I may have to leave soon."

He raised his eyebrows, catching the dodge, a tiny smirk on his lips. "I'm not young anymore. I have to put myself out there instead. And I don't want to see you get hurt by whatever is happening with Paul."

"I appreciate that."

He leaned over and took my hand and then leaned over and kissed my knuckles once. In spite of myself, my body reacted just a little. He slid his chair a little closer.

I wondered if Paul was with his ex-wife right now.

Mark leaned over and carefully kissed my cheek. Then Mark leaned a little closer and I pulled back and shook my head.

"No, no, Mark."

What was I doing? I didn't even know if things were over with Paul. I wasn't even sure I liked Mark.

Mark observed all of this with a gimlet eye, then shrugged, shaking off the spell. "Well, if anything changes with Paul, or goes wrong, I just want you to know that I'm here as a friend, or a date." He stood up and smiled. "Or just as a welcome distraction."

Oh, he's good, I thought.

He grinned, grabbing his coat on the way to the door. I showed him out with a little heat flushing my cheeks red, irritated that he'd managed to get a reaction.

Paul had made me like him, and it made me angry that I was being loyal to Paul even though Mark was offering me a perfectly good no-frills fling. What if it was the wrong call?

Tomorrow I would call Laura and tell her all of this. Well, most of this, anyway.

Even though Laura knew most of my stories, there was one story that I had never told her. Laura knew about Farid, my handsome Iranian-American boyfriend from grad school, the one who helped me get my first job as a journalist. Laura knew Farid had hurt me, and she assumed that he was the reason I didn't trust men.

But Laura didn't know about Colin, the last guy I had actually dated...and the one who put me off dating entirely. She didn't know about Colin because Colin was married, and because throughout the entire relationship, I wasn't sure whether I had found the love of my life, or was a horrible monster, or was just a complete idiot. In retrospect, it was that last one.

In my defense, I didn't know Colin was married when I met him. He certainly didn't volunteer the information. The whole thing happened right before the pandemic, when I was already a financial writer and was still going into the office for meetings. One day at the coffee machine, I found myself chatting with a boyishly cute data analyst who had a desk on the same floor as my boss. It was a casual conversation about coffee pods and the terrible impact they have on the environment and our desire to find alternatives that didn't involve spending five dollars at Starbucks, but he was dry and clever, and I liked him right away. It took two weeks to find out that he was named Colin, and a couple weeks more before I got the courage to drop by his desk when I was on his floor for a meeting. After that, he started tracking me down whenever he saw me in the hallways. We always made each other laugh, and he was around my age, but I tried not to think too seriously about the possibility of dating him. I was such a pessimist at that point that I assumed it would go nowhere.

Then one day, he caught up with me outside the building and suggested we grab lunch together, and then a couple of days later, we got dinner after work on a Friday. He seemed to genuinely like me, and we would text occasionally and send each other jokes. At this point I was telling Laura about the 'cute data analyst,' but I still hadn't told her his name, not wanting to jinx things or make her too hopeful.

After a few weeks of this, we spent a night together, but it never quite became a regular thing, because he only seemed to be available every couple of weeks.

I know, I know.

The shoe fell a few days later when I started joking about a future together, speculating on the names of future kids. He looked at me with a pained expression and told me that he still *technically* had a wife. But it was okay, he said, because they were basically living apart.

Yes, he did tell me that story about how they were still together but emotionally separated. Yes, he did say that they were still living under the same roof but only because they had a five-year-old and were figuring out how to break the news to their child that their marriage was over.

I went out with him for another month, believing that. I slept with him two more times before I figured it out. The thing that's hardest to explain—the thing Laura would never believe, even though it's true—is that I actually believed him when he said it.

"Oh, that's just New York," I told myself, "where it's hard to get an affordable apartment. No wonder he still lives with his ex-wife."

No. He was just living with his wife.

Over the last few years, I've had plenty of time to think about why Colin did what he did, and here's what I've come to believe. Some married guys are sociopaths, planning the whole seduction ahead of time, but I think Colin didn't plan it. He was able to lure me into an affair because he did really like me. He enjoyed our friendship as much as I did. I think he was genuinely falling for me, maybe in some part of his mind thinking that I might be a better fit than his wife, taking pleasure in the brand new relationship phase, where you're excited to send texts to each other and make little jokes and do check-ins—the shiny new relationship stuff that you don't ever experience again once you're married. When he told me that he was 'separated,' I think in Colin's mind, that was a way to lessen the blow, to spare my feelings. He probably thought it was kinder that way, that it would make me feel less used while he decided what he wanted. It gave him options: to run away with me if I was perfect, or to claim that he had worked things out with his wife. He got to date while still being married.

I broke it off, not him. That's the one shred of dignity I have about the whole thing. I broke it off when I realized he was lying not only to me but to himself. He could convince himself that what he said to me was true, in the ninety minutes between when our date started and when it ended, which was why he was so good at lying.

So Colin isn't even what sent me into a tailspin. What broke me was when the next married man hit on me. And three months later, the next one. I started to feel like I must be sending some signal—some vulnerable signal—some flashing light. I am the one you cheat with or the one you cheat on. They sense something damaged in me, and it reels them in. Even on dating apps, I kept getting the guys who said their relationship status was 'complicated,' until finally I deleted all the apps from my phone.

My mother died around the same time, so I was also dealing with that, with a lowkey fear that I was destined to end up the same kind of train wreck, sliding down a path of fancy cocktails until I landed on a cheap bar stool, embittered and alone. I didn't want to date married men, so I might as well not date anybody.

Perhaps that was why I'd attracted someone like Paul, caught in the midst of a messy divorce. Perhaps it made sense that he wanted me only because I was going to leave soon. Maybe the attraction was that somehow, deep down, he knew that nothing real could happen.

He was just another married man whom I'd attracted, in some sense, or at least a man who still wanted to be married. Just not to me.

10

"WHERE COULD WE
HAVE GONE FURTHER?"

PAUL CALLED me early the next morning.

"I'm so sorry," he said. "Yesterday was—I'm so sorry about that. It must have been...I must have seemed really off. It wasn't...I'm not trying to get back together with her. I was just shocked."

"No. Paul, I mean, if you do want to get back together with her—"

He cut me off firmly. "I don't. I really don't."

I said nothing, doubting him, trying not to doubt him.

"Lisette wants to do something today with both of us," Paul said. "Since the weather is so bad, would you be up for going to see a movie?"

"Only a really bad one."

Paul, Lisette and I went to see a ridiculous Jason Statham movie together and sat in the back row where we could make each other laugh with side remarks all the way through, like we were the naughty rebels in a school assembly. It felt like we were team again, and I was glad that the fact that Paul and I were dating hadn't changed that. Then I realized that I hadn't mentioned it to Lisette yet. Had Paul? Should I have done so?

Was I instinctively protecting Paul, in case he might want plausible deniability to get back together with his wife?

It was getting dark when we pulled up to her new house.

"Back to my basement lair," she said.

"You do have other options," Paul replied quietly.

"Nah. I need the history of renting to get a proper lease. Though I think by the time I sign a lease on my own place, I want to formally change my name, so my ex can't find me. And I've picked a name out."

She paused dramatically.

"Celine Dion!" Lisette grinned at us from Paul's back seat.

"Excellent idea," I agreed. I knew this was one of her comedic bits.

"I could be the other Celine Dion," she went on. "But that way if my ex googled my name, he'll just find her show dates in Las Vegas."

We theorized about other names Lisette could choose: Alanis Morissette. Angelina Jolie. Dame Judy Dench.

Lisette paused. "Seriously, though. There's something else I need to say. It's important, and it has to do with my love life." There was a long moment.

"Yes?" I gently prompted.

"I'm not sure this is the right time, but there's something I need to tell you. Or more specifically, something I need to tell Paul." We both waited, watching her struggle to meet our eyes. "I'm in love with you, Paul." I froze at her words. "I'm sorry to do this in front of Abby, but I just needed you to finally know."

Paul stared at her for a long moment, then something in his expression shifted. "Oh, fuck off, Liz."

She broke into a wide grin. "You guys hooked up, right?"

I looked between them. "Oh my God!" I laughed. "I wasn't sure whether Paul told you, and by the time we picked you up, I realized we hadn't discussed it! I'm sorry!"

"So which one finally caved and jumped on top of the other one?"

Paul sighed. "I asked her out."

"I'm very excited about this. I want little babies who look like both of you, but more like Abby because Paul is about forty percent gremlin. This is all my doing, you know that, right? Why didn't you tell me?"

We both looked sheepish. "I meant to, honestly," I said.

"Hahahaha. Your faces when I asked Paul out. That was better than the film!" She grinned and hopped out of the car.

Paul drove me back to my apartment and then sat for a moment in the car without getting out, looking down at his hands. I was trying to give him time to speak before I let my fear shut things down. Saying 'yes and' to life, right? I hadn't entirely expected to see him again after last night, and here he was.

"Can I take you out," he finally said, "on a proper date? This week sometime? Dinner, maybe?" My heart flooded with a dangerous level of joy, and I pushed it down like it was a stranger's dog. Down. No. Sit.

"I'd like that."

He met my eyes, his brown eyes open and serious. "Wednesday? Before we have our improv practice on Thursday?"

"Wednesday works."

"And can I give you a kiss goodnight?"

"As long as you're taking it slow. We're supposed to be taking it slow."

"Oh, I'll take it slow." He grinned wolfishly.

We kissed again, for a long time. A seduction kiss. Then he pulled away and shook his head slowly. "I really want to come upstairs."

"You could. Just for a coffee."

He breathed out a little laugh. "It wouldn't be just a coffee."

We sat for a long minute in total silence. His phone rang, and he glanced at it and groaned.

"Trish?" I asked.

"My mother again. It's like she can sense when I'm happy and activates her missile targeting system."

"You're happy?"

He nodded, without smiling, just gazing at me. "You should go inside. We'll do a proper date night."

"Okay. Goodnight." I got out of the car, my knees a bit unsteady, and went inside, thinking that he didn't kiss me like he was still in love with his ex-wife. Hope rose in my chest, carrying me up the stairs like an escaped balloon, bouncing me into my kitchen, staying with me even as I lay in bed.

THE NEXT DAY, my boss Kedar sent me a meeting request first thing in the morning. I pulled my hair into a ponytail and threw on one of my more professional sweaters, pushing the demolished remains of a cranberry muffin and my 'Tits and Boobies' mug safely out of view.

I could tell something was wrong as soon as I saw his face. He was usually a go-getter, cheerful, a bit of a corporate hustler but basically a nice guy. This time he looked grim.

"Hey, rock star," he said softly.

"What's up?" I asked.

"Pledgemont Funds might be changing its work-from-home policy." I stared at him. I could tell that it hurt him to say it, and I realized in a rush how much I liked Kedar. Sure, he might use annoying corporate speak about whether a particular ball was in my court, but he had always treated me well, always tried to allow me the life that I wanted to live. He had made the last couple of years of my life a lot less miserable than they would have been, and I could see how much it made him unhappy to deliver bad news.

"When?"

"Next Monday," he said. "I got no warning either. I'm supposed to spend three weeks at my cousin's wedding in India, and it looks like I may have to cancel the whole trip."

"How can they do that?"

"They can do that because they can do that," he said.

"Okay." I took a deep breath.

"But hold up. Don't book your flights yet. I'm fighting it. I've told them it's ridiculous. We're writers, not brokers. I think I can push back."

"When will you know?"

"Tonight, maybe. Or tomorrow. They're insisting that it has to be the whole company, or it will pit different departments against each other, but I'll see what I can do, okay? I know this is bad timing for you."

"Okay," I said quietly.

"I'll have more updates soon," he said. "I'm going to have a meeting with them today."

I nodded. "I'm sorry if you may have to miss the wedding."

"I'm sorry if you have to cut your trip short," he said.

The word stung. That's what I was doing in Kedar's mind: a trip. A fun sojourn, a bit of casual travel. I nodded.

"So this is definite?"

"If I make any headway with them, I'll let you know. Maybe I can push it back at least a week or two, but I have to see. I'll call you soon, I promise."

I felt like my heart was breaking. This was exactly what Paul had been worried about, and my job had proved him right. I was always supposed to go back to Brooklyn, anyway. I was supposed to arrive home right when Laura's life with Nick was falling apart, and that might be happening exactly on schedule.

I took out my phone and prepared a text for Paul, tears forming in my eyes as I looked for the right words. Should I call him? Break the news gently in writing? I hesitated. I didn't want to act like I expected Paul to be as heartbroken as I was. And Kedar had said maybe, right? It might be pushed off a week or two, or maybe even forever. There was no point in being sad if I didn't have a definite answer yet. I was going to see Paul on Wednesday night, and we could talk then. I would level with him about where things stood, and by that time I might know more myself.

Jasmine called me that evening.

"Hey, Chica," she said in her musical voice. "When are you back, babe? We're deciding about concert tickets and need to know if you'll be home by October and want to go see a sad gay pop band."

"Is that the name of the band?"

"It might as well be." She named a band I'd never heard of, but apparently, they were playing at Madison Square Garden, which officially meant I was not cool anymore.

I took a breath. "I should be back by October, yeah."

"Amazing. I couldn't handle it without you. Lucas wants to do theme dressing. It's me and three of his other friends, and he's insisting our outfits match. But you and I can cross that Lycra bridge when we come to it. By the way, I looked up pictures of Newfoundland and it is gorgeous."

"Yeah."

"Like, stunning. I mean, what the hell? Why does nobody tell me this stuff?"

"To be fair, I did."

Jasmine started to laugh. "You know what I love about this? You are so far ahead of the curve. In five years, everyone's gonna be like, Oh my God, I have to go to St. John's, and you'll be like, 'I already summered there.'"

"I don't think you get to use summer as a verb unless you make at least a million dollars a year."

"Babe, I'm appropriating 'summer' from the rich folks. It's mine now. I'm summering in Crown Heights."

"Yeah." I was silent for a moment.

"You okay?" she asked.

"I have to come back, and I'm not ready," I said. "The work from home policy may be going away."

"Oh, honey," she said, quietly. "I'm sorry. I'll take care of you. We'll go for drinks, and you can tell me all about your adventures in fairyland. Not that I'm not having my own version of that."

"Thanks, babe." I thought about telling her that I was in the process of getting my heart broken, but what was the point? She would just tell me that I would find someone else. That was what we were always telling each other in New York. Maybe that was part of our problem.

PAUL TEXTED me a few hours before we were supposed to meet on Wednesday. *Hey, I have an urgent family thing that's come up and my mother needs to stay at my place for a few days, so I can't go out tonight. Any chance you'd be willing to host the improv practice tomorrow night at your place?*

Sure, I replied. *I hope your mother is ok.*

I'm so sorry about our date tonight, he wrote back. *I will make it up to you.*

He was already pulling away, I thought. Maybe that was just as well. Less pain for everyone involved. Less pain for him, anyway.

I sat alone at my window, looking out at the city. It was a

beautiful day, breezy and warm, and there were flowers growing on windowsills and people laughing as they passed each other on my street.

And I was leaving.

I decided that I wasn't going to tell Laura about the Paul situation. If nothing else happened with Paul, it was too embarrassing. Not as bad as Colin, but still another humiliation in a long list. She had enough of a romantic saga going on, especially if things didn't work out with Nick. How would I compare Paul's friendship of a few weeks to her years of marriage? I was probably just taking it all too seriously.

I spent Thursday readying my place to host improv practice, and I decided to use it as an excuse to reach out to Mrs. Mahoney one more time.

I knocked on her door on Thursday afternoon, and she opened it, looking at me cautiously.

"Hi," I said. "I am having a couple of friends over tonight—"

"Parties aren't allowed."

"It's three people. But I was just wondering if you knew of any good local Newfoundland recipes I could make for them. Cookies, or dessert, anything nice like that? They are locals and I'm trying to show them that I like it here, even though I'm from the States."

She hesitated, her eyes narrowing suspiciously. "I don't think I know any recipes just for Newfoundland."

"Okay, thanks," I said. "Well, if you think of anything..."

I waved and turned to go. "No parties," she repeated again, but she wasn't entirely frowning when she closed the door. I considered that a parade-worthy victory.

I made chocolate chip cookies from a recipe on the bag, bought some chips and salsa, and provided four bottles of wine, which is as domestic as I get. I hadn't really wanted to cook a Newfoundland specialty; I just wanted to try one last time to warm up Mrs. Mahoney before I left the country. Somebody needed to. She was a version of what I feared I'd become as I grew older: alone, grumpy, resentful of everyone because no one ever seemed excited to see her.

Lisette and Mark arrived on time, chatting and speculating about what was happening with Paul's mother and then evaluating my cookies with an appraising air.

"Could use a little burning," Lisette said, "but I guess they're edible."

"I'll make a note on the recipe," I replied.

"Mark can cook everything," Lisette said. "But he never brings us any of it. He always talks about how he was trying out some new Thai recipe, or some new hummus recipe, but does he bring us a sample?"

"They never turn out well enough to share," Mark said.

"I don't believe it," Lisette said. "I think you're running a small restaurant out of your home and refusing to give us a reservation."

Mark gave her a small frown. "My house is tiny. Not good for entertaining."

"I live in a dungeon, Mark. You have to have us over sooner or later."

Half an hour passed, and then an hour, before Paul finally arrived. When he stepped into the room, his eyes were missing the spark that they usually had. He looked at me and forced a smile, which was more painful to watch than if he hadn't made the effort.

"Hey," he said, and held up a bottle of wine.

"You made it!" Lisette shouted. "You escaped the house of horrors."

"Barely," he said, sounded exhausted.

I walked up to him to take the wine. "You okay?" I asked him quietly.

He nodded slowly. "Wine would be nice."

I squeezed his hand once before I moved to the table to pour him a glass.

"Really, though, what happened with your mom this time?" Lisette asked.

He shrugged. "She's fine. She just starts fights with her neighbors over nothing. This time it was potted plants she put on her front step that she's convinced they stole, even though I'm sure they didn't. It was really windy, and I think her plants blew away. But then she escalated the situation by trying to get revenge on them. I'll let her calm down again and then smooth it out with the neighbors."

Now I could feel Mark's eyes on me. 'You see?' he seemed to be saying.

It was Mark who clapped his hands this time, finishing up the discussion of Paul's mother. "Alright, we have to whip this one into shape," Mark said with a gesture toward me, "if she's going to be on stage with us for her last hurrah."

"Hopefully not a last hurrah," Lisette said. "Hopefully she finds a Canadian to marry and moves here permanently. So that is one of your jobs," she added, pointing between Paul and Mark. "Marry Abigail."

"I'll bring a justice of the peace to our next improv practice, and we can flip a coin," I replied lightly. It was almost as hard for me to force cheer as it seemed to be for Paul. Kedar hadn't sent me the update he promised, and I might have to leave within a few days. I could feel Paul's warm gaze, like I was his port in the storm. When I sat next to him on the sofa, our knees brushed against each other and neither of us moved them away. He took my hand and squeezed it once, out of sight of Mark and Lisette. My heart sped up.

"So let's jump in," Lisette cried. "I made a pick-out-of-a-hat warm-up," and she held up one of her knit caps with papers in it.

"What is this one?" I asked.

"It's simple. Each of us takes a turn. Act out what you get."

I glanced at Paul, and his affectionate look seemed to include everything: that we needed to talk, that we couldn't talk, that we were doing silly games instead, and that it was still better than nothing.

Or maybe that was just what I was thinking.

"Come on, come on," Lisette said, shaking her cap. "Paul, you first."

Paul walked forward and reached into the hat. He handed a paper to Lisette, who read aloud to him the words: "A student who desperately has to use the toilet but is too shy to ask."

"Alright," Paul said. "Fair enough. I have a lot of material to draw from at work." He pulled up one of his low armchairs and clutched the sides of the chair. He raised his hand and then shoved it down again, panting, and then raised it again.

He grabbed a book from a shelf and held it in front of his stomach, then twisted himself sideways, and tapped one foot desperately, higher and higher, his legs twisting across each other. The very picture of desperation to go. It was hilarious but oddly touching, too, his absolute commitment to a ten-year-old child who just couldn't bring himself to say anything, until suddenly:

"Miss! Oh no," he cried, "oh no…" And then he slumped down, with a mournful look of pure relief on his face. "Miss," he said at last, his voice desperate, "can I get a mop?"

Lisette began applauding. Even Mark clapped, slowly, glancing between Paul and me.

All I could think was that this was the real Paul. The one who was silly, the one who could find joy no matter what kind of week he'd had. I wondered what version of Paul his mother saw. No wonder he had wanted to be an actor.

"Mark, you're next," Lisette said.

Mark stood up and took a slip of paper.

Lisette read out, "A person who has never eaten yogurt before and falls completely in love with it."

Mark stepped up and pretended to open a refrigerator, poking around. He was also very funny, but in a darker way. His relationship with the yogurt container took on a sexual component.

"I said love," Lisette cried. "You fall in love with yogurt! Love isn't lust!"

"They are one and the same to me," Mark replied, his tongue licking at an imaginary container.

"Alright, I'm calling time on Mark's porno," Lisette said. "Abby, you're up!"

I stood up, fizzing with nerves that came from nowhere, and pulled a slip of paper from Lisette's cap. Her handknit hat was warm and fuzzy inside, and I felt a strong pull of affection for her. I handed a paper to her, and she read aloud. "A social media influencer doing a paid post for the world's worst hotel."

I nodded, grabbed my cell phone, and pointed it at myself. "Hey guys," I said, "so this week I got a complimentary stay at the hashtag paid post—Puffin Hut Hotel, right inside what used to be the bathroom stalls of this adorable club in downtown St. John's, and it is so incredibly original here, like instead of beds, they have this glamping situation with mattresses on the floor, and porcelain flowerpots that used to be toilets. I'm seriously doing that at my wedding, I'm telling you."

The weirdest part of my whole little speech was that I didn't plan any of it. I was just picking something I knew would make Paul laugh, and when I caught his eye as I finished, he was giving me a look of adoration.

How was I supposed to live without him?

Lisette was up next, and she took a sheet of paper out for herself. "A cow that has found its way among a herd of deer." She immediately got on all fours.

After we had run through all of Lisette's hat ideas, Mark, Paul, Lisette and I wrote a few ideas and put them all into separate piles on the table. We were now going to practice the "storytelling improv" that I had seen them do at their first show.

The story we picked: "Someone tells their family they are leaving to go to acting school." The genre: "Science fiction." And off we went. I ended up playing an overly encouraging acting teacher, Lisette was the kid announcing her plans, Paul the spaceship captain, and Mark the disappointed father who wanted her to go to Space Academy.

When we were done, Paul stood up.

"Let's have some wine and dissect that a bit," he suggested, and then we did, talking about what worked and what didn't. It was interesting to hear his analysis of something that seemed so silly on the surface: how we could have committed more, where we could have picked up the pace. I saw now why they were such a good improv group: it wasn't just Lisette's talent or Mark's dry wit. It was Paul, pushing them to be just better, sharper, riskier.

"Where could we have gone further?" he asked, looking between us. We all offered ideas, and I enjoyed even that. I was going to miss this. I was going to miss Paul and Lisette and grumpy Mark. I might even miss improv.

At the end of the night, as everyone was getting ready to go, I quietly approached Paul. "Hey, can you stay a minute after this? There's something I want to talk to you about."

"Of course," he said. Mark and Lisette both gave us knowing looks as they headed out, but once they were gone, Paul immediately looked ashamed.

"Abby," he said, "I'm so sorry about this week." He leaned against the wall by the door.

"You don't owe me an apology," I began, trying to cut him off. I took one of his hands.

"I do, though. This has been such a rough few days. I really wanted to spend time with you, but first there was Trish, and my mother just...She's awful, honestly. But she needs help."

"And how are you?" I asked gently. I knew I had to tell him that I might be leaving, but it could wait. He so clearly needed someone to listen to him.

He put one hand over his eyes. "I'm furious, honestly. But I have no right to be."

"Of course you have a right to be."

I led us back to the sofa and sat down next to him.

"She really can't help herself." He sighed, struggling for words. "But half the time I want to tell her to get out of my life. That it's not my problem."

I nodded, and he took my hand and squeezed it, searching for words. I said quietly, "I told you my mother was an alcoholic, but what I didn't tell you was that—in the time before she died—she was always calling up Laura and I for a few hundred dollars to get through the month, and the first time she asked us, she felt guilty. But by the third, fourth, fifth time, she started to insult us if we didn't help her. We felt like we were her enablers, and we hated it, but we didn't know what else to do because she couldn't hold down a job. So if you want to talk about how angry you are, it's okay. You have the right."

Paul nodded. "My mother is a difficult person. And I've thought about cutting her off, or drawing the line, but there's no one else she has to turn to. It used to drive Trish crazy. She said my mother was manipulating me, and she absolutely was, I knew that, but if I didn't step in, my mother would have been homeless. She burns every single bridge she has. My father used to keep her in check, smooth things over when she got into it with people, but now she has a massive victim complex and no one to stop her. And she can never see that it's her own fault."

I could see the words hurt him as he said them.

"I understand. Honestly," I said.

He looked even angrier. "I don't want you to understand. I want to take you on a date. I haven't taken anyone on a date in..." He cut himself off. "I still want to take you out, it's just that my mother is at my house this week and she makes things harder."

"Is there anything I can do?" I asked.

"You're such a saint."

"Don't say that. Please. That's so not sexy."

He smiled. "Someone told me nice is sexy." He smiled. "But this isn't your job. I'll sort this out. It's like you said. She expects this. She pushes people away, and then she expects to come stay with me. I think she wants to move in with me, but that's where I draw the line. She's not...I don't like saying this, but she's not a very nice person. She doesn't know how to be."

"You may need to set more rules if it gets worse. I mean, I know how hard that is."

"You know when I said I dreamed of moving to the American Southwest? It's because I knew she couldn't get herself organized to follow me. That makes me a horrible son, doesn't it?"

"You're an amazing son in a horrible position."

He covered his eyes and shook his head. "I'm not an amazing partner, though. I haven't been an amazing husband, or —or boyfriend to you."

I leaned my head against him, and he rubbed my hand, then took it between both of his hands and examined my fingers gently, separating out each one like they all mattered to him.

"Your ex came back."

He shook his head. "That's not the point."

I smiled, and then he turned and kissed me gently. His eyes were very serious afterwards, like he was making a promise.

"My mom—I'm going to tell her this is the last time she can stay with me, and I'm going to stick to it. I can't—if there's any chance you and I, I mean, I know you may be leaving..." My heart was sinking. "But I can't let her do again what she did with me and Trish. I'm not going to let that happen again. Even if it means cutting her off entirely."

He leaned over and kissed my forehead, then my lips. His forehead rested against mine as he breathed in and out. I could feel how much he trusted me. I could feel what it would be like to stay with him.

"Paul," I whispered.

He kissed me again.

"My work says I may have to go back."

He blinked once, then slid away from me by a few inches. He was just looking at me, waiting, and the vulnerability nearly killed me.

"I just found out, and I don't know yet if it's definite. And I really like you, too, so much. But I don't want you to make decisions based on me being here when I don't...I don't even know if..." There were tears in my eyes.

He nodded, his expression turning bleak again. I should have lied, I thought. But I couldn't lie to him. Not when he was like this.

"Thanks for telling me," he said quietly. He shifted to move away.

I wanted to take him in my arms, but I could see it on his face. He was already a million miles away.

. . .

TRYING to distract myself that night, I ended up reading another one of the improv books. This one talked a lot about impulses...about how to trust them, how you had to let them act through you. As long as you weren't molesting your fellow actors, you were allowed to go for it, to try things, to break the rules. In improv, you could talk about things nobody wants to talk about: masturbation, fear of dying, having a crush on your friend's spouse. You could push boundaries, release truths. It was okay to let that stuff come out, because the harder you worked to repress it, the more it killed your creativity.

It seemed to me, though, that maybe improv was the only safe place for acting on impulses. My mother had been impulsive. So was Paul's mom, it sounded like. Impulses weren't all they were cracked up to be. The basic problem was that it was easy to call something 'trusting your instincts' when you just did whatever you felt like—whenever you were afraid, or angry, or lonely, or horny. How could you tell the difference?

I missed Laura. She was the one person who I could listen to when my instincts were sending me badly astray. Because right now, my instincts were telling me to quit my job and stay with Paul forever.

11

"TRY NOT TO GET ATTACHED"

THE NEXT DAY, after not hearing from Paul all day, I finally broke down and called Laura. I picked the evening to call, when I knew Nick would be out playing one of his gigs.

I left a quick message. "Laur? Can you call me?"

Laura called me back a half-hour later, and I wondered if I had interrupted a later-than-usual bedtime routine.

"What's wrong?" she said. She sounded worried enough that I felt guilty.

"It's stupid. I just—I like this guy up here."

"An improv comedy guy?"

"I'm afraid so."

"Oh, honey. Please tell me he doesn't pretend props on stage are his dick."

I thought of Paul's brilliant 'toilet' routine and decided not to bring it up.

"So what's the problem, then?"

"The problem is that I may have to go home. Kedar said the work-from-home policy may be ending, and he's not sure when, but it may be immediately. Next week, possibly. And I don't know what to do. I like him so much."

Laura hesitated before answering. "You could do a long-distance thing."

"To Newfoundland? Long distance works from Boston to New York, maybe. Newfoundland to New York? Two flights away? It's impossible."

"Well, yeah...I couldn't manage with Nick when he went to L.A., and we were married." Laura fell silent. Her silence was thick with something unspoken.

"Are you okay?" I said.

"Just sorting all this out."

I could feel my eyes tearing up. I hadn't cried in months, and now it was coming. "I miss you," I said. "And I miss Hannah. And I didn't mean to fight with you."

"Hey, I'm the one who left you. You were right about that, so I can't get mad."

"Are you going to buy a house with him?" I asked.

"No," Laura said, and sighed. "We're not going to buy a house. I think even he realized that was crazy. I did find a job, though. It's less than I was making in New York, but it's something. And I'll have to get Hannah a babysitter for the days when Nick can't get her from school."

"How are they getting along? Her and Nick?"

"Not that well, actually. He keeps trying to set rules and she doesn't want to hear it from him. She's normally such a good kid but it's like she's deliberately testing him."

"Well, he was away a lot. Maybe she wants to see if he's serious about sticking around."

"I know, it's just hard."

"It may just be a difficult adjustment period. But it will sort itself out."

"Yeah. It may be that." Laura sighed again. "So do you love this guy?"

"Maybe. I mean we haven't even... But I could. I could love

him." I had a horrible feeling that the honest answer was a lot simpler than that.

"Well, don't decide you're in love with him before you decide if you're going to stay."

"I can't stay. I can apply for a visa, maybe, but—even under the best of circumstances, I was always going to be a bit of a tourist here unless I got a visa to live here full-time, and...and now it looks like I can't even be a digital nomad. I'm being dragged back to the office."

"Then try not to get too emotionally involved, right?"

"Right. I know. That makes sense."

Laura had given me the practical answer. I knew she would. I just didn't want to hear it.

PAUL CALLED me the next day, a little after noon. His voice sounded hoarse.

"So," he said. "My mother is gone. I brought her back to her rental apartment. She's not going to be speaking to me for the next few weeks, but it means that I am free tonight, and I would very much like to take you to dinner."

I took a deep breath. He was still asking me out, in spite of knowing I might be leaving. I'd grown so pessimistic that I felt a little shocked. "I'd like that."

"Excellent. Do you have any food preferences at all?"

"I insist on dining on a boat in very choppy water."

"Didn't I tell you all the best restaurants in St. John's are on boats?"

"Perfect."

"Is 7 p.m. okay?"

"7 p.m. is great."

I spent the rest of my free time that day going to shops and trying on dresses, having decided that the only dress I'd brought to Canada made me look like the libidinous spinster in a Tennessee Williams play. I bought a delicate green dress that expressed a lot more optimism than I could muster and put my hair up into something resembling a twist. It felt like I owed it to Paul to suppress my despair until at least the dessert course.

He's probably just trying to get laid before you go, the pessimistic voice in my head said.

I shook it off. If Paul had really kicked out his mother, it meant he was trying to be better. So could I. Lucas had teased me about cleansing my negativity, but it made a lot of sense. Maybe I did need a spiritual Live Laugh Love sign after all. Maybe I shouldn't assume the worst quite so consistently.

I spent so much time worrying about how I should do my make-up and hair that I entirely forgot that Paul would also be dressed up until he showed up at my front door in a tie and his blue woolen peacoat coat. The sight of him made me shy for a moment.

"You look..."

He raised his eyebrows. "Yes?"

Devastating, I thought. Sexy. "Like a dapper ship captain from the 1860s."

He laughed. "I was planning to talk like a pirate for the rest of the date, actually."

"I would hope so."

"Arrr," he began, as we walked down the stairs. "I embody anti-imperialist free trade policies but am part of a corrupt labor system that exploits the marginalized through violence."

"I knew there was a reason I found pirates sexy."

He paused on the first floor to look at my dress.

"Stop smoldering at me," I said.

"Canadians do not smolder. That's strictly an American thing. We apologize profusely while leering at your legs."

"It's the subtle cultural differences that are always the hardest to learn."

I reminded myself on the drive to the restaurant that I was supposed to keep things light, to not get too deep. But this didn't feel like a casual date. When we arrived at the restaurant, which was a beautiful little French spot right near the water, Paul ran a hand along my arm as we waited for a table. He kissed the back of my neck when the hostess turned to find us a table.

"Are you okay after everything with your mom?" I asked, hoping to distract myself from how much I wanted to throw myself at him.

"Fine. I don't want to think about it. My mother and my ex have gotten enough of my energy this week."

"Did you talk to her more? Your ex?" I asked.

"Briefly," he said. "At a coffee shop. She wants to talk again at some point."

"It sounds like her jet setting didn't work out so well."

He shook his head. "I guess not. Let's not discuss Trish. I might say something unkind, and I really don't want to."

"So Lisette," I replied, searching for a subject. "Do you think she really needs to change her name?"

"I'm not sure it would help," Paul said. "She's not a natural blonde, you know. She does that because she wants to be harder for him to spot in a crowd."

"That's so horrible. I wonder if she should go back to Quebec. It seems like he's only a couple of hours away from her here, and she has lots of big brothers who could beat him up."

"Oh yeah. They're all much taller than she is. You should definitely ask for photos; it looks like she's the runt of the litter. But as far as her ex goes, you're right. He's only about a four-hour drive away from here. But she has a community here. Not just me, but the church and so on, and that's been helpful. I'm hoping he gets bored and moves on."

"He's probably tormenting some new girlfriend," I said.

He nodded. "I hate the idea that him abusing someone else is the best we can hope for."

"The best we can hope for is that he's run over by a bus," I said. "But in the meantime...if Lisette ever needs a place to stay, and I do end up back in Brooklyn, she can always hide out with me." Paul glanced away when I mentioned going back to Brooklyn, then looked back with a careful smile.

"I'm going to try not to think about that." He smiled, looking around the restaurant. There was delicate piano music playing, and the distant sound of the city. "It's nice to just be here like this. Quiet. It makes me feel human again."

"You like things calm."

"In my emotional life? Sometimes. A lot of people think deep passion means yelling at someone, but I think it means choosing not to yell."

"My mother was dramatic. She was always telling us stories about her own life, and how unlucky she'd been. She needed attention all the time. I learned to keep her happy by laughing at her jokes. And trying to be funny. To entertain her."

He nodded, slowly. "Things got messy if I stood up for myself as a kid, so I just became quiet. My wife hated that. She was always trying to get me to fight, and I wouldn't do it. So she would get louder, and I would shut her out. She thought it meant I didn't care. But I just couldn't have a relationship where everything escalated."

"Because your mom made you feel like you had to avoid fights. Because fights got ugly."

"Fights got very ugly with my mom. She locked me out of the house one night in winter. I don't know if my father knew. It was below freezing. I slept in the car."

"Paul. That's abuse."

He shrugged. "Well, when you put it like that, it sounds bad," he deadpanned.

"My mom was neglectful. Not abusive, ever. But she was also avoidant. She didn't ever want to hear what a mess she had made of our lives. So she died without us ever confronting her or telling her how much it hurt to grow up that way. And I think that made it hard to grieve. Like we had unfinished business. It's not good to have screaming fights with your parents but it's also not good never to tell people how you really feel."

"I don't yell at the people I love," he said. "I don't yell. It's probably why I like improv. It lets some of the inner chaos out."

"Lisette said she thinks of improv as a way of approaching life. But it feels like, if I was acting on impulse, I'd hurt a lot of people."

"It's different. When we're up there, we're making theater. It may not be *Hamlet*, but it's about finding truths, in some way. But I guess...the way I think of it is, improv isn't about doing whatever you want. It just reminds me to have courage. To take some risks. When it matters."

"So what big risks have you taken recently?" I asked him.

"I'm taking one right now." His eyes were warm and sincere. It took a moment to find words.

"Is this when I tell you about my seven dead ex-husbands?"

He laughed. "Maybe. I'm here even though I may get hurt. And I drew a line in the sand with my mother. She's not allowed to come stay with me again. She's not even allowed to call me."

"Not because of me, I hope."

He shook his head. "Not entirely because of you. I'm not doing a very good job of keeping things light, am I?"

I smiled. "Shall we change the topic to something superficial? Dogs wearing sweaters? Are you for it or against it?"

"For it." He grinned, but then his expression shifted. "Should we talk about the fact that you may be leaving?"

I felt tears prickle behind my eyes. "Not yet. Can we pretend that this could work? For just a little longer. Because I really…"

I stopped.

"What?" he asked.

Now it was my turn to be brave. If he had done it, so could I. "I really like you, and I want to stay. And I don't want to keep things safe now, just because it will hurt more later."

"You're right," he said. "Let's stop being safe."

He took my hand, and I felt the heat pooling in my palm.

"WHERE DO YOU WANT TO GO?" Paul asked me. Dinner was over, and we sat together in the parking lot, taking in the night sky scattered with a thousand stars.

"Your place? I want to see your wood stove in action."

"In the middle of summer?" He grinned.

"This may be my last chance."

Paul nodded, and we drove there in silence. I watched him taking corners, pulling down streets that he had driven a million times. This was a mistake, I knew. Getting close was a mistake, and I couldn't stop myself. We were both going to get hurt, and I wanted it. I wanted to care enough about someone to let myself get hurt.

When we got to his place, he locked the door carefully behind us and bolted it, which I'd never noticed him do before. I wondered if he was thinking of his mother. The living room was in disarray—a broken vase arranged in a corner, a few books off the shelves.

"I should have cleaned up more," he said. "She knocked down a couple of things on her way out."

"Your mother?"

"She was just being melodramatic. I just stood still and

waited until she knew she couldn't get a rise out of me." I stepped forward and then carefully kissed him, my arms wrapping around his shoulders. He was lean, his arms warm even after the drive in the darkness.

"Let me get the stove started," he said after a moment. "I want you to get your money's worth from Canada."

I watched him building up a pile in the stove. Kindling and logs carefully built into a stack. Once it was lit, he turned back to me and smiled, and I could see flames in his eyes, briefly. The room began to smell of winter restaurants and the farmhouses I'd been to for friends' weddings. I thought about one of my mother's boyfriends who had let us build a fire in his fireplace, and how much we'd liked him. He'd been one of the good ones, which meant he hadn't lasted long.

Paul walked up and sat next to me on the sofa. "Hey," he whispered.

"Hey."

He ran one hand along the back of my neck and the other behind my waist, pulling me into a kiss. It was gentle at first, but it seemed to flip a switch inside him. All the passion was at the surface, suddenly. It felt like I was experiencing the real Paul, just for a moment, without all the careful measures of control.

When he pulled back, his irises were darker, his expression intense. Then something shuttered again.

"Abby, I really want to take you to bed," he said at last.

I nodded. "Yes."

"Yes?"

I nodded. He smiled a little, then he took my hand and led me upstairs, leaving the scattered remnants of chaos behind in his front hallway.

Paul's room was filled with floor-to-ceiling bookcases and an old wooden desk with even more books stacked on it. I hadn't considered what a reader he was, but this was a reader's room, piles of books on every available surface. There was a large photo on one of the walls of a Southwestern desert.

He hesitated at the door as I stepped in ahead of him.

"It looks like you," I said. "Your room."

"Boring and steady."

"Smart and sexy."

He closed the door behind us and then leaned back to kiss me against it. He was kissing my neck, my forehead, and then he paused again, breathing hard. It was the same push and pull I always saw from him: desire and then control. Careful, always stopping himself.

"What is it?"

He shook his head and then leaned his head against my shoulder.

"Paul, what is it? It's okay."

"I just want to make sure I get this right."

"You are."

He nodded, but he didn't move. I waited for him to say more. I was pretty sure this was the first time he had slept with anyone since his divorce. Was he thinking of Trish? Regretting this already? I put one hand gently on the back of his neck, waiting until he spoke.

"I'm sorry. Trish told me I was bad at this. At sex. When we were breaking up, she said a lot of hurtful things, but that was one of the last things she said on her way out the door. I know she was just trying to justify what she was doing, but it got in my head. So you have to tell me if what I'm doing is working for you."

"You don't kiss like you're bad at this," I said, rubbing my hand along his shoulder.

"I just start to overthink," he said finally. "I want to get this right."

"You're in your head about it? That's not allowed. You're an improv guy."

"I know, but that's my point. This is exactly the kind of situation where I can't follow my instincts. I don't trust myself."

"Please tell me your instincts aren't cannibalism."

I felt him laugh against me. He shook his head slowly. I thought about what he was saying. I also thought of what a disaster it would be if I started giving him precise instructions, turning this into an exercise where he felt like he was being graded, trying to measure up.

"Alright," I said. "How about this? Let's treat this like an improv exercise. For the next thirty seconds, you follow your impulses. Do exactly what you want, and then you can stop and check in, okay? Within reason, of course. If you have a very specific 50 *Shades of Grey* thing, you might want to run it by me."

"Yeah, of course, I would never…" He stopped. I watched as he considered it.

"And unless I'm uncomfortable, I won't make you stop, and you don't have to stop yourself. And then you check in with me, and I'll tell you if I didn't like anything. Okay?"

He nodded. He took a slow breath. "Does the thirty seconds start now?"

I nodded. "If you want."

As soon as I said it, he pulled me close to him, spun me around, and then gently lowered me to the bed, climbing above me. He leaned over and began kissing my neck, right below my ear, and then moved to my mouth. It was almost too fast, almost overwhelming, but then he slowed down. He moved down to my dress and began to kiss me through the delicate fabric. I arched up to get closer to him, unable to stop himself.

His wife was a fool or a liar, I thought. He was ridiculously good at this. But maybe he hadn't let himself be like this, with her. I knew it could be easy, once someone made you doubt yourself, once they hurt you, to hold back all the time, to keep the most vulnerable parts of you safe. I couldn't remember the last time I'd felt like this with anyone either: like anything I did next would be okay. Paul, not holding himself back, was on fire.

He kissed gently through the dress, down my chest, then below my belly button. He ran his hands along the edge of the fabric, then gently slid both hands underneath, up my thighs. His hands were warm and slow. His eyes were hungry. He leaned over and kissed between my legs through the fabric.

Then he paused and looked up at me.

"When does the thirty seconds stop?" he asked.

"I'll let you know," I said, smiling a little. "Maybe a few more minutes until your time is up."

His eyes warmed, and then his full focus returned to where he was gently running his hands up my legs. He began to slide my dress up to my waist. I pressed closer to him, unable to stop myself. I was going on impulse, too.

LATER THAT NIGHT, I lay awake, wondering if he was asleep. I pulled a handknit woolen blanket around my shoulders and walked to the window. The stars were an epic poem now that the last fingers of clouds had blown away. The Milky Way forged a clear path across the darkness to an unseen horizon.

"Not quite as exciting as New York."

I turned to see Paul sitting up in bed. He looked very handsome, his chest pale and muscular in the half-light, his hair looking chestnut-dark. It felt like he wasn't quite real. "The stars are better here," I said. "You never see very many back home. Growing up in Troy, it was like this, but ever since I went to college, I only see stars when I'm traveling. Which is basically never."

Paul rose and walked behind me, putting an arm around my shoulders. He leaned his chin against my shoulder as he looked outside. It felt right to have him there.

"So how many days did I last?" Paul's voice resonated against me.

"Before what?"

He breathed a laugh into my shoulder. "How long did I manage to keep my distance from you?"

"Taking it slow? About a week," I said, turning around to look at his face. We kissed again, slowly. He ran a hand through my hair, looking at it thoughtfully.

"It's been a few weeks, though," he said. "Pretty much since that first day when you called Lisette a rock star. I knew I was in trouble then. And then I took you on the boat and you got seasick, and I touched your wrist, and I thought, Oh no. I'm not in trouble. I'm completely fucked."

"I thought the same thing. I wanted to kiss you, then, but I also really wanted to vomit, so..."

"I do have that effect."

I pressed myself against him.

"I thought you weren't interested in me."

He laughed quietly. "I wasted so much time trying not to get my heart broken," he said. "And I still ended up here, knowing it's going to happen anyway."

"What are we going to do?" I whispered.

He shook his head against me, wrapping all his warmth around me, head to toe. "We're going to go back to bed."

I woke up slowly to the sight of a hand resting on the pillow next to me: Paul's long fingers curved in an arc. It felt precious to see him so close, still sleeping, and I slid upwards carefully, not wanting him to wake yet. His other arm was draped over my waist. There was light pouring through white curtains.

I let myself take him in, the pattern of freckles scattered across his chest, the breath moving in and out of his lips. It seemed ridiculous that anyone had looked at him and thought that he wasn't worth sticking around for. Softly, I leaned over and kissed the hand that was just within reach.

I still had time. I didn't have to move yet. For this morning, there was nowhere to go. He took a breath in after a moment, his eyes opening slowly. His smile was so tender that I wanted to store it up in my memory, hoarding it to come back to later.

He pulled me back under the covers like I was sinking into a pond. Hands everywhere. Lips on each other's skin.

"Stay," he whispered.

"I'll stay," I whispered back.

HE MADE us pancakes in the ridiculously bright early morning light of St. John's, a slash of light hitting his messy hair, turning light-brown curls into gold like he was the hero in a fantasy TV series.

"You know you're stupidly handsome."

He made a scoffing noise. "Being an actor teaches you exactly how handsome you're not. When I was doing auditions in Toronto, there were all these guys booking roles because they had slightly better cheekbones than I had. And I hated it. It was frustrating watching these model-handsome idiots butchering roles that I would have been great in. But it was even worse when some ordinary guy booked a role, because I couldn't even blame it on his looks. He was just more talented, right? And then half the time you'd find out he was the son of someone famous, or the nephew of the guy who owned the theater company. It's something I hated about being an actor. You're always complaining about how things are unfair. I felt like an internet troll, furiously compiling lists of enemies and wrongs done to me."

"So you never miss it?"

"The part I miss was sharing something with an audience. Making them laugh. But now I'm basically on stage five hours a day as a teacher, entertaining these kids, keeping them engaged. It's not that different, actually. It's a lot of the stuff I loved about being an actor."

I imagined him in front of a class. "They're so lucky. Most of my teachers were chain smokers who gathered for drinks at Fisherman Pub every Friday to talk about their countdown to retirement."

"How many days do you have left?" Paul asked.

"In Newfoundland? I don't know yet. A minimum of six days, and a maximum of who knows. Maybe the end of August. Maybe some angel sweeps in and expedites my visa."

"Can I spend today with you?" he said, tentatively.

"We should probably ask Lisette," I said. "See if she wants to come."

Lisette picked up the phone and told us that she had a church breakfast where she was looking for her next boyfriend, who was going to be at least seventy.

"We can wait," I said.

"Go," she said. "I think I'm about to get a marriage proposal, and that could take some time. First, he has to get across the room on his walker."

Paul glanced at me. "Just you and me then," he said. "What do you want to do today? Tell me what will make you happy."

"Right now? A change of clothes."

"And after that?"

"Somewhere you love," I said.

"Somewhere I love?" He nodded, considering it. "I mean, we already went to the archives. It's hard to top that."

"I could do more archives."

He grinned. "Even I'm not that much of a dork. Do you have hiking shoes?"

"I have sneakers back at my place."

After we stopped by my apartment, Paul drove me up the coast to a parking lot, and from there we began a hike in toward the coast. We were silent at first, listening to the occasional call of birds. I followed him through shaggy coastal woods, down sloping hills, eventually chatting about Canadian wildlife and our feelings about camping and the first time we'd ever climbed a mountain. We didn't talk about anything serious. We didn't talk about how I was leaving.

Finally the woods spilled us out onto a dramatic set of cliffs where a waterfall poured off the edge and down into the open ocean.

We stood there in silence for a long moment. It seemed too huge, suddenly, like a metaphor for something I didn't know I was capable of feeling. I turned to Paul. His eyes were bright.

"My favorite place." He gestured like a host on a nature show, sweeping an arm in a glorious half-circle.

I looked around. "You know how in old maps, they imagined that the world simply ended somewhere—that the world was flat, and eventually you would reach a cliff where the ocean poured down into nothingness..."

"Have we reached the end of the world?" he asked.

"I think so."

We said nothing. Sadness blew past with the wind. I sat down after a moment to look at the view, and I could hear Paul rustling through his backpack, finding the sandwiches that he'd bought for us.

It was a perfect day, clear and breezy, and we ate in silence.

I wanted that. If we didn't talk about it, I could pretend for a moment that there was nothing to say. I rose and approached the edge of the rocks.

"You still have that impulse to jump off cliffs?" he asked.

"Any second now," I said.

He stood up, put his arms around me and held me close. "Don't," he said quietly.

This is going to hurt, I thought. This is going to hurt. This is going to hurt. I turned and pressed my face against him for a moment.

"So," I said. "You start school soon? Are you still planning a trip to the U.S.?"

"Maybe," he said quietly. "I've got some stuff to work out with Trish, first." He shrugged. "House ownership, all that."

My heart sank. Paul knew I was probably leaving. He knew that his gorgeous ex-wife was back in town. Of course he could be romantic with me. None of it had to mean anything. Mark had warned me, and I hadn't wanted to listen.

We went back to my place after the hike so that I could shower. Paul left for an hour or two and then came back with a take-out dinner, and then we sat next to each other, looking out the window. The sun was setting earlier now than when I had first arrived, and it colored the distant water with slate blues and shell pink.

"You never told me much about your father," he said, out of nowhere.

I shrugged. "Never in the picture. He took off and married someone else when I was two years old, and he was never even married to my mom, so…"

"That's hard. Did you miss him?"

"Not as such. She had this long series of boyfriends, and that was harder in a way. It was hard when we didn't like a boyfriend, and hard when we did, and then he left."

I took a breath, looking out at the fading light. "I had a professor in college who—one day I came to class right after a break-up, visibly weeping, my whole face must have looked like a cream puff. And I think she was worried about me, so after class she sat and talked to me, even though it was way outside her job responsibilities. I refused to go to a therapist back then. I thought I was so clever that I would outsmart them, like the goal of therapy was to get to the answer the fastest. Anyway, my professor had been through some of the things I had been through, and after she heard all about my break-up, and my parents, she told me, 'Don't let your father win. He walked out on you, and now you're going to think that everybody will walk out on you. And that will doom all your relationships, so just to spite your dad, you have to try to break the cycle. You can't think, *All men leave.* Because you'll be punishing yourself for what your father did for your whole life. You'll be paying for his crime.'"

Paul nodded. "Very wise."

"I thought so. So when I dated Farid, I decided, I'm not going to do that. I won't doom myself. I went to therapy, and we were together for six years, and I thought. I've won. I've done it. I was so proud of myself for breaking the cycle. Even though he didn't really believe in long-term commitments like marriage, I was still capable of a real relationship. Only it turns out he did believe in marriage."

"Yeah." Paul was gentle. He remembered the story.

I took a breath. "And I think what I concluded was, it's not that all men leave. It's that all men leave *me.*"

He looked at me sadly and then took me into his arms and kissed me. It turned into a breathtaking, consuming, end-of-the-movie kind of kiss. The thought went through my head that we were still at the end of the world.

12

"STILL NOT FUNNY"

THE NEXT MORNING, Paul left after breakfast to run an errand for Lisette, who had nearly run out of milk at the coffee shop where she worked—a fireable offense—and I readied myself for work. Just as I opened my laptop, my cell phone rang. It was Kedar, who hadn't bothered this time with a video call.

"So, Abby," he began. I knew what was coming wasn't good, because he wasn't calling me a 'rock star.' "Bad news. It's official. For everybody. We all have to come into the office one day a week."

"One day a week." There was an irony to the minimal ask having such a maximum impact. "Starting when?"

"Monday. They're going to scale up from there to three days a week."

"Can I have a couple of weeks here to finish out my rental?"

"I tried to get you another week or two, but they know if they bend for someone, they have to bend for everyone. Look, hopefully they try it for a while and realize it's stupid, but there's a new VP and he wants to make some kind of a point. I hate it, too. I was only coming in two days a week. Now they want me in all five."

"This is so stupid."

"I know. I know," he agreed. "But they want to get back to normal, and this is their version of normal."

"So Monday. One week from today."

"They're firm on it. Sorry, Abby."

I didn't know what to do first. I started by texting Charlotte, to give her an update on my schedule so she'd know she could rent out her apartment again. As soon as I'd sent it, I stared at my cell phone, wondering what to tell Paul. When to tell Paul. The right answer was right away, and I couldn't make myself do it.

There was a knock on the door. My heart leapt in my throat. I didn't know if I could face Paul right then. I wasn't ready for good-bye.

It wasn't Paul, though. It was Mrs. Mahoney from downstairs.

"I found some recipes," she said, holding out a set of small, hand-written notecards. "Since you asked about Newfoundland specialties."

"Oh," I said, trying to pull myself together. "Do you want to come in and have tea and tell me about them?"

"No, no," she said. "I have to get back downstairs. I'm baking."

"Oh, okay. Thank you. These look amazing." I looked down at the carefully copied ingredient lists on the lined white note-cards, touched.

I noticed she was watching me as I looked at the pile. "If you come downstairs, I could talk you through them."

I had done it. I had broken through. It made me happy and sad at once. I smiled. "Sure."

Mrs. Mahoney's apartment immediately revealed that she had downsized to her apartment from somewhere larger. It felt like an overstuffed exhibit from a museum about

Newfoundland culture. Every corner was filled with teapots, sewing tables, white enamel basins filled with pottery and bric-a-brac.

"You have beautiful things."

"I don't know about beautiful," she said. "But they've been in my family a long time." I watched her make tea and then check on some bread in the oven.

"I like to make my own bread," she said. "The stuff you buy at the market is garbage."

I nodded, deciding it was not the right moment to tell her that this was exactly why I went to the French boulangerie in New York.

"So where did you come from before St. John's?" I asked her. "Some of this stuff looks like you didn't grow up in the city."

"I hate cities," she agreed. "But it wasn't practical to stay in the country anymore. We used to have a farmhouse."

"Whereabouts?"

She eyed me suspiciously, like I might be a census worker here to ferret out back taxes and then fussed around with dishes as she began to tell her story.

"I spent my whole life in Newfoundland," she said. "Except when I got married and went on my honeymoon to Bermuda for a week."

"Bermuda!"

"It was too hot," she said. "They served us warm soda."

"Nightmarish." I smiled, and for the first time, so did she.

Her husband was a fisherman, and they had one daughter together, who stayed in Newfoundland just long enough to come out as gay and then immediately moved down to Ottawa.

"I wasn't supportive of that lifestyle," Mrs. Mahoney said. "I didn't understand it. And my church, you know, I go to the Catholic Church. You didn't do that kind of thing."

"I understand," I said, quietly. There was regret in her voice, but the quiet kind, and I didn't push at it. I knew there had been a break in the family that she was only beginning to dissect.

"My husband was...he didn't want to talk to Penny at all. I kept in touch, but it was distant."

I nodded.

"And then Al died. And a few years ago, my daughter Penny got married to another woman who worked in the government, and they had a daughter. Sperm donor, something like that. I guess that's how it's done these days."

"One would hope so. The alternatives are alarming."

She snorted a little laugh. "And then, well, I couldn't take care of the farm by myself, and I was having trouble getting to my doctor's appointments. And Penny told me I could come live near her in Ottawa, but I didn't want her to feel obligated. So one of my friends Marie had moved here to St. John's, and I moved here, too."

"Sure."

"Penny wants me to come visit, but..." She shook her head. "I don't know. Ottawa." She said it like somebody had proposed that she hop on a spaceship to Mars.

"It would be nice to see your granddaughter," I offered.

"She'll be four soon. I don't know. I don't know about moving down there, you know? I like my church," she said. "The young people at the church help with grocery shopping, but I don't like..." Mrs. Mahoney waved her hands. "I don't like to be needy, you know?"

I nodded. I did know. "It's easier to be the one doing the giving than the one taking," I agreed.

"But now my best friend Marie is dying, and we have been friends for fifty-eight years."

"I'm sorry," I said. "I know what you mean, though. About trying to decide where to go. I'm doing that right now."

I told Mrs. Mahoney about my sister, and how she'd moved

to Georgia, and I was trying to decide whether to go or not. "I don't even like Georgia."

Mrs.Mahoney considered it for a long moment.

"What's he do? The ex-husband?"

"He's a guitarist. Rock musician."

She nodded. "I would say that's probably not going to work out, but then again, I said my daughter and her wife were probably not going to work out."

"I like being close to my sister. But."

"They're family." Mrs. Mahoney nodded. "Maybe I'll move to Ottawa. I don't know. I don't know if Penny has really forgiven me for how I let Al speak to her. I wish I'd done that differently."

We both sat with that for a long moment.

"I like your teacups," I said, looking at the one in my hand. It was classic and delicate, and tipped with gold.

"Every time I have tea, I have it in a nice cup," she said. "My mother used to do that. Once a day. Fancy tea in a fancy cup. Whatever else was happening, you had your tea in a nice cup. But a few of them broke when I moved, so I only have four good ones, now. You can come back for tea sometime," she added.

"I'd like that," I said.

"I'm sorry I didn't talk to you earlier. Not in a very good mood these days. I'm worried I'm turning into an old bitch."

I laughed. It surprised me. "I'm a bit of an old bitch myself."

On the way out, she reminded me about the buzzer on the washing machine and how loud it was. I told her I could turn it off, and she shook her head, skeptical. I guess it was a pattern she was comfortable with, that warning about the loud washing machine. A conversation starter and a conversation ender, all at once.

I went back to my apartment and sat alone. I knew I had to call Paul. I had to tell him I was leaving.

I called his number quickly and waited for him to pick up. It took a few rings.

"Abby, hi," he finally said, sounding distracted.

"Hey," I said. "Can we—"

"Listen, I uh—I have someone over. I'm dealing with something right now."

"Your mother?"

"No, my—wife. Ex-wife. I'll call you later, I promise."

"Okay."

I hung up. The words, 'my wife...ex-wife' played over and over again in my head. If he was going to get back together with her, at least I didn't have to stick around for that humiliation. The part that left me unsettled was the doubt. Did he still love me? Was he trying to find a way to work things out?

I waited until midnight, and he didn't call.

THE NEXT MORNING, I called my sister first thing.

"Hey, are you at work?" I asked.

"No," she said, "that job didn't start yet, which is good because Nick may be taking a gig out of town."

"What? Wasn't the whole thing with him that he was going to stay in one place for you?"

"It's a really good gig, apparently." Laura's voice was dry. "I mean it's good money, I'll give him that. But."

"But," I agreed. There was a long moment.

"How are you?" she finally asked.

"I'm okay," I lied. "I just found out that my work is getting rid of its work-from-home policy."

"What? Starting when?"

"Next week," I said. "I have to be in on Monday. Every Monday. One day a week, which feels even more insulting somehow. Like it's so obviously just for show."

"Oh, Abby, I'm sorry," Laura said. "I knew you were hoping to stay up there for a while longer."

"It was always a bit of a fantasy in the first place," I said. "Thinking this could work out."

"It sounded like you were having fun, though," she said.

"Anyway," I said, "I'll be back in New York, whether I want to be or not, so…I'll be in a better place if you need me to fly down there or whatever, to see Hannah. I miss her. You too, of course."

"Well," Laura said. There was a long moment. "I decided to move back to New York too."

My heart dropped. "What? I thought things were going okay. Why didn't you tell me right away?"

"I knew you would say I told you so."

"Laurie…"

"It was like he had this whole idea about how things were supposed to be if we moved down here. He picked our neighborhood. He decided we were going to buy a house. And as soon as I wanted to veer from that, he didn't…I think financially, the only way he could make his whole thing work was if I stuck with his plan, and he…" There was a long moment of silence. "He always does this. He always ends up taking a gig, and he lied to me about it. This time was supposed to be different. So the bottom line is, if he wants to see his daughter, he has to come up to New York and make the effort. I can't give up my entire life to try to make this work."

My heart was racing, and I wasn't sure why. "What are you going to do? Try to get your old job back?"

"Maybe. I don't know yet. I gave up my apartment, so I'll have to try to find somewhere else before school starts up there. I just want Hannah to start the year with her classmates. I think she's miserable here. Georgia already started the school year, so it's going to be a rough transition for her."

"You guys can stay at my place if you come back to the city. You know that."

"Really?" Laura asked.

"Really. It's okay," I said. I caught a little sob in my voice. I hadn't even known I was upset.

"Are you okay, Abby? We don't have to stay."

"No, I want you to. I'm just tired. When will you be getting home?"

"We're flying out this weekend. Can we really stay in your apartment?"

"Of course. Don't even think about it. I'll tell the doorman to give you his spare key. I want to see you both. I miss you. A lot."

I felt the tears coming, then, and stopped them with an effort. This was good. I missed Hannah. I was going to get to see her again. This was good, wasn't it? Whatever was going on with Paul, I didn't have to fixate on it, now. The rest of my life could cushion the blow.

A couple of minutes after I hung up, I saw my phone ring again. When I saw Paul's name, I thought about not picking up, but then I did. Whatever came, I wanted to be a grown-up about it.

"Hey, Abby," he began tentatively.

"Hey, Paul."

"I'm sorry I couldn't talk last night."

"You don't owe me an explanation."

"Yes, I do. I want to. You always do that. Act like you're second best."

When I said nothing, Paul continued. "Trish came by. She wanted to have a whole conversation about all of this stuff from our marriage. I didn't—it kind of blindsided me, to be honest. There was a lot of stuff going on that she never told me about. She always said she didn't want kids, but she was actually going back and forth about it, and then she found out she was infertile, and she didn't tell me. Anyway. It doesn't matter."

I said nothing, waiting for him to go on. My heart felt like it was growing smaller in my chest, my heartbeat fading away.

"The important thing for you to know is, it's over. And I didn't want you to think that because it took me so long to get back to you…I mean, she didn't leave until after midnight and that felt too late to call."

"We both have a lot of obligations," I said, thinking of Laura, thinking of my job, thinking of his mother.

"Can I come over tonight and see you?"

"No," I found myself saying. "Let's talk after—we have that show Thursday. With the Newfingers. Can we talk after that?"

"Of course."

"Unless you don't want me to do it anymore."

"Of course I want you to do it."

"I should go." My voice was breaking. "I have to get some work done today."

"Alright. If you want to talk, call me. And I'm here. Okay? For whenever you need me."

Tears were rising, but I could head them off if I was quick enough. "I know. I have to go."

I hung up the phone. I felt like I was floating in space. I couldn't tell him yet. We would do our silly improv show, because I wanted to make Lisette happy, and then I would tell him that this was all falling apart, and I had to go back to New York.

And then what? He would say that we could make it work? That he would fly down to New York all the time, and I would fly up to Newfoundland? That we'd meet for romantic weekends in Toronto or Montreal? That he was madly in love with me?

．　．　．

THURSDAY NIGHT, we met at the Puffin Hut a few minutes before the show to discuss the evening. Paul's eyes lit up when he saw me, and I walked over and gave him a hug, treasuring it like it was the last one, and then gave one to Lisette. Mark was at the bar, buying himself a beer.

"If I just don't jump in, you guys will be okay with that, right?" I said. My heart felt like a solid lump of lead in my chest. I was grieving already, but I wanted to get through this. My last challenge to myself. My last gesture to Lisette. My proof that I was a different person.

"Sure," Lisette replied. "But you will. I know you, and you'll be amazing."

Mark was giving Paul a dark, curious look as he walked over. He said casually, "Trish called me." Paul's attention shot to him.

"She called you? I didn't know you guys were in touch," Paul said quietly.

"She's talking about doing some work for me. You don't mind, do you?"

"Of course not," said Paul. "Why would I mind?"

"She said you really told her off."

"I hope not," Paul said. "I hope we had a good discussion."

"I'm proud of you!" Lisette threw her arms around Paul. "Telling her to take a hike. I never would have seen that coming."

Mark glanced at me, observing how I was taking all this in. He raised his thick eyebrows, his eyes lingering on mine. I looked down.

Then Paul gave me a little smile, and I smiled back. I loved him. I knew it for sure. It felt like someone had taken my insides and shaken away all the residue of other hopes, thoughts, and fears until that was the only certain thing.

It was a fairly large crowd for this kind of show, and I felt a brief sense of panic. I caught Lisette's eyes lighting up at someone's arrival, and then Charlotte appeared at our table with a dark-haired scruffy man trailing behind her.

"Charlie!" Lisette cried. I hadn't expected that the woman I was renting from would want to come to a show, but I realized Lisette had probably asked her.

"Hi everyone. This is my boyfriend Brett," Charlotte said, gesturing to her companion.

"Hmm," he said, shaking our hands. He did look a bit like Ben Affleck.

"So Abby. Lisette told me you had joined up with her team? How did you two meet again?" Charlotte asked, looking between Lisette and me. I realized I had never mentioned that Lisette had stayed on my sofa.

"She forgot something in the apartment, and we met then," I said. "And she became my unofficial tour guide." Lisette shot me a grateful smile.

We sat through another set by Lachlan, which made me strangely sentimental. He had just written a new folk song about the decline of the polar bear population.

"Newfingers, you're up!" came a voice next to us. It was the manager of the club, a woman in her forties named Ellen.

I felt a moment of sheer panic. Now I was going to humiliate myself in front of Charlotte and Brett, on top of everything else. With the exception of Mrs. Mahoney and my taxi driver Rick, everyone I knew in Newfoundland was in this room.

Paul reached over and squeezed my hand.

"No big stakes," he whispered in my ear. "Just be terrible. It's a rite of passage to be terrible in your first improv show." I smiled, wishing that I didn't like him quite so much.

As I stood up, Lisette took both my hands in hers and squeezed them.

"We're doing it!" she whispered.

"We are the Newfingers," Paul said into the microphone,

"with visiting guest Abigail, and we do long-form improv comedy. To start, we will need some suggestions from the audience for a place and an object."

A voice from the back said quite clearly, "The sewer."

Lisette would later tell me that Paul's face went pale when he heard the voice, but I didn't notice anything was wrong. Not yet.

"Okay. Any other places? Ideas?"

"A sewer," came the same voice. A woman's voice.

"Okay, a sewer," Paul said. "Now we need an object."

"A cellular phone," someone up front called out.

"A watch."

"A tomato."

"A gun."

"A tomato. Okay, right." Paul turned to us. There was a look of desperation on his face. I caught his eye, trying to check in with him, but he just gave me a quick nod as if daring me to do this.

I found myself jumping forward, reminding myself not to bring the tomato into the scene too quickly.

"Honey?" I said. "You said this place would be good for hook-ups, but being this far underground is not sexy."

"That's because you're not sexy," came the female voice again. My heart sunk. We had a heckler in the crowd.

Paul seemed determined to ignore the heckler. "Just relax, honey. A lot of people have sex in a sewer. I was conceived in one."

"Still not funny," came the same voice. And then I saw the look of absolute desperation on Paul's face, and I knew what was happening, without him saying a word. His mother had been barred from coming to his home, so she'd come to his show. She was here to humiliate him.

Paul looked at me, determined to keep going.

So I tried. "Well, I just wonder if we should have brought something to lie down on."

"Wait a minute!" Mark cried, jumping into the scene. I could have hugged him. "I can't believe you're here with him."

"Lenny!" I said. "How did you find us?"

"Because this was our spot!" he cried.

"So," said Paul, turning on me. "You've been here before, have you?" The audience laughed.

"Only a few times," I replied.

The voice came from the audience again. "This is garbage," it said.

"Hey, shut up!" Brett, Charlotte's boyfriend, had managed a full sentence. He took a step toward the corner where the woman was heckling us. "Let them do their damn show!" A murmur followed from the crowd.

"Who would want to sleep with her?" came the older woman's voice.

A flicker of anger crossed Paul's face, and suddenly he was walking off the stage. I had never seen him so angry.

My breath was in my throat. I could feel the situation spinning toward disaster. Someone—Ellen, the manager?—had flicked on the house lights, and I got a look at the woman Paul was approaching: an attractive woman in her sixties wearing make-up, with dyed blonde hair. She was more put together than I had expected, and she had definitely dressed up for the occasion, in white jeans and a white top, so that she wouldn't be easy to miss. The room was silent, now, so their whole conversation was audible.

"Can we talk outside?" Paul was saying.

"I'm not allowed to talk to you."

"Come on. Mom. Let's go."

"I paid for a show. Even if it's bad."

Brett was standing next to Paul, now, looking ready to back

him up with physical violence if necessary. Ellen approached them with another heavyset man who spoke to Paul's mother and then grabbed at her elbow.

"Fuck off!" she cried. "Fuck all of you! Fuck you all."

"Mom, please..." Paul's voice was very low.

"I need my fucking coat!" she cried.

"Mom, please come outside. I'll talk to you outside."

Paul's mother gathered her things and left. Paul glanced at me, his expression stricken, and then followed her out.

There was a moment of stunned silence. I wanted to rush after Paul, but I was also scared of making things worse. I could hear his mother beginning to yell at him outside the doors.

Mark took a breath and stepped forward. "Well," he said, "we like to do a ritual human sacrifice at every show, and this time it was Paul. So since that part of the show is over..." Mark met my eyes, and I could see a combination of sympathy and 'I told you so,' in his expression.

"At least she wasn't throwing tomatoes at us," I said, bringing back in the tomato. And we got faint chuckle from the crowd.

I glanced back at Lisette, unsure if we should continue or not, and she stepped forward.

"Folks, our next improv is going to be called 'No Hecklers.'" There were chuckles. "Because there is good and bad audience input, and we need the kind of audience input we can actually use. Here's what we need from you. We want stories about why you broke up with somebody."

The lights lowered again. Things were back under control. We finished the rest of our set in a daze and went to sit down at the little table. I don't know how the rest of it went. It didn't matter.

Raahid got up on stage after us. "Well," he said, "I usually do a set about how Newfoundlanders are way too friendly. But that may not be appropriate this evening, so let me switch that up a bit."

I glanced at my phone, then got up and slipped out during Raahid's set to look for Paul. The street outside was empty. Paul was gone.

I sent him a text: *Are you ok?*

Lisette appeared next a moment later. "No Paul?" I shook my head. We looked out into the empty night, full of stars that I wasn't going to see when I got back to New York. At home, you could forget that this many stars even existed.

Ellen, the manager, came outside. "He left with his mother," she said flatly. "Wow. He's such a nice guy, you know?" She pulled out a cigarette and tapped it against the box as we took this in.

Lisette said, "She's got a lot of problems. He's been trying to set some boundaries with her and clearly, she didn't like it."

"Well," Ellen said, "maybe the two of them can talk it out."

That might have been the most classically Canadian optimism I'd ever heard.

"Or he can just tell her to fuck off," Lisette said.

"Or that," Ellen agreed. She lit a cigarette.

"He'll be okay," Lisette said, putting a hand on my arm.

"I know." What I was thinking was that tonight was the night I was supposed to tell Paul that I was no longer allowed to work remotely, that it was over for us. There was Paul, trying to set boundaries with his mother and his ex, and I was about to abandon him.

HALF AN HOUR LATER, Lisette, Mark and I sat with Raahid in a bar three doors down from the Puffin Hut while the show continued. We were all waiting for Paul to get in touch. Lisette filled Raahid in on the brief outlines of the situation with Paul's mother.

"That's rough," Raahid said. "My mother hates that I'm a stand-up, but she doesn't come and try to ruin my sets. She just wants me to go to engineering school."

"I wish I could run her over with a car," Lisette said. "Her and my ex-boyfriend. I'm not saying I'd enjoy it. I'd feel really guilty the whole time. But some people have forgotten that they owe anything to other people."

Mark caught her eye and then looked at the table. I wondered if we were all feeling guilty for things we should have told people and hadn't.

I finally heard from Paul an hour later, via text. *Are you still out?*

I wrote back right away. *We're all still at the bar. Do you want to come here? Do you want me to come over?*

A moment. *Can you come over?*

I texted back, *be right there.*

I looked around. "It's Paul. I'm going to go talk to him."

Lisette and Mark nodded, with very different expressions.

"Are you two together?" Raahid asked. I wasn't sure how to answer that.

"No," I said, after a second. "We're just friends."

Mark rose and walked me to the door. He looked at me seriously. "If you need to talk later on..."

"Thanks, Mark."

He kissed me on the cheek, and I got a brief whiff of his musk and citrus cologne.

"I'm going to miss you when I go back to the States," I said. "And it looks like that may be soon."

He nodded. "Call me."

13

"A SERIES OF BAD MISTAKES"

ST. John's is not a city with a lot of taxis, so after a futile exchange with my Lyft app, I just walked the twenty minutes to Paul's house.

He opened the door and gave me a hug. "I am so sorry." The words were muffled in my hair.

"It's okay. We were just worried about you."

"I sat her down and told her I was cutting her off. She's not allowed to see me again. At all. And she wouldn't leave, so I ended up calling the police. She left before they got there. She just wanted to see if I'd do it, I guess."

"Oh, Paul, I'm so sorry."

"She said some things at the end, that...about how she wished she'd never had a child, that I'd ruined her life."

"She was just lashing out. You know that, right?"

He shrugged. "I'll probably call her at Christmas, but until then..."

I gave him another hug. He kissed my hair. "Thank you for sticking with me through this."

It was the moment. I didn't want it to be. But I couldn't not tell him.

"Paul," I said. "I've—I just found out that I—I can't work remotely anymore."

"So that means..." His face was blank, which made it worse.

"Basically I've been ordered home. I have to go into the office on Monday. I have to fly back this weekend and show up at work or I get fired."

"Oh."

"And I know this is the worst time to do this. I don't want to go."

"Well, it will make it easier to see your sister in Atlanta, won't it?" he said gently.

"She's moving back, too. To New York. She just told me."

He nodded, taking this in. "Okay," he said, more to himself than to me.

I continued, "But that's not why—it's a change in policy. I've been working from home for two years. I didn't know this was coming."

"And you found out..."

"Monday. After we—after we spent the night. I should have told you right away. You were dealing with so much, and I wanted to get through tonight. It was important to Lisette that I do this, and I thought...I was scared to say it. I didn't want it to be real. I'm so sorry."

"It's okay," he said. He nodded and walked to his sofa and sat down.

I spoke quietly. "You're the best thing that's happened to me in years. Maybe ever."

He shrugged.

"I mean it, Paul. And I'm really proud of you for standing up to your mother."

He was silent again. Then he nodded. "Sorry," he said. "I have this tendency to go quiet when I'm thinking. Trish used to complain about it."

"I don't mind," I said gently.

There was another long moment. He looked up. "When do you leave?"

"This weekend."

He nodded again. "Saturday or Sunday?"

"Sunday."

"And there's no chance anything can change…"

"My boss has been trying. He's trying to get them to reverse the policy, but I think first they have to drag everyone back into the office to prove a point. And I applied—I did apply for a Canadian work visa." Paul glanced up at me. "But the lawyer put my chances around fifty-fifty, so I don't want you to wait on that. Not that you would, but…"

"What a day," Paul said.

"If it matters any," I said quietly, "I want to stay." It was true. I wanted to hug my sister and make her feel better. But I wanted this life. I wanted Paul.

"It matters," he said. "But maybe this is good. We knew things would end, and I—I have so much to deal with right now, and I felt guilty dragging you in the middle of it."

"Don't. You deserve someone who can help you through all this. I want to be that person. You can call me anytime. I just can't expect you to…" I trailed off.

"It's good you're going to be with your sister. She'll need you."

He moved over to sit next to me and took my hand. It was a strange feeling. I felt like I was noticing for the first time how introverted he was, how much trouble he had with talking about things. I thought of the way Lisette had explained their marriage, that Trish walked all over him, perhaps because he was like this, so quiet. He could be loud and funny on stage, but in ordinary life, he retreated. I waited for him.

After a moment, he took a breath, pulling himself together.

"So how was the rest of the show? Was there a rest of the show?"

"It went fine. Everything was fine. We got through the rest of the performance. We got a laugh or two, even. But it was awkward. I wanted to come after you, but I didn't want to make things worse."

"No, you did the right thing." He shook his head a little. "You're so amazing, Abby. To still keep going in the middle of all that. During your first show? You have to do improv in New York, you know. I hear they have some there. Not as good as ours, of course."

"Of course not."

"Can I...can I come over?"

I shook my head. In spite of my best efforts, I started to cry. "I don't think I can handle it. I'll be too sad."

"Okay."

My phone buzzed. It was Lisette.

"She wants to know how you're doing." I showed him the text.

"I'll call her," he said.

"I should get going," I said, standing up.

"You don't have to go yet."

"I do...I can't..." I took a deep breath.

He gave me a sad little smile and nodded, once.

I got up to go, and he gave me a hug good-bye at the door. "You'll call me before you go?"

"I'll come by," I said. "Saturday. I'll bring you back all your books. Okay?"

"I would say you can keep them, but I want to make sure I see you again, so okay."

I wanted to kiss him, but I couldn't. I left. I wondered if he was thinking that he had burned bridges with his mother and his ex-wife because of a woman who was leaving him a few days later.

THE NEXT DAY WAS FRIDAY, and someone rang my doorbell at 9:30 a.m. Lisette stood there, her face bright red like she had been running.

"Hey."

"I left work in the middle of my shift," she said. "And I never leave work in the middle of my shift. So you're *leaving Sunday*? Paul had to text me because apparently you weren't going to tell me."

"I meant to tell you last night, but all the stuff came up with Paul...I just..."

"So when were you going to tell me?"

"After you got off work tonight."

"So you would text me at six, we would hang out tomorrow, and you would leave on Sunday?"

It was the first time I had seen Lisette really angry.

"I'm sorry," I said. "Everything was so messy at the show. I've only known since a couple of days ago."

"And you didn't tell me right away?"

"I wanted last night to be perfect for you. I thought I would tell people afterwards."

Lisette nodded, her face flushed. I stepped back for her to enter the apartment. It took her a long moment to speak. "I am so tired of everyone treating me like I'm fragile."

"I don't."

"Yes, you do. You didn't think I could handle it if I knew you were leaving so you lied to me."

"I was just sad, okay? And I didn't—I wanted you to have one thing—this improv show—go perfectly."

"And look at how that worked out," she said. "Perfect show." Her nervous energy transformed into a different state when she was angry. She was at once perfectly still and also vibrating.

"Listen—"

"But even if...you could still have told me afterwards. You told Paul. In the middle of that total mess with his mother. But you didn't tell me because you don't think of me like a real friend. You think of me like a pet."

"No!"

"I'm not a charity project!"

"You're my friend."

"You don't treat me like a friend! You didn't tell me when Paul asked you out."

"Because I was scared. I was scared it was doomed, or that he'd change his mind."

"Just admit it. You don't take me seriously."

"I'm not used to being important to anybody!" I said at last. "In New York, I was important to my sister, but everyone else treated me like this cool friend they brought along with them to make funny remarks. I'm not used to mattering to anybody."

"Of course you matter!" she shouted. "You're one of my best friends and one of the only people who gets me. And I'm going to miss you, but I guess you won't miss me. I'm just some abuse victim who lives in a basement."

"Not a basement," I muttered. "A sex dungeon."

She shook her head. She was not ready to laugh.

"Lisette, can I tell you something? The last relationship I had was with a married man. And I knew he was married. I thought he was going to leave his wife for me. And I am so ashamed of that I couldn't even tell my sister. I am not looking down on you. You're like me, in a lot of ways, but you're better. You're positive and funny and somehow you don't let life get you down. And I didn't tell you I was leaving because I knew my friendship with you was going to be ending and I couldn't handle how sad that made me. And I couldn't handle making you sad. Or the rest of our time together being sad. I was a coward."

Lisette stared at me. It was hard to meet her gaze, but at the same time I felt lighter. I had told my secret about Colin to someone, and she hadn't recoiled in horror.

"And you think I won't want to be friends with you if you're in New York?"

I said nothing. My friendship with Jasmine and Lucas was affectionate but conditional on my presence. I may have assumed all friendships would be like that. And I wondered if my own fears were the problem. I didn't tell Lucas or Jasmine the really dark stuff about my life. I had assumed all my friendships were conditional on my never being sad. "I'm a mess," I said finally.

"You? I had to sleep on a stranger's sofa this past month. A woman from Brooklyn had to take me in because I had nowhere to go."

"She got lucky."

"She was a rock star, actually. But she doesn't respect me."

"I do. I love you." I smiled, tears in my eyes. "If you want me to, I will keep texting you. All the time."

"I don't need pity."

"Do you pity me?" I asked.

"Only for kissing Paul. That must have been terrible." Lisette grinned a little.

I laughed a little. "Well, maybe this way if he wants to work things out with Trish..."

"Please not that. She's awful." Lisette took a breath. "Okay. I forgive you. And more importantly, I should get back to work, probably."

"Probably."

"I said I was having a medical issue. That's the real advantage of improv. It makes you a better liar."

"Do you forgive me enough to hang out tomorrow?"

"This time. But I will expect constant updates on your New York City life to make it up to me."

"You will hear about every stalled subway train and broken shoe."

"You think that's a threat, but that is exactly what I want. With photos."

I DIDN'T HAVE A VERY productive workday. I forced myself to finish a couple of articles that had deadlines and sent them to Kedar to review. Then I walked over to the windows and stared at the view: this breezy, beautiful city that tumbled down a hill to the coast. I had started to love it here, this practical, stark, beautiful island, full of people I loved.

Lisette turned up after work and threw her arms around me and held for a long moment.

"I should start to pack," I said quietly. "But it won't take me long. I managed to put my whole life into a couple of suitcases. Who knew?"

"Why isn't Paul here?"

"I'm not strong enough. I'll cry too much."

"Does he know you're in love with him?"

I took a breath. "It seems like the wrong thing to tell him right now."

She nodded thoughtfully, still leaning against me.

THAT NIGHT, Laura and I talked about all the practicalities of her staying at my Brooklyn apartment. We were going to be flying on the same day, Sunday, with her arriving at close to 3 p.m. and me getting back at closer to eight at night. I explained how she could get a key to my apartment from my doorman, so she'd have somewhere to sleep. She explained that her plan was to get Hannah settled and re-enrolled in her local Brooklyn school and then fly back to Atlanta to do the work of packing up all their lives while I watched Hannah.

"Nick is not happy with me," Laura said, "and I didn't want Hannah around if Nick and I started fighting."

"Totally understandable."

"I don't want her mad at her dad, you know? Just because I'm not seeing eye to eye with him. I'm not even ruling out ever being with him again, I just..."

"I know, Laur. It's okay either way. Whatever you decide."

"I just couldn't upend my whole life for his version of how everything was supposed to work, you know?"

I was excited to see her again, but a sense of loss still hovered over me. This trip, which had been intended to change my life, seemed to have been a detour. Everything was about to go right back to the way it had always been: me watching Hannah, serving as the side character in Laura's life rather than the main character of my own. But hadn't I wanted exactly this to happen?

LISETTE and I met outside her apartment on Saturday morning and went for a walk in the drizzling rain to buy her some shower curtains for her basement.

"If you ever want to leave the country," I said, "or if the awful ex-boyfriend is giving you are hard time, you have a place with me. You won't even have to figure out a name change."

"I may go see my family instead. You were right. I shouldn't let my ex keep me out of Quebec. And my brother Cedric is back from Florida, so I want to go see him. He's living at my brother Martin's house right now."

"You had a brother in Florida? I didn't know this."

"Yeah. I told you about him. They film in Orlando."

"I thought—when you said wrestler…Lisette, are you telling me you have a brother in the World Wrestling Federation?"

"Why are you so surprised?"

"Because you're so tiny!"

"Well," she shrugged. "Cedric is six foot six. I told you he could beat up Paul." She pulled out a photo of a giant man in tights, growling toward the camera. "They call him the French Revolution."

"This is the best thing I've ever seen. If you go see him, will you send me a picture of the two of you together?"

"I thought we'd established that we are sending each other all the pictures."

When it was time to say goodbye, Lisette jumped up to give me one of her giant hugs.

"You'll be back," she said. "You don't know it yet, but I know."

"I hope so."

"I have faith."

"Well, you inspired me to be brave enough to try improv, so thank you for that," I said.

"It's a way to live," she said. "Sometimes you just have to jump before you know the answer yet. That's how I got away from Simon. I jumped."

I GATHERED Paul's improv books and texted him on Saturday to say that I was coming by. Something about the formality of returning the books had a particular misery to it, mimicking the break-up of a long-term relationship that we'd never get to have.

It was still raining when I walked to his house, just like something out of a sad movie, and I climbed his steps hurriedly, trying to keep the books dry under my coat.

"You walked?" he said when he opened the door. "I could have come over."

"No, it's fine," I said. "I'm trying to enjoy the city while I still can."

"Come inside."

His house was warm. The wood stove was going, and I wondered if that was just for me.

I desperately wanted to hug him, but instead I made myself busy stripping off my coat and putting the books down on a table. Paul stood beside me, looking like he wanted to help and then like he didn't know what to do with his hands.

"Coffee?"

I nodded, once. I knew Paul preferred tea. He had done this for me as well. A small thing. I took a mug and wandered into the middle of the room, staring at his DVDs.

"I gave you so many books," he said, looking at the pile I'd left behind me. "I guess I really am a schoolteacher."

"I read almost all of them. They were good."

He gave a sad smile. "So in New York, you'll still do improv, I hope. I hope we've gotten you hooked."

I shrugged. "Maybe." The space between us felt endless, the hug I hadn't given at the door haunting me. I could step forward into his arms and do it now.

"This is too sad," I said.

He nodded.

I looked at the room, where he had tidied up the mess left by his mother. "You know it's your mother's loss, that you're not in her life."

He shrugged. "I know that, but it doesn't help. It just makes me worry about her."

I went on, because he needed to hear this, at least. "You're marvelous. Maybe when she's burned her last bridge, she'll realize that she was the one setting all the fires."

"I doubt it," he said with a weary little smile. "But I know your sister needs you," he said. "So I'm glad you're going to get to be with her. I always thought that if she needed you, you'd go back."

I stared into the swirling black quicksand of my coffee mug.

"She can survive without me. She's moving into my apartment tomorrow, for a few days. So we'll get back the same day. Honestly, if I wasn't being forced back by work, I might not have gone at all."

"But it's out of your hands."

"Maybe I could find some other remote job."

He gave a quick, pained smile. "Well, you've never lived here during winter. That's when people really decide if they like it up here."

"I like winter, actually. That wouldn't have scared me. I was happy here. You made me happy. You and Lisette," I added.

We were both silent, both good at being awfully grown up about the whole thing. I hated it.

"Paul, I—I loved being with you."

I could see something cross his face, but this time I couldn't read it. "Thanks, Abby. Me, too."

I rose, and he stepped forward. I gave him a hug.

"Abby..."

There it was. The feeling, his hands curving around my back. I was pressed into his shoulder, and I could feel him breathing, feel his heartbeat.

Then slowly we let go. It was like that first kiss: I wasn't sure which of us had taken the step to move away. I put on my coat and took hold of the door handle, the only part of his house that was cold.

"Hey," he said, as he stepped outside with me, "do you want a ride home or anything? It may start to rain again." He gazed up at the clouds, which were moving ominously fast and low across the sky.

"No," I said, glancing up at the dark grey above our heads. "I can handle it."

I walked as quickly as I could and definitely did not look back until I had turned a corner. Once I was out of sight, I paused and took a breath. I had gotten out of his sight before I could give in to the desire to look back at him.

THE MORNING OF MY DEPARTURE, I realized that I had said good-bye to Lisette and Paul but not to Mark. I thought about texting him, but I knew he lived about thirty minutes down the road, and I wanted to see him in person. This felt like the end of an era, and maybe a chance to tell him he'd been right about me and Paul. As a fellow cynic, he might as well hear that he'd been correct all along: we had always been doomed.

I called up Rick, my crossword-loving taxi driver, who was going to take me to the airport and asked him if he could come an hour and a half early and help me find the little donut shop that Mark had said was across the street from his place: Chocolate Heaven. I could surprise Mark with some eclairs.

Rick was happy to drive me because I gave him a few more crossword puzzle clues, and we had a desultory chat as we drove out of the center of the city toward Mark's suburb. It was slowly turning into a gorgeous day. Sure enough, the pastry shop owner knew Mark, and the owner pointed to a house a hundred feet away, just up the street. I took my box of donuts and told Rick to wait for me in the parking lot and decided to walk over.

Mark's house was a nice house. A very nice house, in fact, with a broad, colonial face and high ceilings and a front porch. It felt like the setting for some movie flashback about someone's perfect childhood, porch swings and rose bushes and all.

This was the place he's been hiding from us?

Just after I rang the doorbell, I suddenly knew.

I knew it before a woman in her early fifties walked down the hallway and saw me standing there. She opened the door, wiping flour-covered hands on an apron like she'd been baking a pie.

"Hello," she said, a confused smile on her face.

"Hi, I'm looking for Mark."

"Mark?" She turned. "Mark!" She called into the front parlor, and Mark emerged. He saw me and his expression turned ashen.

"Hey," he said, "what are you doing here?"

"You ordered eclairs? I was asked if I could drop them off by the shop owner." I don't know why I instinctively covered for him.

I didn't say, "You've been pretending you're divorced to live a double-life in the city, sleeping with lots of women, when you're clearly still married."

"Oh, okay," he said gruffly. "I don't think I ordered any. Let's talk outside."

The woman I suspected was his wife gave him a confused look; she knew something was up from my expression, but she couldn't put her finger on it. He stepped onto the porch and closed the door behind him. It was one of those large, attractive front porches that wrapped halfway around a house, with a porch swing laden with pillows and a distant view of the water. It was all so idyllic—that was the irony of it. This was the hellish marriage that he wanted to escape?

"Why are you here?" he asked, flatly.

"That's your wife?"

"Look, Abigail...We're...she and I...."

"You're having problems, but you're still living under the same roof?" I asked.

Mark gave a long, weary sigh.

"It's fine, Mark," I said. "I'm leaving town tomorrow. I have no intention of blowing up your life. I just came to say good-bye."

"It's not what you think."

"I'll bet."

"Hey, listen," he said. "Everything I told you was true, okay?" He glanced around to make sure no one could hear him. "Our kids have left the house. My wife and I aren't connecting anymore. I've been with her since I was a teenager, and I mean, yeah, I was trying to relive my youth for a while. But you were the first person I ever thought about having something serious with. And then you went off with Paul, so you don't need to make a big deal about this, right?"

"I'm not telling her. I am going to tell Paul and Lisette, though."

"Why?" His outrage amused me, like he was a celebrity, and I had threatened to tip off the paparazzi, rather than a philanderer mowing through the female population of a small city.

"So they can warn people."

"Of what? I'm not hurting anyone. I don't go around making promises."

His wife opened the door. "Is everything okay, Mark?" She must have seen us looking tense, looking like we were fighting.

"Yes," he said. "Just a confusing mistake. They want to charge me for these things, and I didn't order them."

"Okay." She looked between us.

"Sorry!" I said. "We almost have it sorted!"

She walked back inside. Mark looked at me. "Thank you for that."

"Best improv I've ever done."

Mark looked at me for a long moment, and then I turned to go.

My driver Rick was waiting for me, happily devouring a donut across the street.

"Hey," he said, glancing between me and his phone. "Seven letter word for misery."

"Despair," I said.

Of course Mark was married. He must have recognized me right away as a potential 'other woman.' Everyone in New York did.

I texted Lisette from the car. *I went to Mark's house to say good-bye. He's married. Tell Paul, too. I don't have the energy right now.*

whattttttttt? Lisette wrote me back.

I texted: *Nice house. White picket fence. Wife in an apron. I guess he didn't tell any of us so he could hit on half of St. John's.*

She wrote back immediately. *Did his wife get upset?*

I took a breath and then texted. *I covered for him. I think she bought it, not sure. I didn't see a reason to ruin her life.*

Lisette wrote again. *He just texted Paul and me to say he quit the improv group.*

So that was his solution. I sighed. *I'm sorry. My fault.*

Lisette wrote back: *Don't u dare blame yourself for shitty men. Ask me how I know.*

I smiled. *I want you to come visit me in New York. I can pay for the ticket if you let me.*

After a long moment, she responded. *I'll have to get a passport. Still deciding on the name to put on it. Thinking maybe Lisette Poulin.*

That's a good name, I texted back. *Only slightly less good than Judy Dench.*

. . .

WHEN WE WERE five minutes away from the airport, my cell phone rang. It was Kedar.

"Guess what, rock star?" he said. "I just got us six more weeks."

"What?"

"And I may be able to get them to extend it permanently. I didn't want to say anything to you until I had good news. I told you I could probably talk them out of this whole stupid back-to-office thing, and I didn't yet, but at least I got us a delay. I knew you wanted to do your trip."

"That's great. You can go to your cousin's wedding." I looked outside the window at the suburbs outside St. John's, speeding past in Rick's taxi.

"Yeah," said Kedar. "And you can stay in Newfoundland for another month if you still want to."

"Wow. Okay...Let me call you back."

Rick pulled up to the airport curb and helped me out with my baggage, and I paid him and stepped away. I needed to think.

This was the moment. I could go running back to Paul and tell him that I loved him. I could call up Charlotte and tell her I was going to stay for the last few days of August, and then I could find another place. Maybe I could even stay with Paul, or find somewhere else, and we could be together for a few more weeks and then...

A sickening feeling was building in my stomach. It all felt like a lie. I would still end up having to go home. I would just be postponing the inevitable, making it all more painful, hurting Paul further.

Laura needed me.

And Mark had been married the whole time. The creepiness of it put me on edge. Of course he was married, and of course those were the people I attracted, and of course it was going to happen again and again.

I sat down on a bench inside the airport terminal and stared at my cell phone. I didn't have the energy to lose Paul again.

I tried writing a text to Paul: *hey, it turns out I don't have to*

I didn't send it. I didn't even finish it.

I thought about Hannah, and I stood up and walked to the check-in area. It was time to go home.

14

"BROOKLYN BITCH"

IT TOOK two flights to get back to New York City, back through Montreal and then another flight to JFK airport. The strangest part of getting off the plane was how little culture shock I felt. When I walked through the airport that my friend Jasmine had nicknamed the world's most overpriced mall, I half-expected to feel overwhelmed by all the people and the noise and the traffic. But instead I immediately relaxed. Everything felt like it was moving at the appropriate speed. Hearing and seeing people from all over the world, with every accent, felt right. Even the brusque taxi driver who tossed my bags into his trunk felt right. He was efficient but not warm. He didn't want to make friends. He drove me back to my apartment in Brooklyn in silence, except for some casual swearing at a double-parked Amazon truck.

My doorman Nash was at his desk, and he greeted me as I came in.

"Hey, welcome back!" he said, and made a feeble motion toward getting up to help me with my bags, which he knew I would I wave off.

"Thanks, Nash, I got it." I hauled my suitcases along the

handicapped ramp that covered half the lobby staircase and then rumbled them along to my elevator. My building had one of those old-fashioned elevators with a small round window like a porthole, and stepping onto it gave me a warm, familiar claustrophobia.

I was home. My heart was breaking, maybe, but I was about to see Laura. I was about to see my favorite kid. My sister and Hannah would already be waiting for me in my apartment.

I still had my keys, and I fumbled awkwardly through my bags to find them. Then I walked up to my own door and opened the deadbolt with a familiar clunk. I could hear Laura talking in my kitchen on the phone, and she quickly stepped into the living room and waved a greeting at me and then kept talking.

"Yeah, I know. I can definitely come in then," she was saying. "Brant," she whispered to me, pointing to her cell phone, and then kept listening; Brant was a co-worker at her old job.

"Got it," I whispered.

I put down my bags and walked deeper into the living room to where Hannah lay watching TV on my sofa, looking half-asleep and sunburned.

"Tabby," she said and made a half-move toward me before her gaze returned to the screen. "We're staying at your place."

"That's just where I want you to be," I said, climbing onto the sofa beside her. She looked extraordinarily tired.

"We were traveling all day."

"Me, too."

"That's my sixth time on a plane!"

"That's very impressive for seven years old."

"I'm almost eight."

"I know," I said.

She looked at me for a long moment as if she was still deciding whether she wanted to hug me, and it hurt my heart to see it. She must have felt like I had left her, rather than the other way around.

Then she flashed a smile at me and crawled into my lap and put one of her soft little arms against my collarbone.

"I missed you," she said as her eyes returned to the television. She was watching an animated show filled with overeager animals debating the nuances of life in a submarine.

"I missed you, too," I said.

I leaned back to watch cartoons with her, trying to tell myself that everything was right again in the world. I was back where I belonged, back in the land of Broadway and bodegas, back with my family all in one place. The hole in my chest would fill soon enough.

After a few minutes, Laura walked into the room and sat next to me.

"I may be able to get my old job back," she said. "Brant is pulling some strings for me."

"That's great," I said.

"And then we'll find a different place and be out of your hair."

"No rush."

A moment later, she said, "I put all the booze in your bedroom." I remembered that Laura was in recovery, and I had forgotten how weird it might be for her to be around my fancy cocktail cart.

"Sorry. I forgot it was out."

"You had the full set."

She wasn't wrong; she would have found whiskey, vodka, rum, tequila, and gin on the credenza.

"Well, you don't come over much." It was true. I almost always went to Laura's house. I would pick up Hannah at school and then we'd go to Laura's and stay there until she got home from work. Laura never went to my place. My life was supposed to revolve around hers, and now she was annoyed that my apartment wasn't set up the way she wanted it.

She shrugged and said nothing.

It bothered me a little that she was implying something about my lifestyle, about how much I was like our mother, but I didn't say anything. She was tired. We were both really tired.

Once Hannah was tucked into my pull-out sofa bed in the living room, Laura and I headed into my bedroom to have a real discussion.

"So Nick," she said at last, perching herself on the end of my bed.

Of course that's what we were going to talk about. Nick.

"I know you want me to say you were right about him," she began.

"I don't want you to say that." It was true. The one thing I didn't feel, right now, was any sense of gloating. "I know it was reasonable to try again with him."

"The thing is, we may work it out. I just need my own life."

"That's fine, Laur."

There was tension between us, but I wasn't sure why. I hadn't said anything, hadn't teased her, hadn't done anything I could think of to make her feel unwelcome.

"I don't want you to think I'm going to live on your sofa bed forever."

"I don't. It's fine. I'm not upset. I told you that you could have the bedroom if you want it. Both of you."

"I didn't want your bedroom." I wondered if Laura's pride was wounded. She was the older sister, but she was crashing on my sofa for the first time. It hit me that she and I both hated acting needy. She was insisting everything was fine, and I wasn't even bringing up that I'd just left behind a man I was totally in love with.

We were fine. We were good. This was how we got through everything.

I wasn't sure what to do with that knowledge. It seemed impossible to do anything but what we were used to.

"You should go to sleep," I said.

"You look tired," Laura said.

"Everyone is tired," I said.

"Are you okay?"

"Yeah," I said quietly. "I'm okay. I'm not an alcoholic, Laur."

"I know that. I'm sorry. I'm just annoyed that I still have to do that. And I had to explain what I was doing to Hannah, you know?"

"Yeah." I hadn't thought about it from that angle. I wondered how much Hannah knew about her mother's relationship to alcohol.

"I'm glad you're back from your trip," she said as she rose from my bed. "I missed you."

"Missed you, too," I replied.

Was I home? I wasn't sure anymore. Why was I annoyed that she assumed everything in Newfoundland had just been a casual lark?

'A trip.' That's what Kedar had called it. A detour. And now it was over.

KEDAR HAD TOLD me not to go to the office on Monday because he was fighting to allow us to work from home and it would undermine his efforts if I went in anyway, so I spent the day with Hannah while Laura ran around trying to get their life back in order and get Hannah enrolled back in a New York City school.

Hannah was not excited that she'd already been in school for over a week, and none of it 'counted,' but Laura had explained that she needed to start back again in New York with the other kids.

"It's not fair," she wailed.

"Well, you'll have at least a few days with me before you go back," I said. "Let's do something fun before I have to go back to getting work done."

We walked to a playground together, but Hannah only spent a couple of minutes running around before she came to sit with me on a bench.

"You remember this playground?" I asked.

"Of *course* I remember it," she said, like I was being silly. "It's not my favorite anymore."

"You like the one in Central Park with the big rock."

"There's a sprinkler playground in Atlanta," she said. "That one is my favorite now."

"I'm glad you had fun."

"I want to move back to Georgia," Hannah said. "I didn't realize I had to start school over again. It's not fair."

"I know, sweetie."

Hannah turned to watch the other kids on the playground with a wary expression. I realized that Hannah looked different. She had gotten new clothes and a new haircut, and I could glimpse the tween that she was going to become. Eight years old was going to be different than seven. I wondered if nine would see her sipping martinis and complaining about her third ex-husband. My time with her was slipping away.

"How was it," I asked her, "down there in Georgia? Was it nice to see your dad?"

"Daddy and Mommy would have all these *discussions*."

"Discussions?"

"Yes," she said wearily. "You should have come. You could

have told them to stop." Then she wrapped an arm around me and hugged me.

"Push me on the swing!" she cried.

"What am I? Your servant?"

"Yes! Come, servant! Obey my commands!"

It was an old gag we had together, and she snapped her fingers for me to catch up. Something in my heart hurt as I stood up. I wondered again whether the time for me to have kids had passed forever. For the last few years, I had been telling myself that I probably couldn't even have kids anymore, like my uterus had closed up shop. Better that than to think my negativity would doom me to spinsterhood. I used to joke to Laura that I was going to pull a Miss Havisham on Hannah and raise her to punish the world of men.

"Push me higher!"

"Okay, okay."

I stood behind the swing and took the thick chain cords in my hands as Hannah adjusted herself, then lifted them toward me and gave her a nice, solid push. Then a gentle shove on her back. I watched her swinging higher, her legs pumping. When I was little, I used to believe that if you pumped your legs hard enough, you could keep going. Nobody was pushing me back then, but it didn't matter because I could pump harder and harder, trying to reach liftoff.

Maybe that was the fundamental truth that you realized as you became an adult: that you would always come back to earth.

I had tried to escape my life in New York, but I had landed right back here: still single, still cynical, still the type who got hit on by married men. I had jumped onto an improv stage, and tried things I was scared of, and gone right back to my old life afterwards. I had tried to find love, and then ended things, too afraid to find out whether he loved me back.

I pushed Hannah harder than I intended.

"Too high!" Hannah called.

My heart in my chest, I let her come down slowly.

"Sorry, baby."

"It's okay." Hannah looked unfazed and took off at a run, but I felt shocked. My frustration had come out of nowhere. I didn't want to take it out on her.

When we got back to the house, I turned on the television for Hannah and fussed with my articles for the rest of the afternoon, finishing a piece on farm subsidies. I tried for humor, pulling out references to movies like *Field of Dreams* and the Zach Snyder *Superman* films, but it read more like a freshman in college banging out their first submission to a humor magazine. Laura got home at five from her meetings about possibly returning to work. She had brought Indian take-out with her, our sisterly equivalent of a dozen roses to smooth over any fight, but I told her that I needed to run an errand.

What I really needed was to get out of the house. I walked the streets of Brooklyn by myself for over an hour, all the way from Carroll Gardens to the Brooklyn Museum, through Prospect Park, past some of my favorite restaurants and vintage clothing stores.

The city was beautiful. It was closing in on September, and the tips of some trees were beginning to be touched with gold. The skies were an endless blue shading into violet, and the whole population of the city seemed to be outside, biking and skateboarding or sitting on stoops listening to rap music.

I took a cell phone photo of the park with the last strains of light in the sky, just when everything was turning purple. I texted it to Paul and Lisette with the words, *back in Brooklyn. miss you both.*

Lisette responded immediately with a long series of exclamation marks. *They have trees in NYC? No one tells me these things!*

Paul didn't respond for half an hour, and when he did, he just "loved" the image. I stared at the heart for a long moment.

On my way home, I walked past an open tea shop and browsed their teas. Shops like this in St. John's would have shut down by six p.m., but in New York, the places that sold caffeine stayed open later, keeping the city going well into the night. I bought a little teacup to send to Mrs. Mahoney with some fancy tea. The teacup looked old and delicate but had 'Brooklyn Bitch' painted in gold leaf. I didn't know if she would love it or hate it, but I figured at least it would make her smile or make her glad she was rid of me. I also bought a coffee press for Lisette because she didn't have one yet in her basement apartment. I knew she worked at a coffee shop, but this one would be something of her own.

In spite of my best efforts, the anger that had been brewing inside me wasn't fully gone by the time I got home. I had a little half-balcony off my bedroom, barely big enough for two chairs, and I invited Laura to sit outside with me and enjoy the breezy night while Hannah finished one last television show before bed. I felt tense and wary.

"You know I'm sorry," she said, out of nowhere, opening a can of seltzer.

"For what?"

"For getting mad at you when you didn't want to move down to Atlanta. I didn't assume you would come babysit, by the way. I really didn't. I just thought you might want to."

"That's okay," I said. "It was just a big ask, and I felt like you didn't really ask. You didn't say I was important to you, and you hoped I'd come. You acted like you were doing me a favor by asking me."

"Well, I meant to ask nicely."

I sighed, nodding.

She paused and went on. "I just freaked out a little. I didn't mean to force you to move to Newfoundland just to make a point."

"Except I did want to move to Newfoundland."

Laura gave me a skeptical look. "Abby."

"Yes, I mean, it's pretty, and there are nice people there…It wasn't just a panic reaction. I wanted to go."

"To Newfoundland. Not Toronto, not Maine, but this island in the middle of the ocean? That doesn't in any way strike you as being an overreaction?" Laura raised her eyebrows at me, and I felt a rush of all the fights we'd had in the past, every little conflict that I'd let slide.

"Fuck you, Laura." She froze, and I pressed on. "Sure, I mean, at first, I just wanted to go somewhere with cooler weather because I hate the heat, but I liked it. A lot. I mean, it's not some backwater, it's a decent-sized city and it's a lot cheaper than other places in Canada. Toronto real estate is as expensive as New York."

"And then you'd what, just never see us again?" There was hurt in her voice, and I wondered if she was being condescending to hide that she was feeling abandoned.

"I could take Hannah for the summers, so you don't have to pay for summer camp," I said. "Camp Abby."

Laura's face was a portrait of incredulity, like I had announced I was joining the circus as soon as I mastered juggling knives.

"I probably can't move there permanently, so I don't even know why we're debating this. I don't know if my application for a visa will be accepted."

"You applied for a visa?" Laura genuinely looked shocked.

"I'll hear in a few months. Maybe in December. But yes. If I got permission, I would move back."

It was the first time I had said it aloud, in such a definite way, and I watched Laura's face. She was waiting for me to say I was joking, trying to come to terms with the idea that she didn't understand me as well as she thought she did.

"You should probably stay there for a whole winter before you decide anything."

"Probably," I said.

She rubbed her face. "But you love New York."

"I like New York," I said, "but the part you may have been missing was that I only stayed here for you. It was like we were married."

Her eyebrows shot toward the ceiling.

"Not in a weird horror movie way. I just felt like you were my family, and Hannah was my kid. I felt like I didn't need a husband to talk about my day with, because I had you. And I didn't need a kid, because I had Hannah. And when you picked up and left, it made me realize it was an illusion. Your family is you and Hannah, and maybe Nick. And I'm just an aunt."

"You are the most important member of my family."

"Fine, but can pick up and leave me anytime, and take Hannah with you. And that's okay. That's how it's supposed to be. But I can't live vicariously through you anymore."

She considered this for a long moment. "Growing up the way we did, I think we always had to be the center of each other's lives."

"I agree. But I need something of my own. I'm afraid that if I don't try, I'll miss my chance. And that means I need space. It means I can't watch Hannah every day. I have to meet people. Date more. And maybe find someone whose life is centered around me, too."

"And you couldn't just go to Queens?"

"I *liked* it there. But I'd need the same thing if I stay in New York. And it's not about abandoning Hannah, or you. I want to be the center of someone's life. I deserve that. And that's not what you can offer me. It's not what you *should* offer me."

She nodded. "Okay. If that's what you need, then okay. I want you to be happy." I could feel my face flushing, like I was getting ready to cry. She was giving me permission to have a life without her. I hadn't known that she would.

"So what do you think about me and Nick?" she asked. "If you were being honest, for once."

I considered the question for a long moment, trying to figure out whether I was tiptoeing into a minefield. "It sounds like he's capable of fitting you guys into the life he already has, but he's not capable of fitting his life around you. So the question is, is that enough for you?"

Laura took a deep breath. "You know how you said you need someone who puts you first? I need someone who puts me and Hannah first. Or at least someone who meets me in the middle."

"Then that's it. That's what you need. If he can't give up anything to keep you, then you're not his top priority. His career is."

Laura nodded, slowly. "I'd really miss you if you move to Newfoundland."

"I probably won't. They're not handing out a whole lot of visas."

"But if you got one, you're going?"

"I think so."

"I want that for you," she said finally. "Your own life."

"Me, too."

As I GOT into bed that night, Paul texted me. My heart leapt, opening it.

What's your address? I want to send you something.

I gave it to him. I wondered if he was going to send more improv books.

I stared at my phone for a long time. Then I wrote him, very late that night, long after he was probably in bed. *I miss Newfoundland.*

I sat there for a long moment, and then wrote, *I miss you.*

I sent it.

In the morning, he hadn't written me back.

I SHIPPED my presents to Lisette and Mrs. Mahoney later that day and got a text from Lisette when I was leaving the post office.

the drama you are missing here is WILD

I wrote back to her quickly. *what's going on?*

Lisette texted, *people are freaking out over mark I swear he slept with half the city*

I wonder if his wife will find out, I texted back, standing in the middle of a sidewalk. People were giving me irritated looks, so I moved to one side and leaned against a wall, just avoiding the dripping from an air conditioner above me.

Paul wants to tell her. He says it's what Mark deserves, Lisette replied. I ached, looking at Paul's name, wondering if I could ask how he was doing. He still hadn't answered me.

anyway we asked Raahid if he wanted to join the Newfingers and he said no but then guess who did?

I grinned and wrote, *please say lachlan please say lachlan*

Lolololol, she wrote. *No that would have been even better, but ellen! the manager of the puffin. So we're trying her out next week. And four other people. And amber did you meet her?*

who writes the sad songs about her boyfriend? I wrote.

The same.

I sighed. I felt jealous of these new people. I wanted to be up there, watching the auditions, listening to Paul give an impassioned lecture about long-form comedy.

My phone buzzed again.

paul isn't sure about the new people. He really misses you, I stared at the words. If he missed me, why didn't he just say so? *I think he wants you to come back so he doesn't want anyone else to take your place*

After a moment, I wrote, *I will come back to visit as soon as I get my sister set up with a new apartment. I miss you all so much.*

Don't forget me, Lisette wrote.

Never. I just mailed you something for your apartment.

It better have porcupines on it, Lisette wrote. *I have a strict theme.*

I walked along afterwards, feeling jealous that there might be a new person joining their improv group instead of me. Did I miss improv, now? What had become of me?

As if in answer, my friend Jasmine called.

"You, me, and Lucas. Dinner tonight. New gastropub Lucas found called the Bone and Whistle."

"Let me guess. Lower East Side."

She cackled. "Worse, babe. Williamsburg. Expect unicycles parked outside."

We met up at close to 8 p.m., which in itself amused me. Half the restaurant kitchens would be shutting down in St. John's by now.

"What is even happening with this place?" Jasmine demanded of Lucas, looking skeptically at the rough-hewn wood doors and post-industrial furniture visible through the darkened windows. "This is very 2010. There better not be Edison lightbulbs inside."

"There are, but you'll love it," Lucas said. "It's a giant throwback."

"You can't have a throwback to thirteen years ago."

"Nostalgia cycles happen in ten-year cycles now, not

twenty. We'll be transported back to our mid-twenties instantly." Lucas was a short, dark-haired California transplant who worked in public relations, while Jasmine was a tall Dominican-American whose fashion choices were deceptively cozy and hand-knit, making her look like a giant fuzzy blanket while she used her razor-sharp wit to tease people. They both gave me kisses that landed somewhere north of my ears and then took my arms to lead me inside like a prisoner.

When we were finally seated at a table, having placed an order for unnaturally large burgers and unnaturally tiny string fries, Lucas turned to me and carefully looked me over.

"So," he said, "I approve of the northern glow up."

"I look exactly the same."

"No way. You've got a color in your face. Don't tell me you've been hiking. Did somebody kidnap you and force you to do a trendy maple syrup diet?"

"There was some hiking. I made a couple of friends there," I said.

"How dare you."

"Male friends?" Jasmine asked.

"One, and I was madly in love with him," I said.

Jasmine and Lucas stared at me for a moment. "And...?" Jasmine asked.

I took a deep breath. This was not the way things usually went between us. I was usually joking about my horrible love life, but never meaning much of it. Maybe after my honesty with Laura, I couldn't stop it from gushing forth everywhere. "He's sweet, and I miss him. And Kedar said I could work from home again, so technically I could go back to live in Newfoundland for a few more weeks, but Laura needs me right now, and I don't know if I have the courage to go back because I don't think I could handle leaving him twice."

"Jasmine," Lucas said, "our little cynic has fallen in love."

I shook my head. "But it doesn't matter, because it's impossible." My eyes were welling with tears, which was definitely a sign that I no longer knew how to behave in New York.

"Maybe he could come here?" Jasmine was not usually this hopeful. I appreciated the effort she was making to avoid her usual snark, but I shrugged. Paul coming to New York felt impossible, too.

"So tell us about your soulmate," Jasmine said.

"He's cute and sarcastic, and he's a schoolteacher who knows a lot about Canadian history."

"So Gilbert Blythe?" Jasmine said. "You're dating Gilbert Blythe from *Anne of Green Gables*."

I smiled sadly. "It doesn't matter, because unless I get a visa, I can't go back."

Lucas sighed and put one hand on mine. "At least you're finally over the last one. What was his name? The one who quoted *The New York Review of Books* to me in an argument about Marvel movies?" Lucas meant Farid, of course.

"So where is the photo?" Jasmine pointed to my cell phone.

I flipped through my camera roll and found one of me, Paul, and Lisette hiking. "There's a moose in the lake behind us, but it's so far away that it looks like a speck."

Lucas examined the photo carefully. "Not bad. He's giving me actor-waiter vibes, like he's a Broadway understudy for a 1960s musical. And the manic pixie dream girl is...?"

"Lisette from Quebec. She's a good friend, too."

"Look at how he's looking at you." Jasmine smiled knowingly. "You're going to have one of those destination weddings in a barn in Newfoundland. And I'm going to have to go."

"He's probably getting back together with his ex-wife as we speak."

"If I go to any event involving farm animals, you're buying me new shoes."

My heart sunk a little at her teasing. They were still my closest New York friends, but Lucas was right, too. I was different.

Paul wrote me back on the way home from dinner: *I miss you too, Abby*.

My breath caught. I didn't move from the sidewalk until someone muttered a swear at me and I managed to get out of their way. Hope isn't dead in New York, I thought, but it better not take up any sidewalk space.

SOME OF THE more famous improv theaters I'd heard about in New York were defunct when I tried to look them up, but I did some digging online and found a little black box space in the Lower East Side that had a biweekly improv show. They had a show the next day, so I decided to go.

It was in a brick building with a couple of small theaters inside and an exhibit in the lobby by a local artist. The lobby art consisted of mouths painted in bright colors, rows upon rows of teeth in blue and purple and yellow. I stood before them for a moment, trying to decide if they were interesting or embarrassing, like I did with a lot of modern art. They felt very improv-appropriate.

Inside, the theater held about one hundred seats and had an audience of about sixty, half of whom would eventually appear in the show. The atmosphere was fun and cheerful, and large groups of people seemed to know each other. A young woman with purple-black hair got up and pitched the theater group's improv classes to the crowd, and then the show began.

"We are asking for help from the audience. Tell me the last time you felt afraid."

I considered it. I could think of a dozen times I'd been afraid recently, but none that I wanted to see performed.

"Almost got hit by a bus!" someone shouted.

"Going to the dentist."

"A porcupine in a tree!" I called.

The woman on stage smiled. "A porcupine in a tree."

The performers were skilled. They were wild. They were loose and funny. They did long-form sets and playful sets and an improv I'd never seen before based around casting a magical spell on the characters to transform them from genre to genre, so that they had to continue the scene they'd started as a romantic comedy, and then as an action film, and then a Wes Anderson movie. I immediately wanted to try the improv with Paul and Lisette.

The performers were great. What they weren't, I realized, was any better than my friends in St. John's. I had not been wrong in my first impression. The Newfingers had been really, really good.

Afterwards, I decided to approach the young woman who seemed to be organizing the event. She was chatting with an earnest-looking young man, but she smiled when I stepped forward.

"Hey, so, how does someone join one of these groups?" I asked.

"Yeah, you should definitely try out!" she said. She seemed nice and warm, her dark eyes twinkling beneath her purple hair. "Just be aware that we don't let people audition for a group without at least a year of classes."

"That makes sense," I said. I briefly wanted to pout and leave, but instead I said, "Sure," and the young woman handed me a sheet of paper with a QR code on it.

Maybe I would sign up for a class.

As soon as I was outside the theater, I wrote a text to Paul.

Hey, I said. *I went to an improv show here and they were great, but the Newfingers were even better, and I wanted to tell you that. The whole time I was watching I felt so grateful for all the times you let me into your group when I didn't really have any right to be there, just to play. And I think improv helped me be more brave, and I think I may try it again back in NY. But more than that, I'm grateful for all the times you took me hiking and showed me how beautiful the world is and made me feel like I was worth spending time with. And I wish things had worked out differently or that I knew how to make things work. But you deserve the best of everything. And you made me a better, braver person just by knowing you. And I wanted you to know that I love you, and I'm grateful that I know you. Whatever happens next.*

I took a breath and sent it.

Then I watched as the ellipses of his response hovered for a long time. Then, nothing.

My heart hurt, but I couldn't be sad that I'd sent it. Sometimes, you were brave just for yourself, not because you were going to get any response at all.

15

"YOU CAN BREAK ME, TOO"

MUCH LATER THAT NIGHT, after I got home from the improv show, Laura got a call from Nick. She had delayed her trip to go back to Atlanta, and I wondered if there was something they were still deciding. Maybe they would reconcile after all.

I offered to step out of the apartment to give her privacy, but she shook her head and just stepped into the bathroom to close the door. It was right next to my bedroom, so I could hear snippets. Things like, "You'll always be her father..." and "That's why I moved down there. That's literally why I moved there."

Eventually I felt guilty for listening and went outside for a walk. I walked to the corner bodega and wandered the brightly lit rows of sodas and overpriced snacks, browsing to kill time. It's rare that I'm sad Laura doesn't drink, but this was one of those times; it felt like bringing her back a bottle of wine would have been a nice gesture, considering how stressful the phone call must be. Instead, I picked up some La Croix seltzer in a mixed six-pack of flavors. Creating mixed six-packs is one of the minor acts of genius of the New York bodega shops. They take six-packs of beer or soda that already exist and blend and sell them, probably with questionable legality, but giving their customers options. It's one of the little pleasures of urban life that is hard to explain to outsiders.

Laura was still on the phone when I got back, so I stood in the kitchen listening to the murmur of conversation until I heard the bathroom door open and heard her broken voice saying, "Okay. I've got to go, okay?"

A moment later she joined me in my tiny kitchen. I could tell she'd been crying. I offered her a range of sparkling waters, and she picked one and cracked it open without meeting my gaze. She just looked at the can for a long moment. Neither of us had to say anything.

"You know what's stupid?" she said. "I actually thought he would show up here and try to win me back."

"He probably will, in a few months, once he realizes he messed up."

She took me in her arms and hugged me.

"I love you," she said.

"I love you, too." I was really glad I was there for her. Coming home hadn't been a mistake.

The doorbell rang and we glanced at each other. "Did you order takeout?" she asked.

I shook my head and walked quickly to the buzzer.

"Hello?"

"Hi, it's Paul, is that Abby?"

At the sound of his voice, I let go of the buzzer and glanced at Laura. She was looking at me, puzzled. Then I pushed it again.

"Paul?"

"Hey! I'm here. Sorry it's really late. Can I talk to you?"

I glanced at Laura. "It's the Newfoundland guy."

Laura stared at me. "Here?"

"He's here." My heart was full of joy, even without knowing what he'd say. Just from knowing I'd get a few more minutes with him. I grabbed my keys. "I'll go down and talk to him."

I rushed out the door. Just as it closed, I could hear Laura pressing the button to the buzzer behind me. "She'll be right down."

I skipped the elevator and ran down the six flights of stairs. Paul was waiting outside in the lobby next to the buzzers and mailboxes. He smiled when he saw me.

"Sorry it's late," he said. "My flight was delayed, and we just got in."

"Hi," I said, my voice sounding breathless.

"Hi," he said with a smile. "I hope this didn't come off as strange, but I wanted to talk to you in person, and I thought I should just come see you."

"Okay!" I sounded ridiculously cheerful.

He took a step toward me. I wanted him to hug me. He looked like he wanted to, but then neither of us moved. "I got your text in Toronto on my stopover, but I'd already bought a ticket to come down here and I thought I should say it in person."

"Say what?"

He took a breath. "So first of all, my mother left a message and said she got kicked out of her apartment complex permanently, so now she's in a homeless shelter."

"I'm sorry," I said.

"She had it coming, to be honest. But the point is, it's not my problem anymore. Maybe she'll realize she can't keep doing this to people, alienating her neighbors and so on. My father let my mother walk all over him, and I thought for a long time that was love. That's what you did for people you loved. I thought I was helping things by being easygoing."

I nodded, listening.

"So when I got married, I kept trying to do what my wife wanted, and also what my mother wanted, and they didn't want the same things. So I tried to be a peacemaker. And it didn't work. But when—when my mother said those things to you during the show, I realized, I don't want her in my life anymore. You were so much more important to me than keeping the peace. And that made me realize, I should have done that for Trish, too."

I nodded. Was that the way this was going? "It's okay if you want to get back together with her."

He laughed, once, quietly. "No, Abby. The point is, I don't think I was ever as in love with Trish as I am with you. Because you let me be angry. And passionate. And you don't try to walk all over me. And you're the one who I cared enough about to finally set those boundaries. So I talked to Trish, and I apologized to her. But the person I want to be with is you. I love you. Completely, and with all my heart. And I want to find a way to make this work."

I was motionless, joy flooding through me in a slow wave.

Paul's face was suffused with a tender, adoring look that I was sure must be reflected in my own expression. "Did you really think I would fly all the way down here just to tell you I was getting back together with my ex-wife?"

"I was hoping not. That could definitely have been a phone call."

He laughed a little.

"And I know you were worried you might turn out like your mother," he continued. "I know you were scared of being bitter and cynical. But you don't do cynical things. Letting Lisette stay with you, was that cynical? Or letting us drag you to improv practice? Or flying home to take care of your sister as soon as she needed you? You're not cynical at all. You look after other people. All the time. And now I want to look after you."

"I love you so much," I whispered.

"Then can we figure something out, here? I know you can't still work from Newfoundland, but..."

"I can."

"What?"

"I found out on the way to the airport. Kedar said I had a few more weeks to work from home. And he's hoping he can get me more time than that. But I still needed to come home for Laura, and I was scared to spend more time with you. I knew I was going to get more and more attached and then if I had to go, it would break me."

"You've already broken me," he said softly. "I still want this."

"What if I have to leave again?"

"Then we'd get married." He smiled at my raw shock. "I know Lisette joked about it, but we could. Eventually. In a few months. And if you can't get a job there, I could always move down here."

"You'd move here?" I looked around at the New York street, the fluorescent lobby lights.

"I'm not saying we get engaged right now, but I did the math, and I figured we've spent about fifty hours together, with all the improv practices, and hiking—I mean if, let's say we were going on a date for two hours a week, then that would be like we'd already gone on twenty-five dates. That's not a completely crazy amount of time to be sure you want to marry someone."

"That's fascinating math."

"I worked it out on a cocktail napkin on the plane."

"I may not be able to have kids. I'm thirty-seven. I don't even know if I even could."

"I don't know if I want kids. But we'd figure it out."

My eyes filled with tears. "You can't be this perfect."

"I'm divorced, I have an impossible mother, and I barely had money to fly here. I am not perfect. I just want to be perfect for you."

I put my arms around him, and he held me tight, pulling me against him so we were pressed together. I felt a bubble of happiness growing again, and this time it didn't feel like it was waiting to pop. It kept growing bigger and bigger, until it felt like it could get so big that it reached outside of us, encompassing everyone around us, too.

It hit me that Laura was upstairs, and that what Paul had just done for me was exactly what Nick hadn't been willing to do for Laura. I wanted to take Paul upstairs, but I was scared that it would make her sad. Paul had made a grand gesture, and her ex-husband hadn't.

But I was trying to trust her. She wanted the best for me. And she would be annoyed if I didn't give her a chance to look him over.

"You should come up and meet my sister."

"Are you sure? It's late."

"She'll give me a hard time if you don't come upstairs. Where were you planning on staying?"

"I hadn't thought that far ahead. I figured I'd get a hotel or sleep at the airport. I need to leave in a couple of days to do school prep. I just wanted to see you."

"Well, if you want to spend the night, you may have to stay in my bedroom because Laura and Hannah have the sofa right now."

"I think I could manage that."

. . .

I LED Paul quietly into the apartment, since Hannah was still asleep. Laura sat waiting for us at the dining table, her arms folded.

"This is Paul," I said quietly, trying not to a grin like a goofy teenager presenting my prom date to my parents. Paul nodded politely, glancing around at my bookcases and the sleeping figure in the next room.

"Hi," he whispered, putting out a hand.

Laura shook it, her expression amused. "Hi Paul," she said. "I'm Laura, Abby's sister. You in town to catch a Yankee's game, or...?"

He grinned. "No, I uh...I wanted to see Abby. To talk."

Laura looked at me, and then at him. "He's spending the night?"

I nodded. "Yeah, sorry. I'll sneak him out before Hannah wakes up in the morning."

Laura shrugged. "No need. We'll figure out something to tell her." She glanced at Paul. "You're okay pretending you're a building inspector, right?"

"Just give me a pen and a clipboard."

"Improv. Right." Then she smiled, and I realized she was happy to see me happy. "Well, I'm going to head to bed," she said. "You two have fun."

I led Paul into my bedroom, and he looked around, taking it all in. The room smelled of my scattered collection of perfumes, the musty ventilation system of older New York buildings, and the city at night.

He took my face into his hands and kissed me, gently. It was an optimistic kiss, like the start of something. Then he took my hands and led me onto the balcony, and he leaned out over the railing to look both ways. The view was nothing too exciting: the glow of an awning lit up on the corner, some mid-century apartment buildings in slow decline, people calling to each other at street level, seeking connection or possibly drugs.

"So," he said, "the Big City."

I took his hand, threading my fingers through his. It felt right, like we were facing this together. He leaned over into my ear.

"Important question about apartment living, since your niece is in the living room."

"Yes?"

"Exactly how quiet do we need to be?"

I started laughing.

LAURA and I ran into each other an hour later as she was coming out of the bathroom and I was going into it, already in my pjs.

"He looks like Tom Hiddleston, Abby. What the fuck? You said improv comedy and I thought he'd be some off-brand Adam Sandler."

"Don't tell him that. He doesn't know he can do better than me."

"There's no one better than you." She put her arms around me and gave me a kiss on the cheek. I couldn't remember the last time that our mother had given a kiss like that: it felt like a blessing.

THE NEXT MORNING, Paul was up and dressed before Hannah got up, and we told her that he'd come over early to show off his pancake recipe.

He demonstrated his cooking techniques in the kitchen while Hannah observed him curiously from one of my stools. He offered to let her flip a pancake and then carefully held her over the stove while she did so, one hand behind hers on the spatula. I watched them, smiling.

Hannah suspected something weird was going on, but she couldn't quite figure out what.

"Are you a real chef?" she said at last, her eyes full of doubt.

"No," he said. "I'm actually a teacher."

"Yeah." She considered this, nodding slowly. "That makes sense."

IT TURNS out that I hate January in Newfoundland.

The piles of snow get taller than the pedestrians in some places, and the stores are stocked with whatever sad, expensive fruit we can get from tanker ships. The coast is stunningly beautiful, bedecked in white and ghostly silent under the frost, but the process of digging out your car every time you want to go anywhere gets old.

So instead, I'm sitting inside next to Paul's woodstove—our woodstove, for the last year—and letting Paul take his turn running errands while I write a letter to Hannah. She likes getting hand-written letters from me, and the more fancy Canadian stamps I put on them, the better. She spent three weeks with Paul and me over the summer, and she has announced she wants us to have an 'official wedding,' since the first one we did was a hurried affair at the city hall which 'didn't really count' because I had neither a princess dress nor sufficient flowers, and more importantly, because she wasn't there to see it.

I've told her that she can come up and plan a better wedding for us herself when she comes back this summer, and we'll have it somewhere along the coast. I've agreed to let her pick the spot, and I'm hoping she'll choose a farmhouse in honor of my friend Jasmine. There aren't really that many people I'd want to invite. I'll start with Laura and her new boyfriend Ollie, who is a quiet tax attorney from Laura's work who seems to make her happy. I'll ask Jasmine and Lucas and whoever they are dating at the moment, which changes frequently enough that they always qualify for 'and guest' on their invitations.

There'll be Lisette, of course, and the rest of our improv group: Ellen and Jacob and Rene. The five of us make a good team, I've found, and you can do much more elaborate scenes and movie re-enactments when you have more people.

I'll invite Mrs. Mahoney and her daughter Penny and her family, if they can make it up from Ottawa.

I'll invite Kedar, who won't come but will be glad to be invited, even though I only freelance for him now.

There'll be a few friends of Paul's, and his cousins, and two of Lisette's siblings. He still doesn't speak to his mother, but she has found a place to live further down the coast, and makes a point of ignoring us, which we both appreciate.

And that's it. My whole world is smaller now, but at the same time it feels completely full of people, because they are all the ones who will turn up no matter what.

Paul comes in from outside with some groceries in a couple of large shopping bags. He prefers to stop in at the local shop on his walk home from his school, and the groceries are often half-frozen by the time he gets them back into the house. It is close to four, so it is already getting dark here, and he shakes himself warm as he comes inside.

I stand up and take the bags out of his hands while he unpeels the long orange scarf that Lisette knitted for him. By the time I've put the groceries away in the kitchen, he is seated by the woodstove, his boots off, looking through a small pile of mail on the table.

I sit next to him, pressing my face to his cold neck, until he wraps an arm around my waist and kisses me, then slides his hands beneath my shirt.

"How are your hands still warm?" I kiss his cold cheeks. "That is medically impossible. Your entire face is frozen."

He laughs. "The miracle of human chemistry."

I kiss him until he decides to stand up to pull closed the curtains. Then I pull him back down onto the sofa next to me.

"Remember that time you kissed me while I was meditating," he whispers.

"During the improv? I thought we agreed that you kissed me," I say.

"I was just being polite."

I laugh and crawl on top of him, determined to completely undermine his inner peace.

Arts and Lovers

Yes, And...

Jack and Jill

Rachel Carey writes satirical plays, serious screenplays, and lighthearted books about characters falling into love or trouble. She grew up moving around between rural Vermont, suburban Massachusetts, and New York City, and currently lives in the Garden State.

A small press bound by the belief that every voice matters.

Sign up for our newsletter to learn about new releases and more.
https://oliver-heberbooks.com/subscribe/

Follow us on social media:

facebook.com/oliverheberbooks

instagram.com/oliverheberbooks

amazon.com/oliverheberbooks

youtube.com/@OliverHeberBooksPublisher